In Good Hands

Bill James lives in his ⟨⟩ ...... Wales. He is married with four children and is the author of a critical work on Anthony Powell as well as many thrillers and crime novels. *In Good Hands* is the eleventh in the highly acclaimed Harpur and Iles series.

'The fun is more ferocious than ever . . . This is a superbly conceived gritty addition to James's growing chronicle of the interwoven sins of cops and robbers.'
JOHN COLEMAN, SUNDAY TIMES

'James's normal, brilliantly portrayed beat is the morally twilight world where cop meets villain. James's skill in exposing the intensities behind police façades is undiminished, and his cop-station dialogue is unmatched.'
MARCEL BERLINS, THE TIMES

'Another movement in the savagely comic, expertly choreographed Jamesian dance to the music of crime . . . Addicts and newcomers will love it.' GUARDIAN

'James has to be one of the funniest crime writers now trespassing on that twilight territory where fuzz and felons make their moves and talk their humorous heads off, with menace constantly rippling the surface.' SUNDAY TIMES

'Quite brilliantly done, with moods expertly modulated and ribaldry kept under wraps.' LITERARY REVIEW

'The restless, spiky style of James's brilliant dialogue was never more appropriate; the rose blooms without a hint of melodrama.' STEPHEN WALSH, OXFORD TIMES

'Dialogue and characters, both criminal and copper, are superb, and the story compelling. This is crime writing at its most honest.' THE TIMES

'James tells the story so skilfully as to make readers alternately quake with fear and quiver with laughter.'
GERALD KAUFMAN, THE SCOTSMAN

By the same author

YOU'D BETTER BELIEVE IT
THE LOLITA MAN
HALO PARADE
PROTECTION
COME CLEAN
TAKE
CLUB
ASTRIDE A GRAVE
GOSPEL
ROSES, ROSES

In Good Hands

Bill James

PAN BOOKS

First published 1994 by Macmillan

This edition published 1995 by Pan Books
an imprint of Macmillan General Books
Cavaye Place London SW10 9PG
and Basingstoke

Associated companies throughout the world

ISBN 0 330 34296 7

Copyright © Bill James 1994

The right of Bill James to be identified as the
author of this work has been asserted by him in accordance
with the Copyright, Designs and Patents Act 1988.

All rights reserved. No reproduction, copy or transmission
of this publication may be made without written permission.
No paragraph of this publication may be reproduced, copied or
transmitted save with written permission or in accordance with
the provisions of the Copyright Act 1956 (as amended). Any
person who does any unauthorized act in relation to
this publication may be liable to criminal prosecution
and civil claims for damages.

1 3 5 7 9 8 6 4 2

A CIP catalogue record for this book is available from
the British Library

Phototypeset by Intype, London
Printed and bound in Great Britain by
Cox & Wyman Ltd, Reading, Berkshire

This book is sold subject to the condition that it shall not,
by way of trade or otherwise, be lent, re-sold, hired out,
or otherwise circulated without the publisher's prior consent
in any form of binding or cover other than that in which
it is published and without a similar condition including this
condition being imposed on the subsequent purchaser.

Without laws the world would become a wilderness, and men little less than beasts; but with all this, the best things may come to be the worst, if they are not in good hands; and if it is true that the wisest men generally make the laws, it is true that the strongest do often interpret them.

From *The Character of a Trimmer*
by George Savile, first Marquis of Halifax 1633–95

'There is no death,' she said. 'No, my dear lady, but there are funerals.'

From *Comfort Me with Apples*
by Peter de Vries

Chapter One

If you knew how to look, a couple of deaths from the past showed now and then in Iles's face. This might be true of many Assistant Chief Constables, maybe even most. What would be special to Desmond Iles, though, was the raw glow of joy and triumph blessing his features at these times. Of course, Iles never spoke about what had happened. That he would see as flashy and dangerous, even to talk about it to Harpur. Just the same, anyone could observe a deep, private thrill occasionally touch the ACC. Yes, anyone would spot that, but could not know where it came from. Harpur felt pretty sure he did know. Nobody worked closer to Iles. Harpur never considered this an out-and-out treat or privilege, just how it was, a harsh, long-life alliance. You could say Harpur sat on the ACC's right hand, except when the ACC was using the right hand and probably his left as well to assist law and order in secret, brilliantly jungle ways.

Chapter Two

Mark Lane said: 'I don't know whether I can talk to you about this, Col.'

Harpur kept quiet.

'Of course, I know I'm isolated here,' the Chief said. They were in Lane's big, light office-conference room, and he waved his hand as though talking about a one-man dungeon. But he meant more than a room. He meant the domain. 'I want Desmond Iles out, Colin.'

For about the first time this afternoon, the Chief looked straight at him. Harpur let the shock get into his voice. 'Sir, is this something you should discuss with me?'

Of course, of course Lane wanted to get rid of Iles. Everyone understood that. A few might even sympathize. It was not something to be spelled out.

Lane said: 'Why I hesitated over mentioning it. I can't act alone, though.'

'Hardly for me to say, but I can assure you, sir, that Mr Iles is among your most committed—'

Lane brought the side of his fist down hard on the desk surface. 'Look, don't think this is just my wife talking.' He did a grotesque yet loving imitation of a woman's voice. '*Get rid of that vicious Desmond Iles, Marky.*'

'Nobody believes you're swayed like that, sir.'

'My wife is a glorious strength to me and sets a tone. Of that I'm proud.'

'We all admire her, as we do you.'

'But I have information which she knows nothing of. I ask you to understand that, Col.'

'Certainly, sir.'

The Chief snarled: 'Certainly? You think it natural that such information should be available about Mr Iles?' Once, Mark Lane was a great detective on a neighbouring patch, and in those days Harpur had carried out good inter-Force operations with him. Now and then the Chief could still dredge up that old sharpness. Thank God he could. It was hellish to watch a man crushed by his position.

Harpur said: 'I mean of course Mrs Lane could not influence you. At your level. On, well, important policy. Sir, everyone—'

'Respects me, and so on.' Lane made the formula words trickle out and disappear, like pissing on parched ground. 'When I say isolated, I mean beyond what would be standard in the post of Chief Constable.'

'Sir, I—'

'So, whom do I talk to, Col?' Lane was in some kind of brownish-beige suit. He had the top button of his shirt collar undone and the knot of his brownish-beige striped tie down on his chest. He liked to believe scruffiness meant relaxation. The Chief bent his head and gazed at the spot where his fist had landed. 'If, for example, we could find Iles with an under-age whore, Colin.'

Harpur did not reply.

'You'll say, is that likely,' the Chief went on.

'Well, yes, sir.'

'Is which likely? For him to be with a child tart or for us to catch him at it?'

'Since he started a family, sir, Mr Iles has—'

'So, why turn to you? You don't want this load. You've got your own pains – recent tragic loss of a wife and so on. Oh, I invoke old times, I suppose. Plus, I believe there are more moments than not when you see things straight and decent, despite everything. Plus despair. In any case, who the hell else do I go to, Col?' The Chief kept this question clipped, almost offhand, but the despair was there, jagged in his words.

3

'A grand team, sir,' Harpur replied. 'People think of you as leading a grand team – the head, yet very much part of it.' He would have loved the Chief to be happy, or at least happier. There was a sort of real greatness to Lane, but the wrong sort for his job.

Lane shoved all this away with another wave. 'Now you'll realize why I have to come to you, Col. I want Erogenous Jones to do the snooping, don't I? Nobody else could shadow Iles effectively. Some routine heavy behind him and he'd know right away and know right away who'd sent him. Iles is a master of our game. Clearly, it's delicate, gum-shoeing an ACC – the disrespect, the slyness. I understand enough about this Force to know Erogenous won't do it unless the instructions come personally from you. He'd tell Iles, or deliberately get spotted, or just refuse.' Lane still had his head and eyes lowered. 'You can see I'm putting myself in your hands. It has to be an under-age girl, if possible ethnic. Just to take him with a whore is not enough. Par for the course and he could brazen it. Why I say Erogenous. It could be a longish, subtle job, with trial and error, waiting for a child. Iles buys a lot of company.'

Lane rose from his desk and walked to the window. He had taken his shoes off, as he often did in the office, and his socks made a very gentle sandpapering sound on the block floor when he moved, like a tame sea on shingle. The socks were to suggest more relaxation. He stared from the window, giving the sense of seeing for a huge distance and wishing he was there. Many times Harpur had watched him in what Iles called his only-a-bird-in-a-gilded-cage attitude. Hanging on the wall alongside him was a framed, multi-coloured diagram giving the command structure. His own post was a thick-lined, scarlet rectangle, solitary at the top, with the letters C.C. in purple at the centre, and an array of delegating green arrows pointing down. 'I've been excluded, Col, that's all. Systematically sealed off,' he said over his shoulder. 'It can be done, given the skill, the poison. Has been done.

4

I talk to you privately, you walk out from here and tell it straight away to— My fate. My fault. I've failed to win you people, get your trust.'

'Oh, sir, I don't believe anyone would—'

'A leadership disaster.'

Yes, a princely man, but unquestionably a stumbling chieftain. Iles reckoned Lane typified a notorious route to failure: somebody with talent promoted one rung above his range, and so to destruction. 'Like St Peter,' Iles would say. The ACC, who worked nonstop to speed this destruction in Lane, claimed he often wept over the Chief's plight, though Harpur had never seen the tears. He said: 'Sir, I don't think you realize how much your people here— We've all learned from you, believe me. It's not easy to come into a strange Force.'

'I should have dealt with Iles long ago.'

Harpur said: 'Erogenous is promoted inspector now. He does little tailing. That sort of tailing.'

'But in your debt, Col.' The Chief did not turn and still spoke towards the window.

'I mean, if it were really so, about Mr Iles.'

'We need him gone, Col. Finished. Yes, *we* need it, not just myself. So I disclose to you.'

'He'd be a terrible loss, sir. But, really, I can't talk to you about an ACC like this. It's—'

The Chief did spin round now, his sallow face a fusion of rage and misery, though Harpur knew misery would win: Lane could not do rage for long, a loveable, sad defect in a Chief. 'Iles, you, Francis Garland, Erogenous, perhaps Sid Synott – that's the real team here, yes? You run us. Meaning Iles runs us. He's killed people, Colin, you know. Yes, you know. In a good cause. But unquestionably killed. Became the avenger.'

Harpur kept his face thoroughly blank and said nothing.

Lane had an apologetic little laugh. 'I feared you might walk out if I attacked Iles like this.'

'You're Chief Constable, sir. I'm a detective chief superintendent. I can't walk out.'

'You've walked out in your head? All I want is for Iles to go elsewhere.'

'If we catch him bare-arsed on docks rubble with a black schoolgirl tart, sir, he's in jail. He'd go down for ever – an Assistant Chief Constable. That's if it were remotely likely, I say again.'

Lane reverted to the window view. 'Oh, no charges. Desmond's a prized colleague, after all. Eminent in his way. Just give the pressure. He'd quit. Col, if he has killed I don't want him here, under me. That's strange, for God's sake? People are niggling about those deaths again. Home Office. The Inspectorate. Possibility of a Parliamentary Question. *Another* Parliamentary Question. That's what I mean. This is the information I mentioned. Am I a chief constable who would tolerate an ACC who's murdered? Can I face that? Can any one of us in this Force face it? This government has the knife out for all police. Rationalization, so called. A smell like this and our Force could get swallowed for ever by next door. Or again, how do I look at home, allowing someone like Iles to continue, Col? Wives don't understand these – these rough complexities of our work. As you know. Knew. They think there are clear moral demarcations. It's sweet in them and ultimately right. Ultimately right, Col.' He went back to his desk and folded weightily into the chair.

'But we've heard such rumours before, sir – about the Home Office digging into those deaths. As you say, we've had the questions in the Commons. Nothing happened.'

'It will now.'

Harpur said: 'So what, sir? I can put it so bluntly because the deaths were properly investigated. We all know you would not have tolerated anything less, especially you. But no luck. The file remains open. We still interview. We'll break it.'

'You see? You instantly knew the deaths I meant. Naturally. Yes, Jamieson, Favard. They kill Ray Street, one of our best undercover boys, are acquitted, and the ACC is maddened and executes them. That's the overwhelming likelihood, now isn't it? Oh, obviously, you're not going to answer. His actions are almost understandable, but— But intolerable. We do not want vigilante assistant chiefs. Also, he thought they'd killed a woman of his, of course. What it comes down to, do we accept that Iles knows better than a jury, better than the law?'

'Never proven or anywhere near, sir.'

'We tried. We tried?'

Harpur stood.

'All right, Col. I'm sorry. But do you want some internal investigating team here, looking at all that? God knows how far it would go. A man's entitled to the privacies of his sex life, definitely, you or anyone else, but you're aware what these clean-up visitations are like. Every corner. In principle one approves absolutely. That goes without saying, I hope. But an outside chief, with a staff of hard noses.'

'They'd discover nothing, sir.'

'I can believe it, Col. You're very capable people.'

'Who?'

'You and your detectives, who did our investigation. Of course.'

'Thanks.'

'But I want Desmond Iles away. Early retirement – some sickness arranged. It can be worked. Or transfer to another Force.'

'That would solve nothing, sir. Supposing there were something to solve.'

'It's all I can do. We'd be wholesome here again. We'd have a chance of survival. I believe you want that, Col.' Lane's voice got up off the canvas. A mild gleam between red and brownish-beige touched his cheeks for a second. He stared at Harpur. 'And he'd know I'd beaten him. I could run this outfit then.'

'You do now, sir.'

'Speak to Erogenous. But, obviously, not if you're going to spill this to Iles. Loyalties will compel you? Or would compel Erogenous?'

7

'My loyalties – all our loyalties – are to the Force and you, sir.'

'Will you report it all to Iles?'

'Oh, I'd be ashamed, sir.'

Chapter Three

On the floor with his skull shattered and a piece of coal jammed into his mouth lay the original very nice guy wearing one of those sveltley cut silver-buttoned double-breasted navy blazers he was so fond of, and rightly famed for, and fine grey flannel trousers that would have cost not less than £250, possibly even custom made. The shoes were slim black lace-ups and, again, perhaps created for him, a kindness to the feet and joy for all admirers of quiet beauty. In talk at The Monty club and around the town generally, everyone used to call him this, the original very nice guy, always in full, including the 'the', and often giving reverential, capital-letter weight, as if: The Original Very Nice Guy. Many had almost forgotten his real name, Raoul Caesar Brace, though that was certainly how he had to appear on charge sheets and maintenance orders, and in newspaper court reports, plus now the death notice. Previously, Harpur had never known the original very nice guy involved in anything that brought him even the slightest injury, but today would obviously make up for that.

Across the room from him, Lester Magellan was seated on a tastefully restored mauve upholstered Victorian *chaise-longue*, eyes wide, as though gazing fondly at the original very nice guy but not. This was Lester's flat and altogether quite a gem for such a rough-house district, the walls a pale ochre wash. Exceptionally vivid Habitat scatter rugs on sanded, varnished boards somehow gave the feel of an art gallery, though there were only framed, old film posters hanging, including *Sergeant York*. Lester

9

wore a pale blue sweat shirt decorated with a flat map of the earth which had angels blowing trumpets at the four corners, perhaps for the Day of Judgement, or just a world-wide gig. The lovingly polished brass poker that had been used to screw a garotte wire very adequately into Lester's neck stuck up erect behind his head like a hussar plume. Lester had quite a tongue.

'Obviously the original very nice guy was loathed more than most, sir,' Francis Garland told Harpur, 'what with the blazers and lordliness and always overmixing the commodity, so customers thought his class rig cost them too much. But, myself, I didn't know anyone had him marked for treatment just now.'

Whizz-kiddery would normally have stopped Garland admitting that gap. The rare sights here might have pushed him askew for a minute. He was authentically bright but did occasionally show flaky. 'No, nor me,' Harpur replied. 'Francis, there was a lot to be said for the original very nice guy. Bee keeper. He recognized all the hive individually.'

Garland had arrived first and was standing near the door, well back from the bodies, as if fiercely meticulous about disturbing nothing before the Scene of Crime people turned up. 'Pockets and so on?' Harpur asked.

'They'd been thoroughly cleared already. Some dental floss in the original very nice guy's trousers. That's all.'

'Had the shoes and socks off? Both?'

Garland glanced at him impatiently, plainly bored by the question. 'Both what, sir? Both legs, both men?'

'Let's say both legs of both.'

'Nothing there.'

'Behind the coal?'

'Mouth's otherwise empty. It took some shifting and shoving back – worse, that – rigor being well on, and he's got excellent teeth, thanks to the floss, I expect: the original very nice guy knew how to take care of himself.'

'Up to a point, copper.'

'And then Lester,' Garland replied, 'such a nothing that who'd waste strength on him?'

10

'Not a kindly man, but he told me once he would only strike a pregnant woman more than three months on, when it's safer, and I accepted that. He had to fight his way up – if you regard where he was now as up. The *chaise-longue* and genuine mahogany-finish magazine rack.'

'I rang you first, obviously, Colin. You'd want to see this ahead.'

'Where did the tip come from?'

Garland let that go, as any decent detective would. 'On my private phone,' he replied.

Harpur himself had been alone at home when Garland called. After Megan died, Harpur decided he should spend more quality time in the house giving companionship to his daughters, so the two girls went out more.

'My own feeling is these deads could have been anyone,' Garland said.

'Some grammar. Well, it's too late to start on the blazer lining. They'll be here any moment.'

'I did consider slashing it, naturally, but that needs your rank, for the level of cheek.'

'Thanks.'

'I had a good feel around the material. I don't think there's anything.'

Harpur crossed the room to see matters from another angle. 'It's all so tidy, Francis. Even the head mess is modest.'

'The original very nice guy could be modest. Everything says there was time to spruce up afterwards.'

'These two weren't fucking each other? Some dalliance variations gone vaguely amiss?'

Garland made a small groan. 'We know what this is about, don't we, sir? Anyway, the original very nice guy's a career straight. Lester could adapt, true, but not with him. I did a quick survey, of course. No signs. Just two insignificants needed for a tableau. My impression. A re-run.'

Harpur bent and had a long stare at the original very nice guy from a couple of inches away. 'As a matter of fact, the Chief was talking to me about all that a day or two ago.'

'Oh, why? Why, sir?'

'Just reminiscing. That happy way he has.'

'These two deaths—'

'Have their resemblances with the earlier two, Jamieson, Favard, yes,' Harpur replied.

'Well, absolutely.'

Harpur straightened up and went to rejoin Garland. 'Not absolutely. Close.'

'OK, Favard was garotted with a broom handle and rope. Now it's a poker and wire. But—'

'Neither here nor there to Favard's and Lester's necks. Fair enough . . .'

A window was open and Harpur thought he heard a couple of weighty vehicles draw up down in the yard.

Garland *sotto voce*d. 'And if the Chief was talking about the earlier ones, did he – well, did he mention Des Iles, sir?'

'Just gossiping generally about the past. No, I don't think the ACC was referred to. Why would he be? Was he involved with that case? No.'

Garland said: 'So, he *was* mentioned? I want to be here when he sees this.'

'Is he coming?'

'He'll come when he hears the details, won't he? If they can locate him. The coal in the mouth, for God's sake. How it was with Jamieson.'

'Jamieson was shot.'

'There are differences, yes. But the pageantry's identical.'

'And then the facial burning to Jamieson. Not repeated here. Wasn't Favard tied to a chair, with a mirror in front of him so he could watch the rope get to work?'

Garland said: 'But you know, don't you, sir, that this refers back? Don't you, though? I can't see the purpose, but it must. Why I say the people don't count. It's the show itself that matters. It's the show that's telling us something.'

'I'm listening, Francis. As ever.'

The Scene of Crime crowd came in and took over with their photography, plastic bagging and print dusting. Harpur always found all that tedious and he and Garland went down a flight and knocked at the flat immediately below. A tough-looking woman of about forty in smart, executive clothes, superior junk jewellery and vehement eighties Thatcher-sweep hair-do opened the door and, leaning forward, felt the material in Harpur's lapel. 'Police,' she stated. There was Ovaltine on her breath.

Garland said: 'We wondered whether you—'

'One hears nothing, sees nothing. But nothing – N O T H I N G.'

'Dear Lester Magellan in number eleven,' Harpur replied, 'the pretty bachelor and nest builder. We—'

'Absolutely zilch,' she said. 'That's how it is here.'

'Noises through your ceiling,' Harpur said.

'You could help us,' Garland said.

'But could you bastards, would you bastards, help me if I helped you? Supposing I could, which I can't,' she answered. 'Am I a mouth, for God's sake?'

'Chief Inspector Garland is a carer.'

'I'm sorry,' she replied. 'You can't protect us. You've written us off. This is the badlands and we look after ourselves, thanks. Who's the star in the Ascot hat and Bonny Prince Charlie overcoat?'

Iles was coming up the stairs towards Magellan's flat and joined them on her landing. He grandly removed the brown trilby and gave a medieval bow. His silver hair gleamed poorly in the feeble lighting.

'This lady unfortunately feels she can't risk talking to us, sir,' Harpur said.

'Quite,' the Assistant Chief replied. 'Madam, if I lived in a shit-heap like this, I'd keep my head very well down, too, oh, yes. Adore the octopus.' He nodded towards a gross purple, yellow and grey brooch on her chest. 'One area never out of fashion is the sea bed.'

'One thinks of it as degentrification of my sort,' she

said. 'One once had all the bourgeois, law-and-order-backing views but if one has to take a place here one also has to take the ambience. And the ambience never talks to police. N E V E R. Traffickers do object. I could show you what's left of people who have spoken, and some I could not show you and nor could anyone else.'

Iles said: 'So true. These lads of mine are poor on subtleties, always have been. Harpur here, with a face like that, I mean, is he going to spot nuances?' Iles had a brief but deep laugh, and the woman joined in. 'Possibly I'll call on you later, dear, in a personal capacity, and who knows how things might seem then?' the ACC asked.

'I promise nothing.'

'One does admire you for that,' Iles replied.

He, Harpur and Garland went up to Magellan's floor. 'What worries me, horrifies me, is how this will disturb Lane,' Iles said, gazing at the bodies. 'He'll hear echoes. Far-fetched, but he will, Col. He's worked so hard to get all that Jamieson and Favard stuff pushed far, far back in his noble little mind, and now this. And for it to happen to the original very nice guy, too. This was a wonderfully amiable man you could scare co-operative just by eyeing his finger nails or screaming in the next cell plus a few coughing blood sounds. What did you find in their clothes and so on, Col?'

'Obviously, we decided we must disturb nothing but wait for the Scene of Crime people, sir.'

'Don't mess me about, Harpur.'

'Obviously, we decided we must disturb nothing but wait for the Scene of Crime people, sir,' Harpur said.

'Lane thought I'd done those other, previous two, you know, funny old eclair,' Iles replied, wagging his head fondly. He did not lower his voice and one of the finger-print gang turned and stared for a moment. 'Hadn't you heard that, Viv?' the ACC asked her, giggling. Abruptly, though, his voice went bleak: 'Those two droppings, Jamieson and Favard, kill one of our best young boys, and then scrape a not guilty. Oh, I don't blame you in the least for that, Harpur. Not altogether. You got them into court, though the evidence could have been so much more professionally plumped. We were faced with some terrorized jury and piss-artist judge, plus the usual defending, libertarian, fee-fat, fat-fee, villains' mate QC. As it happens, Jamieson and Favard had unquestionably done for a certain girl I knew, too, called Celia Mars. By burning. Yes.' Iles had put his hat back on after speaking to the woman beneath. He pulled the brim down for a moment now and swivelled away towards a poster for *Midnight In Miami*, as if to hide his face. For a while he did not speak.

When he resumed, his tone was lighter. Vivienne Aitken, the finger-print expert, had resumed her work, but Iles continued to declaim to the back of her blonde head. 'Yet, purely by splendid fluke, both Jamieson and Favard were later slaughtered in agonizing, picturesque circumstances – well, yes, not unlike these – but with something of a fire motif in Jamieson's case, as I recall. You'll have to put me right on this, Col. When one is not personally involved with a case, memories can weaken. But I think I'm right. Some scorching to the face, and, as here with the original very nice guy, coal in the gob.' Iles chuckled again. 'The Chief put all sorts of two and twos together, primarily, of course, motive, the dear thing, and thought of yours truly. I knew it, know it, though obviously he would never say so, the lovely gent. So, why didn't he have the motive, too, the cream-faced bag of piety? Ever asked yourself that, Garland – when you're not too busy screwing other men's wives? Why didn't Mark Lane want to put things right for Raymond Street, one of his greatest?'

Iles liked answers to all his questions. Harpur said: 'Well, sir, it's—'

Iles said: 'I heard, in fact, renewed Home Office interest in those distant events. That raging conscience, the Chief, will have provoked this in his sweet deviousness. He has a saintly way with a grudge.' Iles never let his contempt for Lane diminish. Far, far back under Barton, the Chief's predecessor, Iles had often acted as Deputy, though still only an Assistant Chief, in fact. Lane never allowed that.

'That's all a closed book, sir, surely,' Harpur replied. 'Not a closed file, but nothing active now.'

'You remember Celia, do you, Col?' the ACC asked.

'Oh, yes, sir. A—'

'Well, I don't need your slimy recollections, Harpur. She was brought out of that torched house unrecognizable, like a piece of turf.' Iles had begun to shout and some spittle flew towards Gary Cooper, crouched in No Man's Land as Sergeant York. Most of the Scene of Crime people knew the ACC's little ups and downs quite well, and took no notice. But Harpur heard a thumping sound in the floor quite near the original very nice guy's destroyed head: the octopus lady must be rapping her ceiling with a brush handle to protest at Iles's din. 'I expect you're very much in the picture on this Home Office move against me, Col,' the ACC said.

Harpur replied: 'Celia Mars – a wonderful, sad face, like an Italian princess grieving over lost terrain.'

'What interests me,' Garland said, pointing towards the bodies, 'is why anyone should want to imitate those killings now.'

'Sod off, Francis,' Iles replied, 'I'm talking to Harpur about a lovely woman who found my soul.'

'Or if we can get whoever did this pair we'd probably have who did the previous ones,' Garland said. 'That would really clear things, sir. I mean generally, and for you. It might not be just copy cat. It could be someone's regular method.'

Iles went across and fondled the original very nice guy's grand shoes. 'You made a slack job with these laces, Francis,' he replied. 'Let me break all this to Mr Lane, lads. He's so delicate. It will have to be put with some consideration. That Sumo wife is wearing him down, unpicking his boyish nerves, though in many ways a treasure, I gather.'

Chapter Four

The original very nice guy's mother had always loathed hearing him called that. Most people close to the family knew it, and when they came to the house to offer sympathy and pay respects they were careful to speak of him and to him as Raoul.

Stanley Stanfield, gazing into the casket with real comradeship, said: 'Well, don't worry, Mrs Brace, we know whose work it was and where to look.'

'I think so,' she replied. 'Am I one to stand in your way?'

Even if the undertaker had not managed such a subtle job, she would still have invited relatives and friends to come to view Raoul in the middle room. You had to make your public statement. You had to tell everybody you still had your pride in him. This room opened on to a small conservatory rich in healthy plants and she had put a bowl of taramasalata dip with crackers on a garden table in there, and set up a barrel of Bass, plus sherry or Pimms for the women. These were good, handed-down procedures for such situations. Some neglected them nowadays, but a community had its tried ways and its own wisdom.

Stanley Stanfield wearing a suit in keeping wept a while quietly, head back, not trying to hide the tears. 'I might have been with them that night.'

'We need you now, Stanley.'

'Count on me. He was the original very – what I mean, he was the original model for so many around here, Mrs Brace. Prototype. His example goes on in us.'

It was exactly because there was such truth in this that she had wanted people to use his true name and still did. Way back, when Raoul was only in his late teens, and acquaintances first started calling him the original very nice guy, she picked up a smear of mockery, possibly contempt or fear, and made it plain she was opposed. Raoul himself had not seemed bothered and believed the title showed affection, but he was a generous boy and optimistic, as life began to open up.

Stan touched the side of the box gently, like getting the tone of a piano, and said: 'He tried to end it with her decently, Mrs Brace. Several times. Believe me, the girl was more than a willing party. Oh, yes, young, yet many of them know a damn sight more at that age than some of us ever will. But fathers – fathers think their little girls are still little girls, and so their appalling rage.'

'Raoul underestimated his own attractiveness right across the board age-wise, the silly, sweet lad. He dressed the beautiful way he did to please himself and me, and didn't realize the golden impression he made generally, cheap shoes being particularly abhorrent to him. Do we expect the police to do anything about his death, anything real? And dear Lester's, naturally.'

'Christ, no,' Stanley replied. He shook his head and a tear flew from somewhere and landed on the shroud near Raoul's face, making a tiny stain for a moment, until it dried. Mrs Brace did not mind that. This was something natural, emotional, true. Stanley went on: 'How could they, even if they wanted to? To be blunt, Mrs Brace, although in his presence, you've heard of wheels within wheels? To me, this looks like someone deliberately using the father's anger to stick him right in the frame. And when I say someone, I mean someone big, someone very big, someone very big police. Someone who understands very well how a jury might be swayed by knowing the father seemingly had a motive. In fact, the girl's father could not do this sort of thing. Beyond him. We both know that, don't we? But because of his anger with Raoul, that father can come in useful – can be landed with these deaths. And then if he's landed with these it can be made to seem he did the other two as well. That's the real point. It's typically clever.'

'This is Iles.'

'Who else is capable?' Stanfield replied.

'Thus, no police help, so we're alone. Have to put it right alone?'

'We're alone, we're together.'

'Right, Stanley. Yes. Just think the number who've fondly come to see him now. This is support.'

'Nobody can ever destroy that spirit. We live and die by it. The work will go on. There could be a pay day around for you soon, Mrs Brace. This was a project devised by Raoul, so I feel you have an entitlement.'

'Thanks. I know you were a fine team.' The dropping of Raoul's given names hurt her more because his friends, Stanley Stanfield and Lester Magellan, were always called Stanley and Lester. Poor Lester, always very secondary, and dead probably only because he happened to be with Raoul that evening. To call a child Stan Stanfield seemed stupid of his parents, as though unable to budge from the *stan* sound, yet people allowed him his due identity, did not make up something different.

Stanley said: 'Yes, in all ways a beautiful man, prime. That girl was nuzzling up to him the very first time they met, Mrs Brace, while he was still concentrating only on general conversation. This was a really embarrassing and avid display by her. But could you tell a girl's obsessed father that? What father would believe his little precious was bed-crazy?'

For all the funeral arrangements, she described Raoul as R. Caesar Brace. Even when Raoul was only a youth she made him sign forms and letters in that way, and he had stuck to this whenever he could since. His name in that shape she had felt was sure to get him noticed. Face to face when he was alive, and now, she never addressed him as Caesar, always Raoul, but used to tell everyone that R. Caesar Brace sounded better than Raoul C. Brace, where the C seemed tucked away and wasted. Of course, the law and courts did both first names, Raoul Caesar Brace, which she had also come to dislike. But this was how the law treated everyone, like the snotty shout of a court usher. The law slammed labels on. It had no feelings.

'What's a man supposed to do?' Stanley asked. 'This was a passably desirable piece, and developed, whatever her age.'

'Raoul would never wilfully take advantage.' And then another of Mrs Brace's main hates was funeral parlours, so she had insisted on bringing Raoul home. This, too, would have been the rule in the past. Lester was *At Rest At Grant's*, as the local paper announcements always said. At Rest meant shoved out of sight at Grant's before disposal and she wouldn't have it and wouldn't have had it for Raoul even if he had died unnewsworthily. Warmth, companionship and loyalty you offered your children, whether or not they could return these, and loyalty above all. For instance, could any funeral home provide such a pleasant leafy conservatory? Emily Brace went in there with Stanley now and they sat for a while on garden chairs looking back through the foliage towards Raoul. She had a sherry, and Stanley took one, too. He had always been a nervy boy and probably thought it would not be proper to swill pints while the body was in the house. Although, in fact, tradition said men drank beer while watching over the departed, Stanley was entitled to take what he wished, and she avoided showing any hint of disapproval or even surprise.

Chapter Five

Only Lester Magellan's death really mattered. Although Stan Stanfield stayed for more than an hour with Mrs Brace among her fat plants, and willingly spoke every fragrance about the original very nice guy, his mind travelled. You did the due thing, that's all, and Mrs Brace had to have consideration, being in touch with the past and full of remarks. Stanfield genuinely thought quite a bit of the original very nice guy despite what many said, but obviously his chief agony now was Magellan was wanted in person to handle the crossbow work on those two fucking guard dogs.

Lester had been basic to this job. In all sorts of ways it was a perfect prospect, except for the Alsatians, which Lester would undoubtedly have catered for with style. Perfect, yes, but only if it was done exactly two weeks from now, Thursday the 12th, some time between 9 p.m. and 11 p.m. After that, and before that, it did not exist. The cash would not be in the house, people would, and one of them Kenward Knapp, the owner, who could be so dangerous. On Thursday for two hours The Pines would be unoccupied. This was the information, and direct from the original very nice guy, as a matter of fact, so probably right. There was a time when he would have come on this kind of job himself. Lately, though, he just provided the insight and left the heavy work to friends, the sweetly shod big-wheel shit.

Driving to Lester's parents' place from the original very nice guy's, Stanley felt rough. Clearly, he would have to come up with true sympathy again, this being, on the face of it, the only purpose of the call. That was all right, because Stanley felt authentically upset about how Lester went, not just over him being abruptly unavailable. Lester certainly did not deserve it, the way that poker made him look an idiot, descriptions spread all over the media. Probably, he did not deserve death at all. He could be exceptionally mild.

But, as well as the full condolences, Stanley had to locate the crossbow and bolts and bring them away without anyone in the house or outside knowing. He needed to get some steady practice with it himself. Stanfield wished it was still the fashion for people to wear black armbands so relatives would see straight off you were grief-stricken and you could think about other things.

Lester had often mentioned to Stanley that he did not keep the crossbow and arrows at his flat in case of possible police visits, or one of his women, or occasional bed boys, or both, running slaughterously amok with the weapon from jealousy or amphetamines. He was wise there, because Harpur's people would be all through Lester's place now, shaking everything apart or 'spinning his drum' as the police heartlessly called it – work they adored. In fact, Lester was almost always an alert thinker on security, although at the end he must have dozed off. His flat was too small and apparently he had a lot of possessions – sports stuff and so on – in a garden shed at his parents' house on the other side of the town. Most of these things were harmless or even healthy, and the crossbow and bolts lay somewhere cleverly concealed among ordinary equipment. Stanley thought he would remind himself of the geography now while commiserating deeply with the Magellans and then come back when it was dark, and neatly get into the shed and forage. To buy a new bow would be crazy if a couple of weeks off two Alsatians shot by arrows were due to be found in the grounds of that fine ransacked property. Shops talked.

When he arrived, Lester's parents were out. They might

be down at Grant's Rest Home fixing the hymns and confirming identification in case Grant's had a sudden glut of clients with heads nearly cut off by wire. Or Mr and Mrs Magellan had possibly disappeared somewhere to avoid Harpur and the Press. To Stanley it seemed very off-key to break into the garden shed of mourners before expressing sympathy, but this *was* a chance, and better than working at night with just a pencil beam and the hazard. Several times he had been to the house with Lester before he set himself up in the flat and knew the garden was pretty well enclosed by a stone wall and a proud scatter of trees. He could probably do it without being spotted by neighbours, although it was light.

Stanfield drove away, parked, put on his long trenchcoat and took a screwdriver and some heavy cord from the boot of his car. Then he returned to the house on foot, went into the rear lane and quickly climbed the wall. It was a risk, but for a primely promising job you took risk. And you looked for the most suitable aids. So, the crossbow. This weapon was quiet and good and if used right a marvellous stopper, ask history. Everyone said folk giving pursuit hated seeing an arrow suddenly sticking out of their chest or throat like the Wild West, and always froze to stare at it with horror then tug. Something similar would most likely apply to dogs. He saw no way this project could work without the bow. Besides, it was too late to change. You could not switch to firearms just like that, even if they were on tap, and this job was not right for guns, anyway. Find the guns, you then had to find silencers to fit, because of neighbours. Hopeless in the time. Naturally, one change there would have to be, a replacement for Lester. But you could not expect to recruit someone in a rush who would be useful in all the general ways and also hold a diploma in crossbows. It had to be Stanley himself.

He waited for a couple of seconds behind a tree close to the back wall, glancing around systematically at the bedrooms of other houses in case he had an audience, and listening for anything that suggested alarm. Things seemed clear and he moved quickly towards the little shed. There was a padlocked door and he unscrewed the hasp plate and went in. It took less than three minutes to find the crossbow beneath a wind-surf board, plus eight arrows and a quiver. He strapped this on under his coat and put all the arrows in. He lashed the crossbow to his chest under the coat with his cord so he would have two hands for climbing the wall again. Taking a quick look around the rest of the shed, he came across a 9 mm Spanish Modelo BS automatic jammed inside a rolled survival tent. The gun seemed to be in good shape and had six rounds in the magazine, though it could hold eight. If Lester had used two somewhere this pistol might be a liability. Would Lester be mad enough to hang on, even if it had been fired in an outing? That was unlike him. Perhaps he had not been able to get hold of more than six. Stanfield put the gun in his trenchcoat pocket – probably best for everyone it should not be left here. He screwed the lock plate back into place, did the wall and left. Walking to the car he felt bulky but sound.

Of course, Lester had said the crossbow was not easy, especially fired standing. Aim could be tricky. It took two hands and was awkward. But this would be that grasping, fly, money-mad jerk making out he was a specialist and worth more, though he swore he had never used a crossbow before in a job, and definitely did not have it on his dossier as a known flair. This could have brought Harpur straight to him pressurizing as aftermath to the dogs, and who could tell whether Lester was a talker? Well, anyone could tell now. He wasn't.

Lester had told Stanley he did a lot of target work up in Dobecross woods and Stanfield decided he should have a few sessions there, too. He loved the feel of the quiver thumping against his thigh. It seemed to put him into the famous military tradition of distant periods. A pair of dogs meant you must be able to get the shots off fast, and they had to be spot on. Part of his practice should be drawing the arrows from the quiver swiftly, not just aiming. He had the idea you could get a kind of double-loaded crossbow, whoosh, whoosh, but it was not one of those. This was why he had brought the automatic, in case things came to the worst, and they often did. These animals would be rushing at you, and you would only have their chest width to hit, not body length. All right, those old-time warriors used to do wonders with the crossbow, but the Alsatians would be attacking in the here and now, not dreams of the sodding Middle Ages. Stanley had seen the dogs on one of their recce trips, and they could definitely turn into spoilers if allowed. Two dogs were more than twice as bad as one because they thought they were a pack and had to act wolf.

He kept his sorrow suit on and in the evening drove back to the Magellans' house to give support and speak regret. That was only right, and he needed to do it, a bond with Lester. They had returned now and seemed really pleased to see him. He parked right outside. This was an open, worthwhile visit. Vernon Magellan brought out some right piss brandy from Ethiopia or Peru, two bottles, for Christ's sake, and they sat late talking of old times, when Stanley and Lester were boys and much more harmless.

'I heard all this somehow involves that questing slice of venom, Des Iles,' Vernon Magellan said. 'Our boy a random victim.'

'There are all kinds of rumours, Mr Magellan,' Stanfield replied.

Mrs Magellan did not cry while Stanfield was there, but her face looked sharp and wrung out. She had on bright clothes, obviously a kick against mourning, yellows, vermilion and blue, and they looked more terrible on her than they would have on most women. If she had been to the Rest Home like that it would hurt staff. 'Tell me this,' she said to Stanfield, 'do you honestly think we could have told him to stay clear of the original very nice guy?

How, Stan? Lester is a grown man, was a grown man. Didn't he move out from this family home where he was always welcome and happy to his own place, although in the same city? What influence could we have on him now? But the original very nice guy is banging the kid daughter of Ralph Ember. This is the tale. And the original very nice guy gets it and so does anyone who happens to be a friend of—'

'Panicking Ralph Ember couldn't do a coup like that, Marie,' Vernon Magellan said. 'Panicking could get het up about one of his children, but not do those killings. Panicking's got a rich image these days, doing a university degree, I heard. Panicking would garotte? Someone like that is going to stick coal in a man's mouth?'

'Ralphy could hire. He owns The Monty club and so on. That place he lives. He's got the loot to afford top-class violence. A man's young, vulnerable daughter befouled. That would enrage anyone.'

'Ember likes a bit of schoolgirl himself,' Vernon Magellan said.

'Not his own daughter?' she replied.

'No, no, God, no.'

'There you are then,' she said. 'Lester wasn't doing something with the original very nice guy, too, was he, Stan, Lester being, well, you know – I mean this way and that in intimacy matters, like so many nowadays, and so what?'

Vernon Magellan said: 'Police. High police, this massacre. A ploy to muddy the waters for those earlier ones. This was resolute, damn it, damn it. This was having the run of the city. We can't do a thing. They smash us and ours and laugh. This is corruption right through.'

'What do you think, Stanley?'

'These rumours really fly. There'll be some sorting out. Lester has earned that much.'

'I suppose that cow's superior she's got the original very nice guy at home, not farmed out, as she'd no doubt call it?' Mrs Magellan asked.

'She spoke very well of Lester, believe me,' Stanfield replied. 'Saw him as fiendishly ruined potential.'

'In his quiet way,' Vernon Magellan said.

'Exactly,' Stanfield replied, 'and certainly no less for that.'

Chapter Six

Harpur had a morning get-together with Jack Lamb, at one of their rendezvous spots. This time, Lamb had nominated a Second World War concrete blockhouse on the foreshore which they used now and then. Occasionally, Jack would inexplicably go off this place, then reinstate it. Harpur always let him choose, and Jack did like the military touch. Often he dressed to suit in superior army surplus. Any detective worth a tip let his informants pick the meeting ground, and Jack Lamb was the world's greatest. Informants carried the risk, so made the conditions. Lamb had phoned Harpur's house early to suggest a talk. 'Re your various grim troubles, Col.'

'Which are they, Jack?'

'Not on an open line.' These were probably the first words Lamb spoke as a baby.

In an elegant old-style cavalry officer's bum-freezer khaki overcoat, and black beret with some regimental badge up, he was already there when Harpur arrived. 'Stan Stanfield's looking for a recruit, Col,' he said. 'Well, actually it's Beau Derek doing the searching, but he teams with Stan, as you know. Searching in a rush, even carelessly. Well, would I hear if it wasn't carelessly?'

'You might,' Harpur replied. Jack needed acknowledgement. 'Recruiting for what?'

'Not known. But I'd note the timing, Col.'

'What timing?' Jack liked to be fed questions. They pointed up Harpur's ignorance or stupidity.

'Stanley did some low-level gangsterism in the South of France then came back and worked with the original very nice guy and Lester. He's lost a couple of partners.'

'The original very nice guy wasn't doing much these days, except the trafficking, of course, which kept him in blazers.'

'The original very nice guy heard much and made his selections. And Lester provided practical skills.'

'Stan's trying to replace Lester?'

'Staffing the kind of job grand enough to interest the original very nice guy and Stan is a sophisticated business, Col.'

Harpur said: 'Lester? That will be high-calibre burglary.'

'Along those lines.'

'Beau the brilliant to open the safe? Who told you he was recruiting in a rush?'

'If the tip came from the original very nice guy, perhaps they're going to do the place of some other big pusher, Col,' Lamb replied. 'He'd know who was taking plenty and when. A lot of cash about in several of those properties, for short periods on collecting days. The original very nice guy might have been able to signal the exact moment. He was talented with information, Col, and naturally tried to fuck up the competition.'

'Who told you Beau was recruiting for Stan?'

'And then what if this target got a hint of the job?' Lamb replied. 'They're all listening to whispers in the wind. He kills the original very nice guy and Lester to pre-empt and *encourager les autres*. There's your case wrapped up for you.'

It was raining and they talked inside the blockhouse, breathing God knew what long-established odours and peering towards each other in the bit of light. Lamb strode to one of the gun-ports and gazed out at the wide mud flats: pink, lime-green and grey with straggling, skipping, wind-whipped effluent, and, far off, the grubby sea.

Harpur had seen him do that before, just as he had often seen the Chief stare sadly into infinity and an uncontrollable future from his office window. Lamb always complained at having been too young for the war, and the tight aggression in his body as he bent forward now said he expected to fling back an imminent invader, despite low water.

'Gang killings?' Harpur said.

'Oh, I know you've got your theories, Col – Panicking looking after his daughter vendetta style, or Iles doing a doubler to confuse the picture, ahead of this outside inquiry from the Home Office or Inspectorate. Could Panicking really garotte, though?'

'Which outside inquiry?'

'Then Lane suddenly finds himself, I hear, wanting to be almighty at last, despite Iles. In its way marvellously brave.'

'Which practical skills, Jack?'

'Lester's? Oh, armament. Very interested in that. The gamut, not just guns.'

'Like?'

Lamb turned his back from his defence duties. With the bum-freezer he had on calf-length black riding boots. Harpur had never understood this taste for vivid costume, mixed with Lamb's almost manic security sense – his suspicion of telephones, the frequently changed meeting spots. Harpur was big but Lamb dwarfed him and in some of his special gear drew wondering attention in any landscape, was unmissable you could say, though that word chilled Harpur.

'A lot of these dealers keep large dogs, you know, Col. There's a new hybrid – Pushers' Alsatian, with twice as many teeth. It could be important to knock them over, but no noise.'

'A silenced gun?'

'Guns aren't the only weapons.'

Harpur said: 'Stan Stanfield—'

'That bloody imperial moustache. He took a taste for

30

my Helen once, wanted her to go back to France with him, and tried to get his hand et cetera forcibly into her knickers, so I owe him something.'

'Well, she *is* a very lovely girl, Jack.'

'What's that mean?'

'Jack, if this was assault, attempted rape, you should have told us, she should have.'

'*She* told *me*. I do it this way.'

Grasses had their ethics, especially Jack. They needed something beyond money and/or favours to make their treacheries acceptable to themselves. Most tried not to damage those who had not damaged them, but those who *had* damaged them they tried to damage for all time, preferably also for gain though not necessarily. It fell short of the Apostles' Creed but was a workable philosophy of life. 'And how *is* Helen?' Harpur replied.

'Brilliant. Further great strides in *l'art fang*. Such a help in the trade, Col.'

Lamb, who must be sneaking towards fifty, lived in his manor house, Darien, with an ex-punk kid, Helen Surtees. She could have been not much over eighteen when she and Jack started and by now probably knew enough about the rough confidentialities of the business to be kept on by him even when she would age into her twenties. Harpur himself tried never to discover anything about the rough confidentialities of Jack's business. That was an element in his own workable philosophy of life. Megan, Harpur's wife, dead now, used to find this 'police blind-eyeing', as she called it, sickening, and what she termed Harpur's 'terminal dependence on Jack Lamb'. But, yes, like grasses, police had ethics, too, if they wanted the information to keep coming. Now and then he missed Megan.

Lamb straightened up and went briskly towards the door, as if about to collect his gallantry medal from a grateful nation.

'Does Stanfield know you know he's recruiting, Jack? He can turn brutal. Where does your tip come from?'

Lamb replied: 'I'm going to look at something very lovely now, Col, which might lead to a deal. A Heckel pen drawing. You're welcome to come.'

'With you in those clothes?'

Chapter Seven

Of course, Erogenous Jones spat and refused to tail Iles, so Harpur decided to do it himself, certain he would be spotted at once. That way, the ACC could be alerted and Harpur would not actually have to tell him of Lane's rancid scheme to save his own soul. Harpur owed loyalties both ways, like any other nobody.

He and Erogenous had visited Lester's flat again and were walking back now. Harpur mentioned the tailing project as soon as they left on the return. Erogenous listened and did not answer then. Perhaps Harpur should have taken the hint, but who took hints from subordinates? Erogenous talked about the work they had just done at Lester's place. It was supposed to have been searched twice already, yet this time he found a couple of unused 9 mm bullets inside a stopped clock. Although they really laboured at it, levering floorboards, digging into mattresses and upholstery, they discovered nothing that could fire the rounds. 'Does it matter?' Erogenous wondered. 'He's dead, and not suicide with a 9 mm.'

'Guns often start a story. We've got nothing so far.'

'Lester had somewhere else to keep stuff?' Erogenous wondered, as they neared headquarters.

'This shadowing – a specific request from the Chief, Erog,' Harpur replied. 'For the well-being of the Force.'

'Fuck him, sir,' Erogenous answered. 'And fuck you if it's a specific request from you.' This was when he hawked and lusciously spat. Erogenous could make you suddenly see yourself as measly, often when you'd felt super bright.

There was no one in the Force Harpur valued higher, and not many in life generally.

'You're saying you couldn't do it unobserved?'

'Probably not, it being Iles. But that's not what I meant, is it, sir?'

'He gave you your leg up?'

'Oh, thanks. I'm bought? Yes, he got me Inspector against the odds, with your help. But just he's Des Iles, that's all. Obviously, he's evil off and on, mostly on, but he's also prime in this confederacy, the authentic tint of the outfit and I'm not in on any shit trick against him. Nor you, are you? Are you?' He shook the heavy heap of black hair and rubbed a shoe on his trouser leg. Inspector Jeremy Stanislaus Jones, Erogenous to all, had the CID man's customary love of beautiful footwear, and was in a grand pair of brown lace-up brogues today, decently polished but not absurdly. Of course, the original very nice guy also revered shoes so much it was mentioned in his file. Once, Harpur used to marvel that police and villains shared so many tastes. But why not? Take also this bias towards young girls: the Chief thought Iles had it, and could be right; and the chat said the original very nice guy did, too; and, apparently, so did the dad of the girl supposed to be involved with the original very nice guy, Panicking Ralph Ember, more crooked than diplomacy, though never convicted on anything major. And then, yes, there was Jack Lamb with Helen Surtees, and yes, yes, yes, Harpur himself, waiting on edge for his sweet student friend, Denise Pointer – as it happened a friend of Helen – to return full of warmth and need from university vacation.

'Who's the loud piece in comic jewellery who came knocking while we were there?'

'From the flat below. She must have heard us. Iles might have given her some quality attention. She was looking for him.'

'Women do, don't they, sir? Well, not his wife. She looks elsewhere. Anywhere.'

Harpur let that go. He said: 'Iles would want to know whether she saw anything, wouldn't he? For peace of mind.'

'What's that mean, "peace of mind"? Talking to neighbours is an obvious part of the investigation.'

'Right.'

'What you saying, Colin?'

'Think back to Jamieson and Favard, Erog,' Harpur replied. 'The Chief suspects the ACC might have—'

'Settled with them. So? Christ, we've all heard that fifty times, Col. The sort of myth to grow round anyone with stature. Lucifer. No evidence. You investigated, didn't you, sir? That's good enough for me. Oh, yes.' He gave that a good boom. 'And even if he did see them off, it was only two cop killers. Best thing that ever happened to them. The whole Force loved it.'

'Except now we've got two more.'

Erogenous winced. 'And the Chief honestly believes he did those, as well?'

Yes, Lane did, or said he did. He still wanted Iles dogged. Suddenly and late and so understandably, Lane was sold on enfranchizing himself. 'The Chief thinks smokescreening – to suggest it wasn't Iles first time but the same gang-war killer, one who leaves trademarks. The coal and garotte stick.'

Erogenous said: 'The chat is it's Panicking Ralph Ember, getting fatherly over his daughter, possessive.'

'There's a lot of chat.'

'Seen Panicking?'

'I will. Some chat says we're in for an outside Force nosing here.'

'Again? You and Iles can see that off. Especially you, sir. Or especially Iles. What's following him to whores to do with it?'

'We don't know it would be to whores, do we?'

'Yes,' Erogenous replied.

'Well, yes.'

Erogenous grew suddenly very concerned. 'Look, you won't try tailing him yourself, now will you?'

35

'What else? Starting tonight.'

Erogenous stopped for a second on the pavement, and Harpur waited: 'Christ, you can't tail, sir. Look at you. Your size. The heavy of clumsy heavies. That huge face and punch-drunk walk.' Erogenous started forward again and imitated a shambling, splayed gait, insulting to his magnificent shoes. 'He'll see you and— Well, see you and think you've gone over. You want that, sir?'

'Gone over where?'

'You really want him to believe that of you?' Erogenous replied and seemed about to spit again, but humanely swallowed it.

That evening Harpur watched Iles's house, Idylls in Rougement Place, but he seemed to stay in. Next night at about ten o'clock the ACC drove out alone and Harpur, in an ancient unrecognizable Astra from the pool went after him. He wanted to be seen, he did not want to be seen. After what Erogenous said it had become important that he could shadow Iles and stay unobserved, at least at first. Damn it, he still owned all the skills. Rank had not addled him, like Lane. The ACC drove down towards Valencia Esplanade, or the Valencia as it had come to be called. Now the area had so coarsened, 'Esplanade' seemed a mockery. Iles parked and then strolled towards where most of the best girls operated, obviously with steam up. Harpur followed on foot, keeping well back, using the shadows and doorways pretty well. It was years since he had done anything of this sort, and it thrilled him to find the instincts still there. The pavements were crowded with people girling or clubbing or just slumming. Pimps, white and black, disappeared quickly when they spotted Iles, and maybe Harpur, but the two of them caused no other stir. Of course, Iles might be a familiar sight.

The ACC turned into a side-street, Dring Place, and, leaving just the right pause, Harpur followed. Two fist blows took him immediately, one just under the right eye, the other square on the chin, though he did not know

36

that until he came round in the gutter. Iles was crouched over him, assuring a couple of women winos in tarnished shell-suits that Harpur would pull through and fanning him with Harpur's own wallet.

'Someone was following me, Col,' Iles said.

'Yes, I was.'

'I know.'

'Christ, well why—?'

'Lane sent you? Clearly. He'll see you marked and know you did your best. But, plainly, Harpur's best will never be enough against D. Iles. He'll realize that now. This will finish it. Can you get up?' He helped Harpur stand and brushed down his clothes.

'I feel appalling,' Harpur said.

'What you need is a girl.'

'Oh, I—'

'Ah, faithful to your student friend? She still bringing you comfort? I suppose you could marry her now. But would she want that? You're in a seedy, very dangerous job, Col, and that luscious kid has to take a lifetime view. Plus, would your puritan daughters wear it?' Iles waved to a couple of women. 'They're rough but they're ready around here.'

'Well, I think I'll—'

'You're not going to desert old Dessy Iles, are you, Col?'

The question was about here and now and tarts and more than here and now and tarts. It needed a deep answer. Harpur said: 'But what age would these girls be, sir?'

'Oh, nothing too old, Col. Don't worry. I hate that myself, as a matter of fact. Though, then again, Elaine is a surprise, yet no child.'

'Elaine?'

'Beneath Lester Magellan. Remember? You've got money? But no worry, they're very trusting. With most you can put it on the slate. Will you want more than one?'

'Sir, as to – look, I—'

'You've nothing to apologize for, Col, gum-shoeing me in your funny way. If the Chief told you to do it, you do it. That's what the job means. Yes, we do have a problem with him, Col.' Harpur was bent over, half leaning against a wall, struggling to recover. Iles took out a handkerchief from the breast pocket of his fine grey pin-stripe suit and held it tenderly against the cut under Harpur's eye. 'I've seen you looking worse, Harpur. You've got the kind of underclass face that *ought* to have scars. Don't fret, the girls won't mind. They're welcoming and put up with all sorts, believe me. Yes, a problem with Lane, the septic lamb. You'll remember that wonderful analysis by George Savile, Marquis of Halifax, in *Character of a Trimmer*, seventeenth century.'

'Will I, sir?' He felt a little less dazed now but could not risk standing unsupported yet. His hearing on one side seemed very poor, though, and perhaps permanently done for. But when he lifted his hand to his ear he found what he hoped was only thick mud from the gutter clogged there, and wiped it away.

'Oh, certainly you will,' Iles said. 'Goes like this, doesn't it? "Without laws the world would become a wilderness, and men little less than beasts; but with all this, the best things may come to be the worst, if they are not in good hands." *Not in good hands*, Col. Obviously, Savile was thinking of Lane. *Without laws*. Do you believe the Chief can uphold laws against the brilliant enemies we now face? *Little less than beasts*, he says, you see, not little more. Would you have us who watch the populace become less than beasts? Not Harpur. So, you and I, but especially I, are sent to counter the Chief, fortify him.' Iles's voice rose, joyously: 'Here I am, girls, and with a dear friend tonight. One of nature's sweetest. They say he looks like a blond Rocky Marciano, but can't take a punch as well. Who's Marciano, you ask. Ancient history to you, kids, thank Heaven.'

Chapter Eight

At first, Stan Stanfield had no luck thinking of someone for The Pines job to replace Lester Magellan. He considered giving up. Not giving up the job, it was too sweet and ripe, but giving up the idea it must be three. Could two handle it, just himself and Beau Derek – more confidentiality, bigger splits? Lester had been in mainly because he knew crossbows, but up in the woods every day, and often twice or three times, day and night, like tonight, now, Stan was learning this weapon, and accuracy and loading speed had really come on. *Lester est mort, vive Stan*, you could say, if you knew French.

First tonight he practised loading, with a smooth, easy arm arc movement, which he reckoned like ballet or a good bull-fighter's best ploys. This crossbow flair he might never have found, but it was in him, waiting from birth, how George VI did not know he could be a decent king until forced when Edward fucked his way out of the job. Stanfield aimed swiftly and put the two bolts twice into the square of brown cardboard fixed to a tree, and then on the third try hit it once and struck the bark with the other, but just above the target. That did not worry him because by the time he made this third pair of shots his arms were tired and he had corrected by tensing, so the arrow went high. At The Pines there should be the two shots and no more, and he could give them his best. For the practices, he wore what he would have on on the night, boiler suit, boots, gloves, to get used to conditions in detail, with the automatic in his pocket. Close familiarizing was vital to him, and he always did it, whatever the job. The soft leather gloves did not hamper him and there would be no mask because nobody was going to be at home. Wearing a mask in such a genuine wood would have seemed ugly, anyway, a crude breach of the surroundings, even at night.

Stanley had always known the crossbow was wonderfully quiet – why it was chosen. What he also enjoyed, though, was the tiny click when you pulled the trigger, and the happy buzzing sound a bolt made as it flew from the bow, like a grouse rising, but much less. Getting off his series of two shots, he always thrilled to the healthy, rural peacefulness, accompanied only by a gentle rustling of branches, and perhaps the rat-tat of growth-giving rain. And then these four tiny noises – click, whirr, click, whirr – so finely full of death.

He opened his thermos flask and gave himself a deserved little rest now, sipping the coffee, seated on the ground. When he first started practising, he came only in the day, but soon realized this was stupid. The job would be night and he must get used to darkness. Also, at first, he used a sheet of paper for his target. Then he saw this favoured him – much too clear. These dogs were brown and black, so he switched to the cardboard. Of course, they would be racing hard at him, not stuck on a tree, waiting nicely. This mobility he could not mimic unless he found a few dogs running in the town, but that might bring attention, what with the squealing and owners' reasonable anger, plus possible difficulty getting arrows back. The point was, the wood was probably darker than the grounds of The Pines, because of security lights, so the conditions should balance out. Also, the pieces of cardboard were only about a foot and a half square, much smaller than those bloody dogs. In his head, he had given them soft names – Fluffy for the long-haired bugger, and Bonzo the other – hoping this would take away a bit of the terror they caused, but it had not worked. Never mind, as well as the bow he would have the gun. He had not fired it, but everything seemed all right, and he did not need practice with that. He brought it with him on these outings, just to feel the presence in his pocket. Exactly how it would be at The Pines.

The wet soaked through the trousers' layers to him. He screwed up the flask, stood and quickly fired twice more. Two hits, smack middle. Could Lester have matched him tonight? Obviously, they had had no choice about including Lester, because this job started with information from the original very nice guy, and he expected Lester to take part. Stanfield recovered the arrows and target, took off his boiler suit and put it with the flask, the bow and his gloves into the suitcase, then made his way down the hill and back very roundabout, very eyes-open, to the car. Nobody lurking, and the BMW all right. Each trip he parked in different spots, nothing tell-tale.

He drove down towards the coast to meet Beau Derek around eleven thirty for a chat about this number three. Or maybe no number three. Usually, the only place for that kind of private night get-together would be Panicking Ralph Ember's club, The Monty, Shield Terrace, with a few good drinks from one of Ralphy's special bottles. In fact, if you did want a third you would find the kind of fit lad at the bar there any night in a suit, ready to negotiate. But now, listen to these crazy yarns that Ember did the original very nice guy to get him off and out of his daughter Venetia, and also Lester because he happened to be around. True, some people definitely turned evil about hot approaches to daughters or girlfriends, but Stan could still not believe this of Panicking. Someone might like the world to think it was Ember, though. Stanfield was sure Ember lacked the rare brilliance so plain in those killings. If he did not, why would he need a degree?

Just the same, some other rendezvous spot tonight. Beau Derek thought they would be all right instead at an old concrete blockhouse on the foreshore from the last war. The Monty would be too sensitive for a while because, if it was true Ralphy did the killings – and if it

41

was not true but being talked – he would expect come-back and might think Stan Stanfield was it, having been so warmly confed with the original very nice guy and Lester. Probably Ralphy had forces ready there, he could afford that, and at this stage Stanfield wanted no violence.

He parked a respectable distance from the blockhouse and looked around. Beau seemed to be standing outside against the wall in what would have looked like thought-fulness if it was not Beau. Why not get out of sight, then, if the idea was secrecy? Beau could use his brain quite well up to a point, but not right through. Stanfield moved his case from the back seat into the boot and made sure he had done the double lock. You could get a second fitted on any up-market new car these days, separate keys. Guarding car possessions was a main skill of the new era, displacing snooker. He walked. It was mucky here and he was glad he had not changed out of the working boots.

Beau said: 'The original very nice guy thought eighteen, maybe twenty.'

'Seventeen maybe eighteen. Let's go in out of the how-itzers, all right?'

They entered the blockhouse. It took some of your breath at first. People used this place for all sorts. Beau said: 'That's still about six grand each, if we have three. Only a night's work, Stan.'

'Except I'm at crossbow-training all hours.'

'You'll have a nice knack there, for the future,' Beau said. 'There's a few who could help us. I'd feel better at the safe if one's in the house with me, Stan, and one outside, or why not two outside? That's good all-round sentry cover, and a driver, ready to go. Kenward Knapp come back too early, Stan, and find an empty car open, ready for the off, he pulls a few wires out and we're shafted. I can't be running over open ground with brutes at my arse, like Devils' Island.'

'The dogs will be dead.'

'Other properties and farms up there keep guard dogs, Stan. This is a rich area. Hue and cry.'

42

'You think Kenward would bring neighbours in to chase drugs money? Christ, a stipe magistrate lives close, why we can't have the Alsatians calling for aid. Kenward wants him to know his business? Cash like that in the house, it's got to be dirty.'

The last time Beau Derek did gaol was through an undermanned job, or so he said – why he wanted three regardless, or even four. Of course, there would have been four shares in early plans, before the deaths. Three would rob, but the original very nice guy had required credit as 'based on an idea by'. Maybe there'd be a token for his mother now. Maybe. A token.

Beau said: 'You've got the confidence, the cheek, Stan, which is great. But I can't work like that.'

'You work great, Beau.'

Derek was called Beau, meaning beautiful in French, not because he was, or horrible, but because of the daft name of some actress, Bo Derek, and his name being Derek. Beau was not an actor, was bald-dark, not blonde like Bo, and dimmish but not girlish. Because of a poor childhood, Beau suffered from low expectations, and he would rather have an undangerous take with a small share than chance of a big share, but extra risk.

'Christ, I wish we had insight on this safe, Stan. A worry, coming to it cold. Kenward, he can afford the best. He needs the best, the bastards who get their eye on him.'

'Us bastards. You'll do it a treat, Beau.'

The darkness in this place and the smells could be lowering his morale. It was a mistake.

'If I can't crack it in the time, Stan. Think. Yes, I'd crack it in the end, but this is damn tight. Why I'd like a good watch outside, Kenward come back too soon.'

Stanfield never thought Beau Derek was wrong to want safety. What use the idea of a fat percentage if it got stuck as an idea? You could end up talking to Harpur in a room stuffed with very adjustable tape-recorders, or tarpaulin-covered on the pavement. Of course, then there would be another fierce civil libs question in Parliament on police firearming, but tarpaulin was tarpaulin. The crux question now, though, was did three operating or even more mean safety?

Stanfield crossed inside the blockhouse to one of the gun ports, careful where he put his feet, and stared out across the flats towards the sea. It was far back and invisible in the darkness. More than fifty years ago men in tin hats must have peered from here, expecting to see what they called Jerry. Life was nice and focused then – you had just one enemy, could shag the women's army and there were guns ad lib. The trouble with trying to find someone for a job too fast— Well, a million troubles, but the main one, you had to start trawling with total willy-nilliness, and how many might hear of it and spread? Then, if you were picking someone quick you might pick wrong, just because he was available and needed fast gain, and was not known to have ballsed-up major scale on some previous sortie. Or, again, choose one and you made an enemy of the other. Enemies talked. They made up for what they were missing by marketing what they had, and Harpur was always in this market. How that bastard Jack Lamb made his fat living and bought his women, such as Helen Surtees, and hung on to them, so long as he wanted. Or that's what he thought.

Beau said: 'I was thinking about Cyrus.'

Stanfield had also thought of him, top of the list, he had to admit, but didn't. He turned to face Beau, or what he could see of him. Beau was nice and small and thin, nearly lost in here or any dark spot, a brilliant burglar quality. 'Cyrus? Well, Cyrus is pretty solid, I'll give you that,' Stanfield said.

'And he drives. I'd do the talking to him. You, busy with the crossbow.'

Beau had rights to an opinion despite his mind because he was a gem with safes, and there would be a sticky one at The Pines, like he said. The original very nice guy told them an under-the-floorboards model in the so-called gallery-room, with a key lock, not combination. He said it like he knew but that was his style, yet he had never been inside The Pines, for sure. Would Oliphant Kenward Knapp invite another maxi pusher home for sherry and a talk about the safe, and what was the usual in his firm's collection plate? The original very nice guy might say key lock because if it wasn't he ought to have the combination, fucking know-all. He was not going to be there, in The Pines, when Beau got the boards up and took first look at the problem, with Kenward not far enough away. Well, of course, now, the original very nice guy was not going to be anywhere, the deeply missed coal-sucker.

'Cyrus can be very silent,' Beau said. 'He's not earning, and not with current fanny, so no chatter or questions there.'

'This is big money for him.'

'Some would be scared lifeless to try Knapp's place, but Cyrus has the valour.'

'Not try. Do.' Stanfield wanted to get out of this place and home to bed. He was growing fed up with the wilds and mud. Stepping away from the gun port, he said into the stinking shadows: 'All right, Beau, talk to Cyrus, but very oblique at first.' Was there a choice? A safe breaker in a tremor would be no use.

'Oh, great, Stan. I know he'll be OK.'

'How? Beau, you've been talking already?'

'Only put out a feeler or two. No detail. Would I, before we discussed, Stan? Just general, on availability.'

'Beau, the spread, for Christ's sake. Think of Lamb, think of Knapp himself. They're in networks, get signals. Did you say it was me?'

'Only in general terms, Stan. You're a selling point.'

'How, general terms? My name or not, Beau?' This bunker gave a big, blaring echo and Stanfield heard fright crackle in his words.

'I didn't say you, but Cyrus asked if it was. He knows a connection, you and me. I could see he wanted it to be you. He knew it would be a good job if it was you. So, when he asked I—'

45

'Didn't say yes, didn't say no?'

'Said I could not disclose at that stage.'

'But he knew?'

'He seemed happier, Stan. Happier than when all he knew it was me. Cyrus will be keen. He could be better than Lester, God rest his soul.'

'Anyone could be. Lester was just a famous fart.'

Chapter Nine

They drove out with Cyrus in a hired car to see the target. There would only be time for one recce visit, so Stanfield allocated a whole afternoon. Familiarity was important, especially when the next view would be in the dark and pressured. Geography was important, especially for the driver.

When they were a couple of miles away, Cyrus said: 'Kenward Knapp's got a place somewhere up here. You heard of Kenward at all?'

'Right,' Beau replied.

'Knapp, that's right,' Stanfield said.

'Quite recent,' Cyrus replied. 'He's very profitable now.'

Stanfield said: 'I thought you'd been told, Cyrus.'

'What? Told what?'

Beau said: 'To date as much as possible has been left general, Stan, like you wanted.'

Stanfield said: 'But I thought you told me you'd—'

'I said Cyrus would—'

'Christ, you mean we're doing Knapp's place?' Cyrus asked. 'Itself?'

Beau said: 'One property's like another, you ask me.'

'It upsets you it's Knapp?' Stanfield replied.

'I told Stan it wouldn't,' Beau said.

'People have tried,' Cyrus replied.

'Not with Stan organizing,' Beau said.

'This is six, seven grand each, Cyrus. Off-the-street notes, no story to tell. How often you heard of something like that, from an empty house? Equal thirds though

47

you're only just in. Here's The Pines now. I'll drive past slowly but not loitering. Three in a car, all male, hungry, is advertising. You can take a bit of a look, Cyrus, not too much, not at this stage. Beau not at all. I'll go up around the back lanes and we can get other views. No sketching, though. Memory's better every time.'

'Is he going to be there?' Cyrus replied.

'Now?'

'No, the night.'

'Of course not,' Beau said. 'This is not some— This is a prepared operation. This is information. Stan and I thought a long time before bringing you in, Cyrus, why it could seem lateish, but we know we were right. I mentioned valour to Stan.'

'Kenward's a bit mighty,' Cyrus replied. 'Wide domain.'

'He might be there now,' Stanfield said, 'not a collecting day, so we don't make a show, even in a not-known car.'

'Well, there's this tale Kenward did the original very nice guy and Lester because he knew they had something cooking for him,' Cyrus replied. 'Look, Stan, Beau, I—'

'It's balls,' Stanfield said.

'Fence either wood or wire right the way around the property,' Beau said as they passed, sing-song and almost enthusiastic, like some estate agent. He was in the back with Cyrus, and Stanfield saw in the mirror that Beau gazed ahead, speaking from recollection not gawping at the house but Cyrus stared out, taking it all in. How it should be. Now and then, Beau did it like he had been told, but you never knew when. In the mirror, distorted a bit, Cyrus looked older, say thirties instead of twenties, but a good tight-up face, hard, though not loony hard, and with a streak of dread in it now, boyish collapse, suddenly hearing of Kenward. No bother. That could be scared out of him later.

'There are dogs,' Stanfield said.

'I heard of them,' Cyrus replied. 'Kept sort of, well, wild. Well, Kenward, he's got his Mother's Day side, but jaw-lock dogs is what you'd expect.'

48

'Very fortunately, these can be dealt with,' Beau said.

'When Kenward's out, which he will be, the dogs run loose in the gardens, grounds, contained by the fencing,' Stanfield said. They were drawing away from the house. Six bed, three bath?

Cyrus asked: 'We get through the fence and they come at us? They're gunned down? You've got some pieces? I'm keen on shooting dogs, they look so bloody betrayed when they're hit.' He had a good chuckle, seemed much easier suddenly, so it was heartening to hear him.

'Not like that,' Beau replied. 'I told you, subtle preparation.'

Stanfield said: 'You'll go around the side to where there's a wood section and make out you're climbing in, some noise. You won't be. Your place is outside with the car, as vital as any other, ask Beau. The dogs hear and come and try to get at you, but the fence is too high, just snarling, harmless leaping, nothing to it.'

'Bound to be or these dogs would be out and a public menace,' Beau said. 'Kenward has to be civic up here.'

'I'm a diversion?' Cyrus asked.

'While they're with you, Beau and I cut through the wire and get in towards the house. We need that few minutes. We'll be quiet at first, but then we start calling to bring the dogs from you to us. "Here doggie, doggie, come on lovely fellers, see what Uncle Stanley's got for you, Fluffy, Bonzo." You go back to the car then, keep an eye all round and be ready to bang the pedal. You'll be there half an hour maximum, and probably less. Trouble and you use the horn twice. Trouble is any vehicle comes off the motorway on to their side road, that's any vehicle at all that time of night. Don't wait to see Kenward's gold fillings.'

'It will be much, much less than half an hour,' Beau said. 'Stan sees off the dogs.'

'The information – it tells you about the safe as well as the rest?' Cyrus asked.

'Location, exact,' Beau replied.

'But type or combo?' Cyrus said.

'Beau can handle anything.'

'Half an hour's the worst scenario. Ten minutes,' Beau said.

'Entry has to be quick,' Stanfield said. 'They're going to bark at you, but it mustn't be for long. We don't want notice.'

'You said sees them off,' Cyrus replied.

'This is very sweetly, very silently, hail and farewell,' Beau said. 'Perhaps just a couple of whimpers.'

'Crossbow?' Cyrus asked. 'Lester was good with crossbows, yes?'

'You don't have to worry,' Beau said. 'They won't be coming out through the broken fence. Anyway, you'll be all right in the car. Get there fast.'

The BMW was climbing through narrow lanes. 'No alarms on The Pines, obviously,' Stanfield said.

Beau laughed. 'Alarms!'

Stanfield said: 'Alarms mean police. Kenward wants them on the property? Think what he might have about the house. The product. And receiving. Cameras, microscopes, precision gear. Cyrus, don't forget he could drive the last bit lights-out. He's on edge nonstop, and might cater for problems every time he comes home. If the window's down he'll miss the dogs noising a welcome.'

'Why not get them to a section of wire fence and do them through it from outside, no peril?' Cyrus asked.

'Fair question,' Stanfield said. 'One reason we picked you, Cy, you're a thinker. One, the mesh is too narrow. Second, we can't have the corpses in view. This house has lights around. Cars pass. Dead dogs with arrows sticking up are a sight. They've got to be further in, near the house.'

'Good little surprises for Kenward,' Beau said. 'He'll think Sioux.'

They had almost reached a spot Stanfield knew where there were grand, overall views of The Pines. Cyrus said: 'If the original very nice guy and Lester got it because

50

Knapp knew they meant to do him, will he be waiting us? With friends. He won't believe that's the end. He'll expect replacements. Once he's a target.'

'Stan told you it's rubbish,' Beau replied. 'Stan's sure those deaths are Iles, like the others. Or maybe Panicking Ralph for these last two.'

'Oh, Iles,' Stanfield said. 'Done by someone with a huge and gorgeous soul, never Ralphy. You've got to consider the psychology profiles. The coal – Ember couldn't think of that touch, not even imitating. These deaths are top-rank political. Those two boys just happened to get caught in it. Ralphy's charming, but only a lucky nobody.'

They reached the high ground from where they could look down on the spread and stay well hidden by farm buildings and hedges, because, now he'd gone landed, Kenward Knapp would have very good binoculars to study wagtails. Stanfield had good binoculars with him, too, and, after a quick survey, passed them to Cyrus. The lad's hands looked pretty steady when he took them and he located his eyes all right. These were cruxy elements in a driver. He might earn his third.

From here you could see the size of The Pines and the shape and roll of the gardens, which would be, yes, grounds, more or less. The house was modern, say seventies, but not too ugly, and built around a very classy little grass and paved quadrangle with fountain where Kenward and boys from his firm would probably stroll, taking main-board decisions on crack. The gallery was along the west side, for sun in the afternoons, when Kenward might want to relax there totting up. Stanfield heard Knapp bought The Pines from a failed rag trader in 1992 when £50,000 plus came off the price and including all carpets and curtains, bringing it to £315,000.

Binoculars still up, Cyrus said: 'You're all right with the crossbow, Stan?'

'All right.'

'Stan will be prime,' Beau said. 'Whatever he starts he does it prime.'

'Starts? Stan, how long since you started?' Cyrus asked.

'It's something you've got or you haven't,' Stanfield replied.

Cyrus handed the binoculars back and before he gave them to Beau, Stanfield took another, longer look. He moved his angle slightly because there was good sun today, and if you were careless the lenses gave a glint. Kenward would know about glints. The house and surrounds looked quiet and he could not make out the dogs. Maybe in one of the stables eating foals. Mostly, big pushers had nothing properties, because how did they quote income for a mortgage? They bought top cars cash and gold medallions on thick chains and did Eton or Roedean for the kids instead. The tale went Knapp had coughed a fine donation to one of the best schools where his son was and had his name italicked on a board by the head's study. It would look great in gold lettering, Oliphant Kenward Knapp. Probably half the kids in that school and more than half the staff smoked stuff Kenward marketed, but he would not brag there about this. Kenward was getting some of that upper-class reticence.

'I'm the new Lester?' Cyrus asked.

'We wanted, want, you as you, Cyrus,' Stanfield replied. 'Beau spoke very highly – various earlier sorties. Mind, I didn't need converting. As I said, the thinking, the steadiness.'

'But you must have changed things around at a rush,' Cyrus said.

'How's that, Cyrus?' Beau asked.

'Lester was never in on this,' Stanfield said. 'This isn't some patched up, slapdash operation. You couldn't do something like that against O. Kenward Knapp, for God's sake.'

'Crazy,' Beau said.

'If Lester was the crossbow, he would be the one to go in with Beau, not handle the diversion. You would have been the outside guy then, Stan, banging the fence, nursing the car.'

'If, if,' Stanfield said, laughing. 'Lester Magellan had no role at all, going in, diversion, whatever.'

'Why should he?' Beau asked.

Cyrus said: 'The original very nice guy comes up with the information, so he wants Lester in, being mates, and to keep an eye on his cut.'

'You've got it confused through this tale about Knapp doing those two to stop them,' Stanfield replied. 'What it is, a tale. Was the original very nice guy the only bugger with insights? I don't think so, Cyrus.'

'We don't think so, indeed, Cyrus,' Beau said.

Knapp must have been brilliantly liquid when he bought the house, or knew a really fancy bank that would help, which would be screwing him now. Luckily, pushing and habits took no notice of recessions, so it was probably cash, maybe not even a cheque. Some of them thought police had an any-time way into bank statements, and that could be right. If cash, why didn't the original very nice guy get the tip when that little fortune was waiting at Kenward's previous place, a much more burglarable hole in Arthur Street, close to where Harpur lived, as a matter of fact? Six figures was so much more worthwhile and dignified than five, and he could not have kept these sodding fangs there.

'You bought a crossbow for the job, Stan?' Cyrus asked. 'That going to be remembered?'

'I've always had one or two. Hobby as much as anything. Nice weapons, and all the history in them. I just needed a little refresher course.'

'Here's Kenward now,' Beau said, with the binoculars to his eyes, 'inspecting the estate. The twat's got jodhpurs on, Stan.'

'There going to be switch cars?' Cyrus asked.

'Again a sharp question I don't resent,' Stanfield replied. 'We think over-elaborating. This is not police pursuit – nor any pursuit at all. We don't have to beat a squad of vehicles, even if things went wrong.'

'They can't,' Beau said. 'This money's filthy. He can't make any show.'

'We know you could lose anything that was behind us, Cyrus.'

'Want to look at him, Stan?' Beau asked, offering the glasses.

'I know him already.'

'Cyrus?' Beau said.

Cyrus took the glasses and gazed at Kenward. This time Stanfield thought not just the boy's hands but his body shook. 'Leaving aside losing the money, the story is he really loves those dogs,' Cyrus said.

'We hope you're going to stay with us and accept this clear-cut role,' Stanfield replied. 'You see, we've told everything now. Plus our one hundred per cent belief in you which it would be very sad to let go.'

'Of course he's going to stay with us,' Beau remarked.

Cyrus handed the binoculars back. Stanfield said: 'All right, I will give him a glance.' He watched Kenward for a while. 'Yes, a takeable-looking commodity. Our luck is he's at a big charity auction on the night. Can't miss it because he's Mr Generous and has to set the pace. Attempting to go respectable. Oh, sure, there's a positive side to Kenward, but, obviously, it would be very wrong to let him keep what can be taken.'

'So true,' Beau said. 'Sometimes you sound just like the New Testament, Stan.'

'You mean, "But the greatest of these is charities"?' Stanfield replied.

Chapter Ten

At a bit after midnight, when her father was still working at The Monty and her mother asleep, Venetia Ember let herself quietly out of their house, Low Pastures, and set off on her mountain bike for Harpur's address, which she had found in the telephone directory. She was astonished he appeared in the book. Police should keep their homes secret for safety. But there it was: C. Harpur, 126 Arthur Street, 705141. In any case, his wife was murdered in the station car park not long ago, reported on TV, obviously, so perhaps he did not believe in safety. D. Iles, the other high officer she had heard of and also needed to see, was not in the directory, perhaps too important. C. Harpur would do. At first, when she saw his number, she thought about telephoning. But this had to be face to face, for urgency and depth. Also, she did not know whether the phones at Low Pastures were bugged. Her father had all sorts of tricks. She wore an old black track suit, a black bobble hat over her fair hair and black school shoes, to merge in. She was weeping as she went down the drive, but quietly, and after a couple of miles put a stop to it altogether.

This was about the right time to go. Usually her father did not come back until after 2 a.m., so she would not meet him on the road. And police probably went to bed late because of night crime, so C. Harpur might be still up. This could not be done in the day or at a police station. When they lived in the flat over The Monty, she would see C. Harpur and D. Iles sometimes on calls at the club. Her father hated it. They seemed both the same, Harpur and Iles, hard and big headed the way police were, and in dark suits, but she had to find them now. Who else? She thought she would begin to cry again, and fought it again and beat it. There would be something dim about being on one of these tough mountain bikes and crying like a kid. She enjoyed cycling so late through quiet streets, but watched for police cars because they might pull her in if they saw her dressed so black, like a burglar, even though she had lights on and was on her way to a police officer.

The house in Arthur Street looked dark, and that badly upset her. During the ride she had decided that even if Harpur was asleep she would wake him, but now she wondered. It would be a cheek. All the same, she forced herself to go into the little front garden and wheel her bike up the path towards the front door. She could re-decide there. And then, nearer the house, she thought she heard music coming from the front downstairs room, volume low, although she still saw no lights. The curtains were not across and she tried a glance but could make out nobody. She was afraid to stare in. For a couple of minutes she listened to the faint music. Yes, it could be The Red Devils, rhythm and blues, playing in that world-famous LA bar, King King. One day she would get to LA. When she knocked on the door there was no answer, but after a while she thought she glimpsed for a second a face come almost to the window of that front room, someone checking, perhaps a boy about sixteen, no shirt on, keeping back in the shadows. She did not knock again, but waited, holding the bike to her like a shield. Suddenly, a light blazed in the room and a bit later she heard a door open inside and then the hall light was put on and through the glass panel she saw a girl coming to answer. She looked about Venetia's own age. Venetia seemed to remember the television said Mrs Harpur had a daughter, or maybe two, at school. When the girl opened the door, there was no chain on or anything like that, which also seemed shocking. Venetia made out a boy standing behind the girl, half in, half out of the room. They were both dressed all right now, but looked surprised.

'Please, I want Mr Harpur,' Venetia said. 'I know it's late, but—'

The girl said: 'I'm afraid he's not here. I can take a message, though.'

She sounded like she was used to telling people this at all hours. How to deal with the customers if C. Harpur was missing.

'It's very important,' Venetia replied. 'I'm extremely important in an important case of crime.'

'So, is it important?' the boy replied.

'I don't know when he'll be back. Not for a few hours. I can get a message to him,' the girl said.

A light came on upstairs and Venetia saw another girl, younger, in pyjamas, on the landing, staring down to the front door. 'What's happening?' she called.

'Someone for Dad, that's all.'

'Oh, that.'

'Go back to bed, Jill.'

But the young girl disappeared into a bedroom and immediately came out with a school raincoat over her pyjamas, then descended the stairs.

'Is the CD Red Devils?' Venetia asked. 'So deep.'

'Yes, called *This way up*. I'm Mr Harpur's daughter, Hazel. I can take a message. Jill's my sister.'

'You should ask her in,' the boy said.

'Is your father engaged in detection on an important case?' Venetia asked. 'Telly said he was in charge of the double murder.'

'This time of night? He's at a party,' Jill said. She was standing by Hazel now.

'Yes, do you want to come in, listen to the Devils for a minute?' Hazel asked. 'I expect you like Lester Butler singing?'

'Well, yes. But that name, Lester—'

'Like the one who was garotted,' Jill said.

'Is your father out enquiring into that matter?'

'We told you, he's at a party,' Hazel replied.

'A party? When it's so serious, and their funerals are this week,' Venetia said.

'Going?' the boy asked.

This one had to be so clever. Yes, yes, she longed to attend one of them. That boy would be amazed to hear this, probably. Her father would try to stop her, for sure. But it was her duty, a final act of loyalty and love.

'Police don't bother much about funerals, except their own,' Jill replied. 'There wouldn't be time for anything else. Bring the bike inside. This area. A model like that, they could get eighty-five for at Alfie's Mart.'

'Seventyish,' Hazel said.

She came out and helped Venetia bring the bike into the hallway.

'Do you want to say who you are, but not if you don't, obviously,' Jill said. 'We're used to that. You're not at our school, John Locke Comp, are you? Don't recognize you.'

'Venetia.'

'This is Scott,' Hazel replied.

They went into the big front room where the music was playing. Shelves full of books, mostly real, not paperbacks, took up three sides of the room and there were a lot of pictures.

Hazel nodded towards the books: 'We'll be getting rid of this lot as soon as ... Soon. Dodgy. They were our mother's.'

'I heard about that,' Venetia said.

'Yes, well,' Jill replied. 'Private school?'

Hazel straightened up the cushions on a settee and they all sat down, Venetia on the settee, Hazel and Scott on the floor, and Jill in a big armchair.

'Ralph Ember's my father, as a matter of fact,' Venetia said.

'Is this to do with Dad's work?' Hazel replied. 'He doesn't tell us a thing. Police are like that.'

'But if there's vital information, we could put you in touch, now, if you want,' Jill said.

The girls seemed quite kind and perhaps even the boy was not so bad, but it hurt Venetia the way they treated her like they were used to all sorts, even in the middle of the night. They did not seem to realize. They could be immature. 'More than information,' she said.

'We can let him know anything,' Hazel replied. 'Or give us a number and he'll call. Is your old man in the book?'

'Perhaps I shouldn't tell you why I'm here,' Venetia said.

'Tell Dad,' Jill replied.

And then Venetia could not stop herself weeping again. This time she sobbed noisily, really flat out, hopeless, gushing. She felt ashamed but also really deep. Hazel stood at once and went to put an arm around her shoulders. 'You're all right, here. What is it, Venetia?'

'Or don't you want to say?' Jill asked. 'A lot of these things are private.'

'Shall we send for Dad? He would come right away if he knew you needed him.'

Venetia fought to control herself again, but failed this time. She put her wet, snotty face in her hands. 'I am so very, very unhappy,' she said through her fingers.

Scott said: 'Jeeze, big suffering.'

'Button it, Scott, smart-arse jerk,' Hazel said and held her closer. 'Jill's going to make some tea, and then we'll take you where Dad is, or get him to come home. He won't mind.'

'You see, oh – perhaps a man I love has been murdered by my own father,' Venetia replied.

'Go make the tea, will you, Jill?' Hazel said.

'What people say,' Venetia went on. 'How can I—? Well, why I must see Mr Harpur.'

'Of course,' Hazel said.

'Does he know who killed Raoul?' She took her hat off.

Scott said: 'Is this the one they call—?'

'Raoul Caesar Brace,' Venetia replied. 'Yes, in the papers and on television. He was older than me. People didn't understand what he was really like. Honestly. Daddy didn't understand what he was really like. Especially Daddy. And now this terrible death I expect you heard about, having shocked the whole city, even the whole country. Or it could have been someone else did them. Someone important. In school some say it—'

'Are you at Corton House?' Jill asked.

'If Dad's handling the case he'll try everything he can,' Hazel said.

'Will he? Honest? Hazel, I expect you understand about love.'

'Well—'

'All so fine and true, but Daddy—'

'How much older?' Jill shouted from the kitchen, doing tea.

'Yes, older than me. That didn't matter. Why should it? Why? But Daddy—'

'What do they know about things, fathers?' Hazel asked. 'Too busy chasing it themselves.'

'Called him evil. I don't know what he meant. Do you?' Venetia asked.

Hazel said: 'Well . . .'

They listened to the music for a time. Jill came in with the tea on a tray. Venetia said: 'If you had seen Raoul I really believe you would have liked him. People said terrible things about him, I know that, but it was because he was so beautifully dressed always. Yes, jealous, that's all. Do you know, Hazel, he never even mentioned I was only fourteen, well, nearly fifteen. He treated me like twenty-five, even twenty-eight. Lovely grown-up gifts, especially a sapphire ring, yes, genuine. Dad threw them all out, I don't know where. Mummy? She would never go against Daddy. She's not afraid of him, but she believes in him. Sometimes I have to think – I just have to, Hazel – that he is the one who's evil, my own dad. You see? I don't want to believe that.'

Jill gave her some tea and she sipped it. She had stopped crying again.

'So I don't know who I can talk to. Not my dad or mum. I don't believe I was too young to be really in love, do you?'

'All kinds of crazy rumours about those deaths, Venetia,' Scott said. 'Some even say the Assistant Chief Constable, Mr Iles himself.'

'I heard that, too,' Venetia replied. 'This is everywhere, I know my dad says that. He hates that Iles. Says he's Satan with braid. Also girls in school said he did it. It's the big buzz. Will police really look then, or look the right way? Dad always says they take care of one another. I don't mean your father, but mainly. Or they'll blame my father, even if it was this Mr Iles?'

'Of course they'll look,' Hazel said. 'If it's our dad, he'll look properly. Of course he will. Don't talk like that.' She started to yell. 'And, Scott, I told you before don't speak of Desmond Iles in that stupid, evil way, spreading shit and pretending to be shocked.'

'Oh, you and that Iles,' Scott replied. He tried to yawn, being cool. 'Older than your father, for fuck's sake, and grey.'

'What?' Venetia said.

'Nothing,' Hazel said. 'Nothing at all. Scott, I won't have this. It's so mucky, so false. Venetia, don't listen to them all. Desmond Iles is ... oh, a bit mad, but deep down OK. Listen, we can take you to see both of them. Put a stop to this rubbish now. Now, now, now.' She punched out towards Scott, though not meaning to reach him, only a sign. 'Dad's at a party in the Iles's house.'

Venetia felt sick. 'At Mr Iles's? I mean, regardless? Is this to show they couldn't care less, the two fingers? Just before the funerals?'

'You could be right there, kid,' Scott said. 'You must know Iles already.'

'Des Iles has been elevated to some top rugby referees' panel, that's all,' Hazel replied. 'Rugby's one of his things.'

'Tell us about the others,' Scott said.

'He heard yesterday, and they're celebrating,' Hazel replied. 'Refereeing, fairness, are so major with him.'

'Is that it, really?' Venetia said.

'Come on, we'll go now, all of us. We'll get our bikes.

There's an old spare one for Scott, if he wants to come, bitter sod. Jill go and dress.'

'Will they mind?' Venetia asked.

'Iles is always hot to see Hazel,' Scott replied.

'Oh, get stuffed, Scott,' Hazel said. 'Didn't he lend you a suit for my mother's funeral?'

Chapter Eleven

Harpur had thought from the start that violence was likely at Iles's party, but never a killing. For God's sake, this was the home of an Assistant Chief Constable, with the Chief himself present and the Chief's wife. It could be seen, *was* eventually seen by the court, thank God, as part accident, with the verdict manslaughter not murder. But the death was a death, just the same, and the knife a knife. That should never have been brought out of its hiding place, should never have been brought to the party at all.

Erogenous Jones's live-in girlfriend, Jane Vanteaux, did not even see the dying or the death, because apparently she had drifted upstairs with Sid Synott during the political charades and they only reappeared when it was too late. This one had been like most of Iles's lively parties, but with the sudden, terrible deathly extra.

An outside inquiry into the Force was certain now. COP KILLS COP AT BOSS'S MIDNIGHT MANSION RAVE, the *Star* said, and the party turned symbolic. You had Sarah Iles naked to the waist giving him mouth-to-mouth for more than ten minutes on the wide front lawn, both thick with blood. Some of Iles's appalled big-wheel Mason and sporting guests in leisure clothes stood grouped around watching with their women. The rest huddled inside, comforting one another. They drowned trauma in malt and wondered where was safety now, if police knife attacks happened at a senior officer's first-class property. Probably neighbours tried to gape through the trees from upstairs windows all over Rougemont Place, intrigued by yells and ambulances. When, eventually, Jane Vanteaux did realize what had happened, she was unstoppably loud with sorrow and guilt.

Inevitably, as the stories were passed on, people would ask deep questions about police behaviour, and this uneasiness was bound to spread. Harpur feared Lane could fall on the lawn with a stroke or heart attack through shock. He was always a grubby colour, and lately had come to see ruinous signals everywhere that law and order were done for and the dash to chaos quick-ening. For him, this shambolic knees-up at Iles's house would scream that message. At Lane's rank they looked behind the immediate to themes and it brought stress.

Iles himself attempted to get between the two on the lawn and stop it, and was cut in the arm by a stray blow. This pair were nimble and strong and skirted him easily. They were determined on each other and long past caring about orders. The knife, only one of course, had appeared very late. Until then, everybody let the fight bang on: just routine, unspecific rage and boozed, way-off punching. Parties at Idylls often went like this – 'hump and thump soirées', folk in the canteen called them, and Iles liked the physical. But it was the ACC who also sensed first the weapon was coming – realized that Ned Bixton in his sort of work might always have it on call – and, so, suddenly sprinted to intervene, squawking genialities. Harpur, slightly slower on the uptake, followed. Half a minute later Erogenous was dying, and in a minute he had gone.

Iles went down on his knees at once alongside him on the grass, and tore at Erogenous's shirt to get to the wound. Blood rolled like a spring and Iles struggled to fold the front of the shirt into a plug. Harpur joined him. The ACC was weeping, first time Harpur had ever seen that, or even close. He pulled his own shirt off and made a ball, but in a second or two it was sopping and useless. Erogenous wheezed feebly, coughed feebly, seemed to try to speak a word, maybe 'Jane', maybe 'insane', dredged for breath through a helplessly bubbling throat, and then went silent.

Sarah Iles shoved Harpur and her husband aside, snarling some sort of bright abuse at Iles, and both men stood up. As though imitating Harpur, she removed her expensive lavender-blue lamb's wool sweater and would have handed it to him, then saw the mess he was in and flung it from where she was crouched up at one of the rugby wives. 'Take a pass, hooker,' she said. Bra-less, she got her face down to Erogenous's, neglecting the flow from the wound, and jammed her lips on his. What it might look like from one of the bedroom windows in Rougement Place God knew. And what it was was worse than anything they thought.

Discreetly split from Sid now and tidied up again, Jane Vanteaux came out alone from the house on to the lawn, smiling decorously in search of her partner, and also misread the scene. She bellowed a chapter of filthy curses at Sarah, Erogenous and, what could have seemed to her, *exhibition* spectators. Then, abruptly, she cottoned and the shouting turned to agonized wails. 'Me, I should be doing that,' she howled and lunged to get Sarah off him, tugging at her bare shoulder. Sarah swung a fist, trying to punch her in the knee, and did not move her mouth from Erogenous's. After a little while someone pulled Jane away, still keening. Harpur's shirt fell from Erogenous's chest and lay alongside him. Sarah broke off to spit a great mouthful of his blood on to the grass, spattering her breasts, belly, arms and hands, then went back to him, occasionally turning her head aside again to clear her mouth. Was it what was needed? But nobody else came forward with anything else. Presumably none of Iles's non-police guests was a doctor or even rugby cuts man. Afterwards, the Chief's wife said she was sure she heard Erog – Inspector Jones as she called him – speak Lane's name just before death, indicating his grand, unwavering devotion.

Of course, Iles had deliberately laid on conflict, but not

this much. As soon as Harpur arrived at Idylls in the early evening he could see the picture. The refereeing leg-up, if it existed at all, was nothing. Iles had called this do to flaunt and extend the gulf in the Force; and to show that, as ever, Iles was happy and supreme on his side of it, possibly unbeatable. He had almost all his people there – Erogenous, Mike Upton, Tarr, Vivienne Aitken, Diamond, Sam Oxford, Sid Synott and Harpur himself: Iles would think of Harpur as being on his side, probably, and most likely that was fair. Yes, most likely. Garland was looking into new aspects of the original very nice guy murder tonight and absent. This might be lucky because nobody could say where his loyalties went, except to himself in tubfuls: what being a whizz kid meant.

Iles's party said, 'Up Yours Then' to the Home Office, 'Up Yours Then' to the Inspectorate of Constabulary, 'Up Yours Then' to any investigating officer from outside and above all 'Up Yours Then' to Mark Lane. It was what you would expect from Iles, one of his standard, blazing gestures: harsh, somewhere between foolish and crazed, unflinching, brave, pathetic. Life-threatening, as it turned out. Some of these Iles groupies were low ranking for one of his parties, but the rugby connection let him bring in Sid Synott and Carl Diamond, both good players, and Vivienne because she did the food for the Force club. Among the other guests were some useful wire-pullers from local life, including an editor.

In the middle of the lawn, lit from all the uncurtained downstairs windows, Ned Bixton had staggered from a left jab, then suddenly produced the knife. It was a mad, nearly unbelievable act. Probably, he had genuinely never meant to use it. The show would have been all – anything to scare Erogenous and subdue him. But, of course, liquored up, Erogenous could not be scared or subdued. Even when sober it was famously difficult to frighten and subdue him: why he had been such a titanic cop. Anyway, now, he had glanced at the knife and then immediately moved forward to try to disarm Bixton. The move forward was a lurch, though. At the trial, Bixton's defence would say a drunken Erogenous had virtually fallen on to the knife, and the jury believed it. Harpur half believed it, too, and wanted to believe it altogether. Of course, the knife should never have been there at all, so Bixton still had to go down for something.

Bixton revered the Chief, and naturally Iles had invited some of Lane's backers as well as the Chief and his wife themselves. Iles abominated unfairness and peace, and it would have saddened him to see no hope of confrontation. Some had come who hated and feared him for all kinds of meaty, cogent reasons. For months or longer they had pressured Lane to get him out any way he could. They were Rowles, Chat-up Charlie Hill, Bixton, Seabourne and Cave, sometimes Lane's *aide*. It would be these who had finally influenced Lane to move against Iles, in his own skulking, doomed style.

Bixton's life would have depended a hundred times on immaculate self-control, and Harpur did not understand at first how he went the way he did tonight. Ned spent great stretches of his time working out of touch under cover, mostly anti-drugs, and was normally one of the most disciplined and calculating people Harpur knew, a great detective. Like Iles, Harpur did understand, though, how Bixton came to be carrying a knife. Self-preserving habit. In interrogation later, Bixton said not very much, but perhaps just enough. 'I would never have used it, but I couldn't let him win, not in public like that. The sight of it was supposed to stop him.'

'Not Erog,' Harpur had said.

'No. But they're traitors who help a devil and hinder the man holding decency together. I work in shit, see not much else, so I fight for good when I find it – shit-scared shit will win.'

'I've heard Mr Iles say the same.'

'Good's not what Iles was about, nor Erogenous, except off and on, and that's not enough any longer. I don't know about you, sir, or Francis Garland. Fistwise, Erog was going to beat me. It couldn't be, Col. That would have signified too much. Why didn't he just back off, let it rest? Did he want suicide?' *That would have signified too much*. More symbolism. Now and then even Harpur felt sanity was on holiday, let alone law and order. Chaos had already moved in and put its feet up, maybe.

Sarah abandoned Erogenous and stood, exhausted. She began to weep now, too. Her fair hair on one side was matted and stuck to her cheek. Iles took off his ripped jacket and helped her on with it. He would loathe the smell of gallantry in that. His shirt-sleeve was bloodstained from the elbow down and a droplet hung dark from his gold cuff-link. 'Oh, how can this be, Colin?' Mrs Lane asked, her kindly face full of pain. 'Desmond injured, also, look. And you – your own face marked.'

He explained away the bruising done by Iles at the Valencia, as he had already explained it to the Chief in the office. 'Some trouble with a prisoner in the cells. I fell. My own fault.' In addition, he had reported to Lane that Erogenous tailed Iles unobserved several times and discovered nothing of use to the Chief, only ordinary social visits with Sarah and their child and a trip to his shrink.

And then, as Harpur was speaking to Mrs Lane, he was astonished to hear Hazel's voice. 'Dad, what's happening?' He had not seen her and the other three approach behind him. Their bicycles lay piled near the front gate. 'Your shirt? This fancy dress? You're a tramp? What's Sarah doing in that coat? Oh, God, God, is that Erog?'

Sarah, recovering a little, said: 'He was a lovely man.'

'Well, we know,' Jill sobbed. 'Is this the foul, cruel, cruel feud?'

Sarah put the arm in Iles's sliced jacket sleeve around her, good serge fluttering. 'Something's gone haywire, yes. Don't be too upset, love,' she said.

'Feud?' Mrs Lane replied.

Hazel turned deliberately away from the body and said: 'We came because this girl wanted to talk to you and Mr Iles urgently, Dad. She's Venetia Ember. Was that all right?'

'Yes, of course,' Harpur replied. 'I know her dad well.'

'To ask whether you knew or cared if my father did Raoul Brace, or was it Mr Iles,' Venetia said.

'Good questions,' Sarah replied. 'Col, Des, how say you?'

Venetia asked: 'You see why I worry? Why I don't know what to do?'

'You youngsters should not be out so late, not at all,' Mrs Lane said.

One ambulance had already arrived and another now made its way up Iles's drive with a police car behind. Poor cop sods called out to this one. Harpur felt relieved he had come alone tonight. Denise was back from vacation, but he was not ready to bring her to this kind of function yet, even if it had gone better. An ambulance moved slowly across the lawn towards Erogenous.

'Does Ralph know you're out, Venetia?' Harpur asked.

'I hope not.'

'You three should get her back to Low Pastures,' he said.

Jane climbed into the ambulance with Erogenous, looking scared that Sarah would want to go. Harpur saw Sid watching from the edge of the lawn, but he kept well out of things now. Sid could be sensitive and had a great marksman's smart reflexes.

Venetia said: 'Mr Harpur, did my father—?'

'You can rely on Mr Harpur and all the police to get to the truth, dear,' Mrs Lane replied. 'This is what they're for, isn't it?'

'I've heard of that,' she replied.

'Who you with tonight, then, Dad?' Hazel asked.

'Well, I'm with you now,' he said.

Chapter Twelve

When Venetia reached Low Pastures with the other three she could see that her father was home and still up. Sometimes on return from The Monty he would watch a television movie or video to relax himself for sleep, and there were still lights on downstairs. It could be tricky getting back in unobserved. He did not always close the living-room door to the hall, and she would have to pass that. She was not a climber, and in any case had not left her bedroom window open. The problems gave her an idea. She got rid of the two Harpur girls and Scott, telling them it would take her a little while to sneak in and they need not wait. Once they had gone, she turned the mountain bike around again and made her way back down to the city to see Raoul. It was not the kind of rather intimate trip to take police kids on, although they seemed nice and perhaps Hazel knew about full love.

This could be her only chance to be close to Raoul again, and she must do it. He would definitely have wanted that. She was his only love. Frequently he had told her this. Her father might be able to think up ways to stop her going to the funeral, especially if he had discovered she was out now for some secret reason. He was clever and nervy and might have checked the bike shed, even her room. She did not think she would ever find again the ring Raoul had given her. It was taken with all his other gifts by her father in that fury, but if she could be personally with Raoul for a while now, only the two of them, it would show they were bound together for ever, even without the ring. The ring was lovely, yet only a thing, only a sign, whereas they were linked in a deeper way, spiritual, and so it was a duty for her to be with him during his last days on earth. It might have been better to go to the funeral and show everyone her grief and loyalty, whatever people thought. But her father could be so negative, perhaps so destructive. She wanted to love him because he was still her dad – oh, she must, must love him – but it grew so difficult now.

Although Raoul lived with his mother and had not married, this did not mean he was immature, or anything like that. He had never taken her to the house, naturally, but she knew where it was and quickly found the street, and there was his lovely Daimler outside the house, so powerful yet smooth, deprived now for ever of its owner from new. How many girls in her school had had sweet love in a white K Daimler with cries of curlews through the open windows, not that she ever boasted? Also, Lester would sometimes lend them his lovely flat with great old movie posters on the walls, which were so atmospheric. The woman in the flat below pulled a sour face at her once on the stairs, such disapproval, but the ill thoughts of the world had to be gladly faced for love. Sometimes she thought that maybe Lester liked that neighbour, rather.

Venetia was careful again now, in case the police put a guard on the front door of those murdered, the kind of useless thing they would. Life had begun to seem such a horrible mess to her, the death of Raoul and Lester, and the awful sight on the lawn at Mr Iles's house just now, with that woman, maybe his wife, smeared and in a man's coat that could not cover her bare breasts properly, regardless of spectators. When everything was so bad all around you you needed somebody to be yours alone, somebody you could really rely on whatever happened. This was why she had to be with Raoul. She could not trust her father now, and perhaps not even her mother, because she would agree with him.

This was a house with a back garden and a lane entrance. She put her bike against the rear wall and used it to climb over. Raoul's hives stood against the wall. He had loved his bees, despite some stinging, so admiring the way they organized themselves and produced honey by discipline. One downstairs room of the house room seemed to have a conservatory with plants in at the garden end, and she thought this would probably be a nice place to keep Raoul, the greenery near by cool and restful. She tried the conservatory door but although it did not feel too secure she could not open it. Perhaps a bolt. She took a stone from the garden and very gently broke a pane of glass in the door, managing to hold the big pieces before they fell inside and made a noise – something heard from girls at school who did shops. When the hole was big enough, she reached in and pushed back the bolt.

Yes, here was dear Raoul, and she knew she had been so right to come. She had thought that perhaps a candle would be burning at all times close to the body in reverence, but it did not matter. They did not need it. There was some moon and it shone in through the glass roof of the conservatory so she could see him very well. The best thing was, he did not look damaged at all, his lovely face as she recalled it from their grand times together. In the future when she remembered him – and there would never, ever be a time when she did not remember him, even if eventually she wed another – she would be able to picture these handsome looks, like the photos she used to have of him, until her father took them. If she had not come tonight she would have always had the thought in her mind about the coal and the injuries to him, as in the Press. Now, she could forget that.

'I am here, Raoul,' she said. 'You knew I would come, darling. Shall we ever find who did this?'

There were garden chairs for those visiting. She considered it great that his mother had not sent him to a funeral home. Many would call in tribute. She sat down and watched, almost happy. When the dawn came she would be able to see him even better, and she would leave then. Her father would have gone to bed. This was called a vigil.

Someone, a woman, said: 'Who are you? Why are you with my Raoul?'

'What time is it?' Venetia replied. She opened her eyes and the room was full of sunlight.

'After ten. Who are you? You slept with Raoul?'

'What?'

'Slept here all night?'

'Some of the night.'

'Did you know him?'

'Oh, yes,' Venetia replied. 'Oh, yes, Mrs Brace.'

'You slept with him? You're Panicking's babe?'

Venetia stood up. The sun was brilliantly on Raoul now and the white material he nestled in. The oak-type coffin also shone, but in its own, good, darker way, like genuine wood.

'We'll have folk here soon,' Mrs Brace said.

'So many friends.'

'Have the police talked to you, darling?' Mrs Brace replied.

'Not at all.'

'They will. Did Raoul say much to you?'

'What about?'

'Businesswise? I think you should watch what you're saying, that's all. They've got some clever sods, dirty sods, and a lot to hide. They're engineering something for one of them.'

'Raoul often spoke of you, Mrs Brace. He said he owed it all to you. Did he speak to you of me – of Venetia?'

'Often. Always with real affection and respect.'

'With love? Wasn't it with true love, too?'

'You're right, he was very, very close to his dear mother. I'm going to do you some breakfast,' Mrs Brace replied.

They ate together, sitting on the garden chairs alongside Raoul, with trays on their laps: bacon, egg, sausage and black pudding with tea. It made her feel even nearer to him, a meal in his home, with plants giving atmosphere.

'For instance, if Raoul ever mentioned Stan Stanfield,' Mrs Brace said.

'I think I met him. Big moustache? He looked at me like – I didn't really like him, Mrs Brace.'

'Stan thought such a lot of you, love, I mean in the nicest, most wholesome way. But if the police talk to you it would be better not to mention him. You wouldn't want to hurt him – any friend of Raoul. Stan doesn't think your father did it – doesn't think he could, if you don't mind me saying. That's the sort of kindly person Stan is, under it all. But Raoul and Lester worked with him sometimes, and it would be best not to talk about him now. They find all sorts of mucky connections – make them up. It's their job.'

'Plus I've seen another terrible death tonight, Mrs Brace.'

That shocked Mrs Brace and her knife fell with a clatter to the floor. 'Seen? You? I heard about that on the news. What I mean, they'll be trying to tie it all together. Their training. You were actually there, at Iles's place? Who are you with now, then? My God, not a cop? Not Harpur? I thought he already had young pussy.'

'There by accident, with Mr Harpur's children.'

Mrs Brace took away the tray and tea pot. When she returned she stood looking into the coffin and Venetia joined her. 'I don't like it, my dear. Raoul would not like it, not at all. Police, police children, it's all the same, you see. They can't be mainstream. These are people Raoul would never trust, and I hope you don't. They're the people who killed him. Direct or roundabout.'

'But why, why?'

'Because he was Raoul Caesar Brace. They have to smash the best. Why we can't trust them.'

'But what can we do? How can we let them do this?'

'Stan has it in mind. This is why he must not be interfered with now. And a project created personally by Raoul.'

'I was the only one he wanted. Often he told me that. Absolutely nobody else.'

'Don't you fret yourself about having broken the door glass, Venetia,' Mrs Brace replied.

Chapter Thirteen

Stan Stanfield took Cyrus with him to the wood to watch some crossbow practice. Stanfield did not like the miserable way Cyrus went through so many parts of the job analysing on that trip to see Kenward Knapp's place. This boy was terrified of Kenward, anyone could see it. That hard black face hid pulp. Beau Derek was supposed to have let him half know it might be Kenward before he was told too much, feeling him out. This was some mistake by Beau. Cyrus had the whole lot now in his head. The choices on what to do with him if he looked shaky had closed down. A kid in this state, it could be first stop Jack Lamb.

Stanfield had brought not just the bow but the Spanish automatic again. He could tell Cyrus was scared to go there with him at night, but Stanfield said it might do him good to see how Kenward's little pets would be taken care of. Cyrus was a jumpy, bright kid and of course he would wonder about going up to a wood late when he had really only come in off the street to this job yet suddenly had so much information on it. Cyrus did not know about the pistol, but a crossbow could be bad enough. The way Stanley asked him to come, though, it would have looked like Cyrus was backing out of the whole commitment if he went on saying no, and he would be afraid of that as well. He knew he knew too much. He was a kid, but he knew how things worked.

Stanfield set up the brown cardboard and let go three pairs of shots, all right on. Cyrus made a couple of little whooping noises, praise. Cyrus wanted to be liked, especially out here at night.

'And this is farther back than I will be for the dogs,' Stanfield said.

'We'll be great, Stan. Watching you, the stance and aiming – well, I know we'll be great. I mean, I knew before, but watching you – well, a great idea to bring me here, see for myself. Not just a performance, Stan, this has meaning. Lester—'

'Was bugger all to do with it. Who needed him? Why we always talking about Lester?' Stanfield recovered the arrows and did three pairs again. Five hit, the last missed the tree and Cyrus went to look for it. 'It's all right, Stan,' he said. 'Doesn't bother me.'

So fucking generous. 'What I need is a couple of good snarling furry throats to bring out my best,' Stanfield replied.

'Eleven of twelve is some percentage, Stan.' Cyrus found the bolt and brought it back. They sat for a while and Stanfield produced the coffee from his duffle-bag. He gave Cyrus the cap cup and drank direct from the flask himself as host. This bugger, who'd miss him? Beau said he was not living with a bird now, and Stanfield did not know of any family. He still thought this could be a two job, and maybe better a two job. This boy would be driver and with drivers you had the famous little problem that if they chickened they left early and solo, *with* the vehicle. You could not wait for a bus at Kenward's place. This was the part of Cyrus's analysis that Stanfield hated above all – when he kept on about Beau and Stanfield going in, while he stayed outside in the vehicle. He really pinpointed it. He was checking he had it right. That could be his scheme – keep everything nice and calm and safe for himself now, then exit when the other two were busy. He would lose the money, but maybe he was too worried to care, could not take this level.

The other thing Stanfield did not like was how Cyrus thought they did not know enough about the safe. You could see he was afraid it would take time. This kid, sitting out there on his own, scared witless because of Kenward Knapp, could crack after ten minutes, put his foot down and disappear. Better have an empty car waiting than no car.

When Cyrus went looking for the arrow like that and was bending, eyes down to the ground, it would not have been too hard to put right these perils. Stanfield did not think it could be done with the crossbow. You would need great luck to finish someone with one or even two hits. Dogs were different. They did not have all that body space and protective bone quantity. In any case, the first arrows would stop the Alsatians even if they did not kill them. This was all that counted, and you could get right over them then when they were twitching and helpless to give the merciful finales. He would not want to do that to a kid like Cyrus, firing arrows down into a human's chest from no distance. This would probably be a boy still conscious, maybe looking up at you, not really under-standing. It had to be the automatic from the start, so much sprucer. He did not owe Cyrus any pain or indignity with arrows sticking out of him. It was not his fault. He should never have been brought in. After the coffee, Stanfield could have another series at the target, and maybe miss on one again. That dud with number twelve just now might not have been a dud at all. It threw up ideas. This was what leadership meant, finding good, new opportunities even in errors, apparently.

When they had finished the coffee, Stanfield stood and fired three more pairs. The sixth went wide. 'Sod,' Stan-field said. 'Always the last.'

'Still great shooting, Stan,' Cyrus replied, and moved off to search for the bolt, like a good retriever.

Stanfield put down the crossbow and walked quietly after him, his hand on the automatic in his pocket through the dungarees. Especially to the head, arrows could do nothing like the damage a 9 mm shell would from a couple of yards. Cyrus kicked at some undergrowth, searching, then suddenly bent down, all the back top half of him on offer. He was excited again, so clever finding it. Stanfield had the gun three-quarters out, really cosy in his hand, or more than three-quarters, goodbye Cyrus. Then he let it slip back. Christ, you could not shoot a boy like that, helping you, doing his best, no enemy and among these fine, age-old trees. He was not a dog. Probably he would be great on the night. Cyrus stood up, sparkling with pride even in the dark, and handed Stanfield the arrow. He brought his hand off the gun to take it.

They went back down to the BMW. 'We'll be great, Cyrus,' Stanfield said.

'I see it your way now, right through, Stan. Where else to find twenty grand in untraceables like that? And the timing – so beautiful. The police all messed up, killing one another, and two teams at war – Iles against the Chief, as ever, but so beautifully worse, now. Too busy gutting each other to bother with us.'

'I told the original very nice guy's mother I'll think about that Desmond Iles, when I've got time. And I might. Can we have him running outlaw, for God's sake? Who's next with coal in his mouth? Who stops him but us? Imported big cops on an inquiry? Against that Iles and Harpur? Don't make me laugh. That confed nobody cracks.'

'You could handle Iles, Stan. Or Kenward, if he did it. I know you didn't think so, but suppose. Either. There's something mighty about you. It can scare. Really give the shivers. Honestly. Well, don't mind me saying, but I felt it up at Kenward's and just now, in the woods.'

Stanfield laughed. 'You, scared? Of me? Not you. You do me good, Cyrus. We always knew you were a general thinker, but now brill on nitty-gritty tactics, too – like to spot about the timing. You warm old Stanley's spirits. Not straight to the car. We do a bit of a detour, a scan.'

He put Cyrus down near his place off Stipend Road and watched him as he walked the rest, that stupid, hard-man strut some of these kids had, all shoulders, trying to hide their bloody uselessness, making things worse by drawing attention. See the type of help you had to take and risk yourself with when there was not much time. This job had to work, two on it, three on it, whichever. How would he get close to a girl like Jack Lamb's Helen if he did not have a pocket full of money? She had made him feel so cheap, that one, accusing things when he had only tried to show devotion. Her kind could smell bad cash flow. Of course, even if The Pines went beautifully, he would not pick up anywhere near Jack Lamb's sort of money, a mansion and antiques, especially as it might be noble to push something Mrs Brace's way: she had a good side to her which made up for a lot in the original very nice guy. But six or seven grand, if you used it right, free-handed not flashy, could make a girl think this might be only the surface – night-out money from a real basis. You could buy temporary style with six or seven grand, say a few months. He would have loved to think he had a hope of something long time with Helen, but knew he didn't. Girls these days were sure of their worth, and particularly someone as all-round great as Helen, with those bonny tits and ballet ability, plus growing knowledge of art, they said. So, you went for what you could get.

Chapter Fourteen

Lane did not instantly go under with a stroke or heart attack as Harpur had feared but left work early on the day after Erogenous's death looking very rocky. That evening the Chief was diagnosed as on the brink of stress-related depression and forbidden from resuming duties for 'at least weeks'. When Harpur heard, it struck him that the body had humanely set off its own safety mechanism, and felt almost relieved. The Chief used to gaze from the office window, as if hopelessly yearning to flee this shitty bailiwick, and now his chemicals had forced a kind of escape.

Of course, he might think his removal would let in the chaos he dreaded, and had struggled to stave off. Iles took over. Alan Missay-Noaks, the Chief's Deputy, was still on protracted secondment, helping a couple of newish African states tidy up their police forces. Home Office rules said that, if no Deputy were available, the senior ACC stepped up in such a crisis, and that meant Iles. Although the Chief had almost always managed to exclude him from the Deputy aura, the Home Office could not, nor bar him from the supreme post. Iles might come under inquiry any day, but it had not happened yet, and the rules took no account of rumour, nor of an in-house knifing on his lawn. Anyway, among the home talent, probably only Iles could do the job. Lane had wanted him out, and instead he was in charge. Harpur more or less approved.

'Clearly, one will try to run matters exactly as the Chief

himself would,' Iles said, 'though it is a daunting order to emulate that kind of leadership, I'd say, Col.'

Iles liked his questions answered. Was that one? 'Oh, indeed, sir,' Harpur replied.

Tobin, chairman of the council police committee, said: 'I'm afraid I'm going to be very blunt, Assistant Chief.'

'Maurice, that's your style and is – well, simply your style, a grand feature, and I think I can say understood and respected by all, wouldn't you, Col?'

'Oh, indeed, sir.'

'Maurice, we go back a long time together. Am I likely to demand you call me "Acting Chief", not "Assistant", for Heaven's sake?'

Tobin had insisted on the meeting at once. Harpur could sympathize. The three of them were in Lane's suite, Iles comfortable behind the Chief's desk, and possibly more comfortable than Harpur had ever seen Lane himself there. Iles was not big by police standards – he might have been an accountant or dentist – yet seemed easily to fill Lane's chair, and to dominate the room just as easily, his grey hair richly shining, like an altar light. The Chief probably never sought this kind of distinctiveness for himself, and if he did he missed it. Maybe as a testament that he might truly model his reign on the Chief's, Iles had so far kept the framed photograph of Mrs Lane on the desk. Now and then he pretended his eyes had accidentally fallen on it. He would wince and lean forward to double-take for a second incredulously, then turn sharply away.

'I have to tell you, Desmond, the Chief telephoned me before he left yesterday,' Tobin said. 'We spoke at length.'

'That would be so like the man I know,' Iles replied. 'The bond between you two, almost mystical.'

Tobin said: 'His only concern that—'

'That the integrity of this Force, so secure and expanding in his care, should come to no harm. What I meant about the difficulties facing a mere stop-gap such as one's self, even aided by Col.'

Tobin said: 'The Chief seemed agonizingly aware he

was withdrawing at a time when his colleagues confronted appalling problems, even incredible.'

'The killings? Appalling, yes. Thank God we have someone like Harpur here to deal with them. Rigorous but even-handed. Not brilliant, certainly, yet hardly stupid. Progress is being made, believe me, Maurice. My main wish is that when the Chief returns restored – and let it be soon, oh, soon, soon – that then we can present him with a concluded, water-tight case against the murderers of the original very nice guy and dear Lester. And then the matter of Bixton? Well, signed and sealed already, I fear.'

Tobin crouched forward in his chair, stymied by this politesse, one hand on the desk opening and closing in growing anger. He stared at Iles. 'Desmond, I've said I meant to be blunt. I and my committee are now faced with a situation where the Acting Chief Constable is—' He lowered his head for a moment through embarrassment and determination. Then he faced Iles square again. 'Look, I have to ask you straight if you feel you are the right person to head up a Force whose main current activity is the investigation of these murders.' Tobin had the roaring energy, fine egomania and aggressive features vital for his kind of career, but, as Iles once said, he could at times look deceptively wholesome. Now, an honest sort of anxiety, even civic care, was in Tobin's face and you could have believed him selfless. He wore plimsolls, a decently faded denim jacket, jeans and an open-necked black shirt. Uniform did get a hold of people.

' "Right person to head up a Force whose main current activity is the investigation of these murders",' Iles semi-chanted slowly. He gave a soothing rhythm to the words. Iles liked taking over people's words, the way cannibals thought they could take over the strength of someone they ate. 'In what particular sense am I or not the "right person", Maurice?'

'What I and my committee have to keep in mind, Desmond, is that—'

'Are you saying I killed those two bit-part crooks, and

the previous two, Jamieson and Favard?' Iles asked. 'Really? An ACC? Now an Acting Chief? Did Lane suggest this in his death-bed call to you, the dear suffering slice of brain frailty?'

'My God, no, no,' Tobin replied. 'Could Mr Lane conceivably suggest such a thing—'

'On an open line. Fair point. So who did suggest it to you, Maurice? I gather this is supposed to be some kind of baffle tactic, to divert any Jamieson and Favard inquiry away from me.'

'Desmond, listen: there is the law, obviously, but everyone understood the police feeling against those two at the time, especially yours, myself very much included.'

'Of course. They murdered a talented boy cop and were acquitted,' Iles replied.

'A court said they did *not* murder a cop,' Tobin said. 'Nor, incidentally, your beautiful woman friend.'

'Yes, sick, wasn't it,' Iles said. 'Did you ever hear a niftier lawyer than their tub-o'-guts QC? We were rather fortunate those two died as they did so soon afterwards, while the lesson could still be drawn. Courts are very properly the only law, but not the only justice. Trite, but that's my view. I don't know about Colin.'

'The file's still open, sir,' Harpur said.

'Certainly it is. Harpur's not one to throw in the towel, Maurice.'

Tobin folded over on himself and spoke fiercely into his shirt. 'Christ, Desmond, can't you see the position I'm in, I and the committee? We have a responsibility to the public. To them, now, we appear to be presiding over, tolerating—'

The door opened slowly and Lane, wearing one of his suits and a rabbit catcher's brown-beige cap came in. There was quiet nobility to him, as well as sickness. He seemed to glance around the room as though it were already unfamiliar, lost. In one hand he carried two empty Marks and Spencer carrier bags. Iles stood immediately, went round the desk and walked quickly to take the Chief by the arm and bring him to a chair, like a VAD with the shell-shocked. 'This is marvellous, sir. But you look grand. Colin and I were just trying to convince Maurice that between us we can keep the machinery turning over, despite our loss. I'm afraid he's understandably sceptical. Your reputation. Plus, he thinks I killed the original very nice guy and Lester, not to mention Jamieson and Favard, so as temporary police chief I start fairly far back, even by, say, the Met's standards. Just four deaths, I ask you! But he swears on his dear mother's grave it wasn't you fed him those ideas. You've a real friend in Maurice, sir, damn loyal.' He gingerly removed Lane's cap and put it on his lap.

'Should you be here, sir?' Harpur asked. He had also stood now. Lane looked as he had looked late in the night at Idylls; worse than pale, beaten, dodderingly brave, a valiant relic. Iles could easily set him back another few months, if he really worked at it. Why wouldn't the Chief simply rest?

Lane said: 'I left in a hurry. A few personal things I would like to pick up, Desmond.'

'Please,' Iles cried, and waved his hand towards the desk and cupboards, like feeding the five thousand.

'And I wanted to say face to face, Desmond, Colin, Maurice, that you must regard me at all times as being available. Only a phone call away.'

'Thank God,' Iles replied. He was standing near the Chief's chair, and jerked his arms down straight at his side in a movement of convulsive pleasure. 'I thrill to that phrase, "only a phone call away". You hit these things so effortlessly, sir.' His voice soared. 'We're not alone, Col. In a sense, we would not have been, even without that offer, Chief: the pattern for us to follow is already clear and established. You are here, even when not. But to know you are always available in actuality is such an extra, isn't it, Harpur?'

'Indeed.'

'So, what's all these addled "indeeds", Harpur?' Iles

replied. 'Feel absolutely free, sir. I have not opened any desk drawers, in case of intimate materials. And then the picture of Mrs Lane. But perhaps you will not need that now, since I'm sure she will be very close to you at this time, in the as it were flesh. If I may say, I rather hope you will leave that photograph. It is a kindly reminder, should I ever for a moment forget, of whose this room is, whose is the rightful presence here. But did you drive yourself here, sir? Is that all right? Should Harpur run you back?'

'My wife is with me,' the Chief replied. 'She did not wish to come in.'

'Oh, dear. Yet, that I understand, sir,' Iles said. 'Your dear domain, which very temporarily, is not your domain – is occupied.'

'Particularly in anything involving the Home Office or the Inspectorate of Constabulary,' Lane replied. 'Should you require guidance. These people can be very searching.'

'I'm going to make a note of all this, sir,' Iles said excitedly.

Lane wiped his face with his free hand. His tone had been slack and quiet, but picked up bite now. Often the Chief could give a glimpse of how he used to be before the attrition of this job. 'Desmond, you of course realize the spot you might be in?'

'I've pressed him on this, Chief,' Tobin said. 'Which is reflected on to all of us, unfortunately. My constituents begin to see me as soiled.'

'My God, I don't believe that,' Iles replied. ' "Soiled"? Maurice Tobin? Col doesn't consider I have any real problems, do you, Col?'

'No, sir.'

Apologetically, Lane said: 'But Colin is, in a way, involved with—'

'Not that I'm anything but grateful for your and Maurice's concern, sir,' Iles replied. 'You honour me in believing, however wrongly, that I might have seen off

Jamieson and Favard. Flatteringly, you suspect I alone, yes, alone, was conscious of the duty on this Force to blot out two recidivist louts who'd done to it foul, fucking injury by slaughtering Ray Street. Quite apart from charring a lovely, serious woman who had found my merits. And they thought they had got away with it! That's the eternal treat, isn't it, sir? While they were still giggling, this lump of coal is, wham, in the kisser and a garotte cord doing the necessary. Sweet. Shall we gather up your little possessions now?' Keeping his aura well focused on Lane, Iles had remained near the Chief's chair and bent to help and support him to the desk. 'I wonder if I might offer you some of your own tonic wine, sir?' he asked, pointing at the drinks cupboard. Lane refused, and Iles did not bring the bottle out for Tobin and Harpur. 'Harpur's a gin and cider soak and Maurice would not compromise himself,' he said.

When Tobin had taken the Chief back down to his car, the carrier bags loaded with his things now, Iles, behind the desk again, said: 'They'll chat over their mad, dirty little plots in the lift, Col. That will be a therapy for Lane, the bemused, honourable prick. I see so much greatness in that man, even crumbling. It's best he should talk about all his poisonous notions to someone. Tobin will do. Not good they should putrify within.'

'Did you get anything out of the woman living under Lester Magellan's place, sir?'

'Out of? Elaine? She said little, regrettably, Col. Oh, she did see the child there, love-nesting with the original very nice guy once or twice.'

'Venetia Ember.'

'Panicking would be very upset about that – when he's trying to establish the family as city bulwarks. I find quite a bit in women like Elaine, occasionally; boisterous, exacting, older. I won't be going back there now. Oh, you'll think I had to check if she saw me getting into Lester's to do him and the original very nice guy. Believe me, I felt a genuine warmth for her, Col, while it lasted. Her executive clothing. If she comes looking say I've had to give myself over entirely to beef-teaing the Chief *pro tem*.'

'Do you think it's smart to alienate her, sir?'

'She might lie about me? Place me at Lester's place around the time of the deaths? Elaine's not like that. A good creature.'

'I've known some. They dislike being dropped, sir.'

'You're so worldly, Harpur.' Iles went and gazed through the window, as Lane used to. 'What the hell did he see out there, Col?'

'We think one or both of them – the original very nice guy and Lester – could have been in some project,' Harpur replied. 'Probably Lester. The original very nice guy might have given the information but he didn't do rough-and-tumble himself lately. Stan Stanfield's been recruiting, in a bit of a rush, probably to replace Lester.'

'Stanley's a persistent lad. The target got wind and pre-empted by wiping out those two in an established style!'

'It's a possible.'

'More than that, Harpur. Who? This looks more likely than Panicking? Would, could, Ralphy garotte? He'd get his fingers caught.'

'We don't know the target.'

'A tip? Who from?'

'Lester did crossbows, so probably dogs,' Harpur replied.

'Are you really looking?'

'Indeed, sir.'

Iles spoke to the window. 'They're seriously trying to snare me for this lot. You do understand? Have you been got at, Col? Frustrated, ageing whizz-kid, menaced by younger whizz-kids like Francis, and so looking for a career relaunch?'

'Kenward Knapp has dogs, and Pastron.'

Iles turned to face Harpur. 'I've always liked Kenward. The Pines? Disgusting modern property, lovingly looked after. Yes, he could garotte.'

'There'd be collection nights when his house is stuffed

with old notes. Rupert Pastron's probably not a big enough tickle for Stanley, and not cash, mostly musical instruments and bulk cigarettes. Stanley hates boxes and lumpy stuff in general, and if he's still working with Beau they'll want something he can use his pretty fingers on.'

Iles stood and strolled to a street map on the wall, near the hierarchy chart, which still showed the Chief in charge: Iles would probably do something about that shortly. 'And then these sodding funerals, Col. Are we going to get a big villain turnout for the original very nice guy and Lester, messing up traffic half the day? In this job I have to think of these things. I've had Stinchcombe in here talking about "potential by-pass embolism". It's all right for you, getting your youthful comfort unstinted. Do you take her home, since you're a widower?'

'Mrs Brace will probably be able to organize a crowd for the original very nice guy, yes. She's a community figure.'

'I admire that – the way these folk, men and women, can live in or near criminality all their lives, yet still hang on to a bit of status. JFK.' Lane had left behind the picture of his wife for Iles and the Acting Chief glanced at it now. 'Is he going to be all right at home with that continuously, Col? No chance for him to come here and seek solace from myself. Well, and from you. I felt the sweet man's structure was going, didn't you, just now? He needs very tender treatment. Such a holy nincompoop to think he could take me on, wouldn't you say, Harpur?'

'Indeed, sir.'

Harpur went down to his room and talked for a while with Garland about the case, then drove home. When he turned into his street, he immediately had the feeling his house was being watched. A grey Metro stood about five or six doors down from his, with a man at the wheel. It was dark, and Harpur could not identify the man or the car. He decided to act as if he had not spotted it and parked and entered the house. His daughters were in the kitchen getting a meal ready. Harpur went into the big front sitting-room and stood at the window without the lights on. The Metro was still there, but it looked empty now. Hazel entered and saw Harpur watching. She left the room dark. 'Someone out there, Dad?'

'I thought so.'

'So did I. But not for very long. Is this work? You ought to get out of the phone book.'

'People who want to call a cop need the cop's number.'

'And address?' she asked.

'Don't tell me you're getting jumpy in your old age,' he said.

Someone tapped the front door. 'Shall I answer?' Hazel asked.

'Of course.'

In a moment she came back with Tobin and put the lights on. He must have been home since the meeting and had changed into a svelte dark blue fur-collared anorak, like some American author on an arts programme telling how he beat alcoholism. 'Harpur, I have to see you. I mean alone, not in the presence of Mr Iles. I didn't want to disturb your children until you arrived.'

'You run a Cavalier,' Harpur replied.

'My wife's Metro. I thought discretion. This is a lovely room. The books.'

'We're getting shot of them,' Hazel replied.

'Could we draw the curtains?' Tobin said.

'They don't go right across,' Hazel replied, but tugged them as far as they would. 'Are you pro Iles or Lane?'

'Councillor Tobin's not into all that, thank God,' Harpur said. He brought some drinks, and Hazel went out of the room.

'I'm not eager to be seen here,' Tobin said. He stood shielded from the street by one of the curtains. 'Harpur, I don't think you realize how deep you're in. But you could still get out. That's why I'm here.'

Harpur poured a couple of good gins, put tonic and ice in Tobin's and cider in his own.

Tobin drank and said: 'Protecting Iles. If it came to anything, accessory.' With Iles not present, Tobin seemed stronger, more designing, clipped, high-handed. 'Suppression of evidence.'

'What evidence?'

'I know you're close to Iles and would normally report this kind of meeting to him. But I hope you appreciate it is not in your best interests.'

The Chief had spoken to him like this. Why couldn't they see he was not available, even if what they said made sense?

'We have to move against Iles before this inquiry begins,' Tobin said. 'That might put you in the clear.'

'And yourself? Mr Lane has been talking to you?'

'Of course he has. But long before that, I— I have a responsibility for the integrity of this Force. I will exercise it, regardless. I hope with your help, but without it, if I have to. I have to purify this outfit, Harpur.' Purify: the word sang.

'Bixton thought he was purifying it,' Harpur replied. 'It's an impulse that turns people crazy. Are you talking about the original very nice guy and Lester Magellan? We have good lines of inquiry going. Garland's confident.'

'And previous matters.'

'They've been thoroughly looked at.'

Tobin sat back in his chair, held the drink at his lips and crossed his legs. He had stillness. 'Harpur, I am offering an alliance.'

'That's not how it works, councillor.'

'If I am called by an inquiry, I can say either that you helped me or that you obstructed me, in my attempt to make this Force answerable to scrutiny.'

'You would not be called. It wouldn't be an inquiry into political control.'

'But, Harpur, you're not naïve: I could, must, somehow exert an influence.'

'That would be improper, councillor.'
'Oh, my God, who's talking proprieties?' Tobin yelled.
'I am.'
'But this is about Iles, for God's sake.'

Chapter Fifteen

When the original very nice guy's mother heard from several of the last callers to see Raoul that Iles had soared into the top job she knew it meant he had killed her son and Lester. This was how police worked. If one of their people was in trouble or going to be they promoted him, to show how brilliant and clean he was. They hoped trouble would turn tail then.

Her view was some big struggle had gone on inside the police and Iles had won. Iles was the kind who always won. Raoul, Lester and probably that detective knifed at Iles's house were all part of this battle. She did not see how, and perhaps they had not known how, either. It did not matter. Her certainty was what mattered. Those three had been swallowed by it, that was all. A disgrace.

Sitting alone with her son two days before the funeral, she thought how sad it was that the young girl, Venetia, should believe her own father might have killed Raoul. Might have killed Lester, too, of course, but Lester was only on the edge. The girl's real pain came from the dread that Panicking Ralph had murdered what she regarded as her dear love, Raoul. This meant she had suffered two terrible losses at once. Now, she could see her father only as a cruel enemy, and her supreme sweetheart was dead. A child like this would never understand that Panicking lacked the oomph to carry out two such stagey killings.

Mrs Brace decided she must see the girl and her father and tell them she was certain it had been Desmond Iles.

She had more or less known it from the start and now there was no question. Stan Stanfield was sure, too, even before Iles's dirty leap to the top, and Stan heard a lot and had a bit of a brain – Raoul always said that about him, 'a bit of a brain not totally stifled by the moustache'. Stan reckoned also he was descended from a marine painter last century called Clarkson Stanfield who had a letter from the novelist Charles Dickens, which could mean inherited class.

Raoul would not wish the girl to suffer in this awful way, nor even Ralphy. Of course, Stan said Raoul never really wanted anything to do with Venetia. The child had pursued him and would not let go. Mrs Brace could certainly believe that. Raoul was so wonderfully content to live at home. All he desired from life he found there with her. Yet women and girls did adore him, it could not be helped. And he would be kindly to some and, yes, responsive, because that was his way, humane. He would wish his mother to be kindly now, also, no matter how little this pathetic dick-mad infant meant to him. There was a duty. Raoul hated all unnecessary pain and would often go out of his way to stop it. That was why the manner of his death had been so foul and heartbreaking, especially the disgusting coal insult. This was exactly Iles, an evil signature.

She was unhappy to leave Raoul in the house alone among all those smug plants, but had to see Panicking and the girl today. She wanted to press them, both of them, to attend Raoul's funeral the day after tomorrow. If they wished, they could go to Lester's also on the day after, though he was very much an also-ran, even as a corpse. All would admit that, his parents included, though, naturally, their grief was quite real. True, he, too, was a son, but it was inevitable his funeral came second.

She took the Daimler and drove to Panicking's club, aiming to arrive at about six thirty in the evening. Raoul used to take her there occasionally around this time, when things were quiet with no punch-ups or whores, and she quite liked it. The Monty had aura. Once it was a very select businessmen's club, and Ralphy had cleverly kept the dark mahogany and brass fitments, which seemed to carry on the distinction. When the juke box was not on, it was as if you could hear the murmur of old conversations by important professional men, happy on gin. Panicking gave distinction, also, despite that name, because he looked like Charlton Heston, when Chuck was younger. In fact, it could seem brutal and foolish to call him Panicking, just as she hated that sneering name people gave Raoul.

The club was almost empty. A couple of young men played pool and Panicking was behind the bar, looking at some accounts near the till. Good music was playing, reggae, not *The Messiah*. The point was, if Panicking and his daughter attended Raoul's funeral it would be seen and widely known, and it would signify. The police would certainly hear who was there, make a bloody list for their terrorizing files. Associations, they called it. Perhaps one of those police might even come. They did that sometimes for murder victims. This was supposed to be respect, but in Raoul's case it would be to crow, obviously. If Panicking and Venetia were present, it would shout a message that Ember was naturally proud of his kid's relationship – association, if you like – with Raoul and would never have committed that filthy act against him. By being at the funeral, they would tell Iles that they and everyone else knew he was responsible, and none of the braid and big pay could hide it.

She noticed that the two young men stopped their game for a second when she entered and looked towards Panicking. Perhaps they were there to take care of him. Panicking would usually be at the club early and late in the evenings, taking the rest of the time at home to deal with his university studies. The child probably would not be here. Ralphy had cornered some real money lately and moved the family out from the flat above the club to a fine country property, Low Pastures, which used to belong to another operator. But it was Ralph she most wanted to see and reassure. It was Ralph who would have to say whether they would attend the funeral. He might take her to see Venetia when he went home.

The men playing pool looked what Raoul would call '*fauve*', meaning wild. They went back to their game when Panicking gave her a smile and said, 'Mrs Brace,' then came and stood where he could serve her a drink. The smile was tiny and meaningless. She could understand that. He could not know why she was here. He was asking himself did she believe he had killed her boy. So, in answer, she put on the biggest smile *she* could offer, to comfort him, keep him from one of his panics.

'Ralph,' she cried, 'Kressmann armagnac on me, absolutely. Bring the bottle to a quiet table, yes? A chat.'

She took a place far from the pool table and he joined her with the bottle and glasses. He seemed to look more like Charlton Heston than ever before: the ruggedness, the great nose, his fine, bony head. It was hard to think of him falling into helpless terror. She could imagine him in a disaster movie being repeatedly brave.

'I've sent her out of town, Mrs Brace,' he remarked. 'Are you here to invite her to the original very nice guy's funeral? No fucking way.'

'I don't hold you responsible for Raoul's death,' she replied. 'Never.'

'She's become uncontrollable. Out all night recently with her bike, no explanation. My sister in Wales agreed to take her, until after the funeral, at least. She's missing school.'

'The dear child came to see—'

'I don't want to hear it,' Ralph replied. 'It's over.'

'But, surely, Ralphy – I mean, look at the terrible situation we're all in. That Iles, top dog, and so on. He'll persecute us. Wouldn't it be better if we united now, all of us, against—'

'I put my daughters into a good private school – classical studies, damned expensive vacation trips to the Holy Land, you name it – and give them a sound home upbringing, Mrs Brace. Then Venetia turns to a— Turns to your son.'

'Raoul thought so much of her, believe me.'

'The original very nice guy, thirty-four, a low-to-middling career villain in good shoes, was having a child of fourteen, Mrs Brace.'

She leaned forward over her goblet and said quietly: 'I could believe you're glad he's dead.'

'He's dead.'

'I thought that if you and your daughter could be present at the funeral—'

'Me as well. You're joking.' Ember stood. 'The Kressmann's on the house. Which car did you come in?'

'Well, Raoul's Daimler.'

'They had it off in that.'

'How can you know this? You interrogated the poor wee one?'

He spoke to the men at the pool table. 'Mrs Brace is leaving.'

That really upset her – the coarseness of the language used about Raoul and the car, and the bum's rush. This club and the bit of wealth Panicking had stacked somehow was turning him arrogant. It also showed in becoming a university student at his age. They used to say he looked like Charlton Heston without the money, but now he had the money and that country spread, Low Pastures, bought cheap from Caring Oliver's widow, Patsy. There was even a story Ralph might have seen off Caring and had some time with Patsy. Panicking adored himself. Perhaps all the success had altered him – got rid of the panic and given him a hardness that would make even the murders of Raoul and Lester a possible after all. If he did Caring, it might have started a taste. People like Stan Stanfield thought Ember too feeble for gaudy slaughter, but they might not have considered how possessions could transform a man, give a burnish, even to Panicking. Someone had touched his little girl and done dishonour to the up-and-coming Ember clan. So, he would put it right, would he? Stanfield said the girl had been the pursuer, and she could believe it, but, of course, Daddy would not have that. His child had been polluted by – what had he called Raoul: a 'low-to-middling career villain in good shoes'? What did Ember think he was, then? She could tell him – a through-and-through villain in a slum club that was supposed to take on quality via a couple of bits of mahogany and brass and a past when accountant and company owners used to meet there to fix rough deals and allocate women. The fact was she always felt scared to sit down in there in case she caught something, and not just off the toilets.

As Mrs Brace drove quickly back to Raoul, the weight of those insults dragged at her. She had abandoned him for nothing. It was gross to spit on her invitation to the funeral and talk as if Raoul had corrupted that girl. This lad, Panicking, had to be dealt with. Even if he did not kill Raoul and Lester, he must be punished for his bitter treatment of her just now and the soiling of Raoul's memory before he was even cremated.

Perhaps she could create extra motive for Panicking to have done the killings. It would be easy to say Raoul told her he was going to take the girl to live abroad with him, really break her from her father and family. She could suggest Panicking had found out and stopped them in that savage, monstrous way. Of course, the idea of Raoul actually going was absurd. He would never consider leaving his mother and lovely home to make a distant life with some tarty scrap. But people would not realize this, and especially police would not: they believed all men at all times thought of nothing but getting it away with young girls. It was because they behaved like that themselves. Think of Iles, think of Harpur. Raoul would never have been such. Yet she was sure that as a way of repaying Ember for those miserable attacks Raoul would not mind her releasing such a tale. She parked and looked carefully, angrily, at the back seat before locking up and rejoining Raoul. He would be gone very soon. She brought a Polaroid from his bedroom and took some favourable snaps.

Chapter Sixteen

Stan Stanfield was jubilant. He called a meeting of Beau
Derek and Cyrus down at the foreshore blockhouse. It
might be the last get-together before they did the job.
Especially he wanted to see Cyrus and build him up with
good news. Oh, yes, Cyrus had sounded so positive and
ready after the last trip to the woods, but could you believe
it? He was the sort to say anything if he was scared enough,
and maybe in the woods he had spotted that moment when
Stanfield thought of killing him for silence. People were
quick at picking up this kind of flavour.

The big danger with Cyrus was still he might run –
either disappear any time now, before the job even
started, or in the middle of it. The last would be worst,
of course. Then they would be out in the wilds with no
transport, heavy with Kenward's cash and festooned with
dead dogs. But it would be bad if Cyrus went ahead of
the project, too. This stayed planned for three, because
of Beau, and he could turn useless if there was a change.
Beau seemed nervy enough, as it was. In any case, if
Cyrus ran now there would be the traditional danger –
he could talk. People of his level might give up the chance
of good money through fright but would still look for a
snitch tip.

Stanfield's good news would put all this right, though.
In the blockhouse, he said: 'Iles has moved up. It's bound
to mean he did the original very nice guy and Lester. We
don't have to worry. It couldn't have been Kenward. He
hasn't been forewarned.'

Beau said: 'I heard the Chief was sick, that's all.'

'Of course he's sick. How they work it,' Stanfield replied. 'Some major ferocity has gone on there, your usual police hate-tourneys, and Iles won. Probably Lane wanted him looked at for these killings, and the two before. The old Chief did what he could, lost, so sees the helpful doctor. What hope, with Iles and Harpur against him?'

'Harpur?' Cyrus said.

'Most likely. A mate of Iles,' Stanfield replied. He wished there was more light so he could get a good look at Cyrus's face, to see if he had real hope in him now instead of that mock-up. 'What always happens if a cop's in the shadows through allegations. They promote him above it all. That fight at Iles's place would be part of it. The war was still on then. Erog was Iles's man. The lad who killed him would be Lane's. It's like champions in history. Things must have looked bad for Iles then. He'll always come through in the end. He coached the Serbs.'

'This is great,' Cyrus said.

'But I think you've still got your worries,' Stanfield replied.

'How do you mean, Stan?'

'Afraid Kenward's going to be waiting for us – something like that.'

Beau said: 'No, Stan. Cyrus knows when you plan a job it's planned. No gaps.'

'Right,' Cyrus said. 'What Stan Stanfield is famous for. I don't join any old combo, Stan.'

'Great,' Stanfield replied. 'You're going to be there?'

'Where?' Cyrus asked.

'The job.'

'Christ, of course he's going to be there, Stan.'

'Of course I am,' Cyrus replied, giggling. 'This is six, seven lovely grand – plus a chance to see some great boys at work. Yes, please.' He shouted and got a heavy, wowing echo. They all laughed full out.

'We've heard plenty about your own style, too, Cyrus. All top class.'

'Or would I have invited him?' Beau said. 'You going to the original very nice guy's funeral this afternoon, Stan?'

'Myself, I thought get out of sight until the project,' Stanfield replied.

'So right,' Beau said.

'Naturally, I've paid my respects privately. What I have to think is— Well, Iles's moving up is a lovely thing, but there's the other side. If he's got himself in the clear, he'll want someone else for the killings. They'll be working at the original very nice guy's colleagues, won't they, pretending to look for motives.'

'Associations,' Beau said.

'That,' Stanfield said. 'I don't want to talk to them just now. Obviously. Or ever. That funeral – it would be an invitation to Harpur. The original very nice guy was such a nothing, anyway. Do I traipse after him to the crem with a load of small-timers and innocents?'

'No, I'm not going either,' Cyrus replied.

'Flowers, yes, with some non-names on the cards,' Beau remarked. 'But not the parade.'

'This is your usual meeting spot, is it?' Cyrus asked, glancing fondly around, like a show-house.

'Why?' Stanfield asked.

'It's good, Stan,' Cyrus replied. 'Out of the way.' He went to the observation slit.

'A vista,' Stanfield said. The tide was high today and the sun gave the sea a really healthy glint, not blue or green, but definitely lighter than usual. You could believe a daredevil cod might risk going through it on the way somewhere else. Waves broke with a bit of force instead of that usual lurch and collapse. Everything seemed livelier.

'We don't always use the same place,' Stanfield said.

'That's good, good,' Cyrus replied. 'Where else?'

'Why?' Stanfield said.

'I'm just learning how big boys work.'

'You'll be a big boy yourself after The Pines,' Beau said.

'We're lucky to have found you, Cyrus, that's a fact. Don't worry. No fang mementoes in your arse.'

Chapter Seventeen

Cyrus drove from the blockhouse first. The other two stayed on – supposed to be security. Car windows shut tight, sound-sealed? Great. Let's go then. He yelled, full volume: 'Christ, Cyrus, get out of this job, out, out, out. Exit, now, now, now.' It was like a frightened kid. Well, that was how they saw him, a frightened kid, so act like it.

But now and then kids asked the right questions, the big, simple questions that saw right through. Stanfield hears Iles is into the big job, so this proves he did the original very nice guy and Lester. Who says? Who fucking says? Where's the link? That's big-boy thinking? He had been so pleased to be brought in by these top veterans, but now – bollocks. Cyrus could see Stanley had a mind, and he heard it all the time from Beau, anyway, but people, bright people, experienced people, would get into the run-up to something sweet and shut their brains right off in the excitement, or bend them to suit. That lord, the grand scholar, who just knew, for a day or two, the Hitler diaries were right. This was an ACC they were talking about, an Acting Chief. They really thought he did four killings? God, you did not need to be a scared kid to wonder.

And then, something else that might push Stanley's great brain far off beam. A right giggle, this. He had this crazy hope for Jack Lamb's girl, Helen Surtees. All sorts knew how he felt, but nobody ever mentioned it to him. They couldn't. They were afraid they'd wet themselves laughing. Did the daft sod really believe he could creep into Lamb's league and Helen's pants by getting his hands on six, seven grand, and with a yard-brush moustache like that?

Cyrus glanced in the mirror. Those two famous, long-term operators wanted to talk about him on their own – talk about him on their own again, after what had just been said. Stanfield obviously had some thoughts, and maybe Beau did, too. Beau was always defending him, telling Stan how great Cyrus was. That would be only because Beau picked him, though. Those two could be saying now, *He's a feeble seen-nothing kid, he's not going to turn up, he'll run, he'll talk, so snuff him.* Up in the woods, there had been a moment like that. Cyrus had felt it. Anyone would have. Stanfield brought a crossbow for the practice, yes, but there was a pistol in his pocket, no question, and he had put a hand on it when Cyrus was searching for the arrow. One thing about kids, their eyesight had not begun to go, and he spotted that. The first time Stanfield missed up there it was genuine, probably. You could see his rage. Maybe it gave him the idea for the next, though.

Cyrus stopped the car, climbed out and walked to the back, as if checking whether he had a flat. He wanted to have a proper look at them, not just in the mirror. They were standing just outside the blockhouse, watching him. Beau half turned away fast when Cyrus glanced up, pretending to admire the crummy sea view suddenly. Cyrus kicked the rear off-side a couple of times and then waved to signal no problem. Stanfield waved back, very friendly. *He* was the problem. Cyrus climbed in again and drove on.

If they decided he might run they would come looking for him, no delays, scared he would talk. *You're going to be there?* Stanfield had asked it like that, straight bloody out. Beau jumped in immediately, yes, to put it right, but the question hung all the time in the dead air of that blockhouse. Then Stanfield jumped in, two feet, when Cyrus tried to make some decent, pass-the-time chat about the blockhouse and their other rendezvous spots.

Why did he want to know? Stanfield thought Cyrus was charting their work patterns to market somewhere? Stan was a lovely partner.

Best run now, not even go home and pack? He had one credit card that still worked and a bit of cash. He could turn on to the motorway in a couple of miles and be in London by this afternoon, and farewell Stanfield, farewell the original very nice guy's funeral. He knew two or three people in London around his own age, more kids, but kids who would give him a dug-out for a few weeks, one a very wholesome girl. There might even be some small jobs to thicken his money. He would not be choosy. It was an idea. He kept it alive in his head for a while as he drove.

Two things held him back, one basic: he was not a runner. If he said he would he did. His career was only just beginning, but already he had a reputation for that, and a black had to be whiter than white. His father used to say something about if you put your hand to the plough forget about the lunchtime piss-up. Once, he had a lot of time for his father. Probably Stanfield could find him, anyway, even in London. He had ears everywhere. Cyrus did not head for the motorway yet, but went home. He could still make his choices, though.

The other factor was the money. Of course, the money. This was six, maybe seven grand in street notes, a very meaty pick-up, a better pick-up than he had ever seen before. Naturally, he would not tell Stanfield this, but, yes, better five or six times than he had ever had from one job. Probably Stanfield knew it, so wise and bloody mature. Also, it was better than anything Don or Justin or Debbie could put him on to in London, mostly off-licences. Stanfield could be right and The Pines might be easy. Everyone knew Stan was good on planning and research, no shit.

He reached home and immediately packed a couple of bags. There was nobody to say goodbye to except the landlady, and he would not bother with that. She would want to know where he was going and when he might be back. She would require rent, to hold the place.

If he was going, he ought to go at once, he knew this. But it came back to he was not a runner. He could go, but he would feel like a rat. Instead, he looked for some sort of middle way. This was always one of his things, find a balance. He had a reputation for that, too, although young. It would be something safe but also something with a bit of consideration in it for Stan and Beau. They were diabolical in many ways, yes, but in this kind of life you expected that and he must regard them as mates. After all, Stanfield only fondled the pistol that night in the wood, didn't blast off.

Himself, he still thought Kenward did those two for self-protection, and he would never believe an ACC could commit such crimes, not even Iles in trouble. But then there was Panicking Ralph Ember. Of course, Stanfield said impossible, and Cyrus thought he could be right. Panicking lacked. Yet there must have been times when he pulled some pretty ripe acts, or he would not be so rich. What had happened to Caring Oliver, for instance? Ralphy might still have some dirty power hidden there inside him.

Cyrus thought that tonight he would go up to The Monty and look for a police presence. This was how they would do it if they thought it was Panicking, or if they didn't think it but had decided to prove it *was* Panicking for convenience and old times' sake. Their first move would be to put a few heavies into the club and to watch his house in an obvious way, crowding him, working on his nerves. Panicking had a lot of those. Then they would move in with the questions, and their own answers if his weren't what they wanted. Erogenous would have handled this, but now it might be Garland, Chat-up Charlie or even Harpur himself. He was hands-on management.

Cyrus decided it like this: if he saw plainclothes lads jostling Ralphy, he could believe Stanfield had it right and

Kenward did not kill those two, and would not be waiting with a battalion in the property for whoever took the project over. Police would love a chance to get Kenward, so if they did not nail him now it must be because he did not do it. If Cyrus saw no police, and if Ralphy looked full of his glories as usual, it meant Panicking was not in the frame and Kenward might be. And Cyrus would find a nice little gift for Debbie at the service station, then the motorway. If the police moved on Kenward there would be no job worth doing anyway, because how could he make his collections? And if they hung back and waited, Kenward might be there, in The Pines that night, waiting, too. Maybe this was a simple, childish way of seeing things, but it was the only way Cyrus had.

Chapter Eighteen

Harpur drove out to Kenward Knapp's place, The Pines. He wanted to see if it was the sort of target Lester Magellan might have thought he could handle. Harpur went to a spot up behind the house to take an uninterrupted view with binoculars. There was some sun, and he must be careful of glints. Kenward's kind expected observation, and Harpur did not want him warned.

Lester would not have tried anything he thought too much for him. And the original very nice guy would have fed him only tips that looked manageable by Lester, and possibly Stan Stanfield and Beau Derek. Those two were up a division, but the weakest usually conditioned the grade of job.

It was not a bad spread, The Pines. Knapp might be doing his own shipments if he had that kind of money, and something pricier than cannabis. Harpur could see the dogs, sleeping close to the house, and possibly on long leads. He lowered the glasses. Probably a three job and definitely not too big for Lester to believe he could be one of them. It would have been Lester to do the dogs and go inside with Beau, if there was a safe. Who outside? Possibly the original very nice guy, though he did not risk his shoes much these days on site. Stan Stanfield, organizer, recruiter? There would have to be changes now. Perhaps Stanley was teaching himself crossbow. He had the nerve. It was those distinguished genes.

Harpur went back to his car. Had Kenward heard somewhere that the original very nice guy, Lester and company were going to visit him one night, and so did two of them first? Kenward had a fine information system that told him all sorts, and in good time: one reason he had stayed free so long since his last trip away, and one reason he now had The Pines and grew big in charities. It would be such a treat to get him for the killings: Kenward out of the way for years, and an intact police image. Well, almost. He must work on Kenward.

On his way back to the office he called in on Erogenous's girl, to see how she was taking things. Jane wandered a bit, but had also looked after Erog really well, and accepted his weirdnesses. They had had something as genuine as you could get between two adults.

'I don't want Lane at the funeral, Col,' she said.

'The Chief's ill.'

'The *noblesse oblige* sod is still liable to turn up for one of his troops, on a stretcher if necessary.'

Yes, possibly she had it right. Jane and Erog had shared a decent flat off Grant Hill, with fishing-boat prints on the living-room wall and a bar, though apparently empty, because she did not offer a drink. Her grey synthetic sweater and black trousers were oldish. She looked full of fight now, not grief.

'You – maybe I'll let you come, Col, but I can tell you it's touch and go.'

'Erog was my friend.'

'Whose side are you on, Harpur, ordering him to shadow Iles?'

'He shouldn't have told you that.'

'Whose side are you on?'

'It's a Police Force, not soccer teams.'

'A Force whose Chief spies on his Assistant.'

'Lane's not well. He's been making odd decisions.'

'So, why did you tell Erog to do it? And why is he dead? For liking Iles?'

'A good man flipped.'

'Why did a good man flip?' she grunted. 'Because this Force is cutting itself to bits.' The rightness of the words made her stop for a moment and deep-breathe. 'Lane still wants Iles for Jamieson and Favard, doesn't he? The original very nice guy and Lester might be a route.'

She was a squarish, square-faced woman with slow movements, though she could move fast enough when she wanted, and had some sex to her. Jane's eyes were small for such a large face, making her look a bit malevolent, which Erogenous always said she was not. Harpur had never known where he stood with her and was finding out.

'It's a long while since Lane thought straight,' he said. 'Why he's gone sick.'

'You – do you want Iles for the original very nice guy and Lester, and so a link with Jamieson and Favard?'

'I can't talk about these things now, Jane.'

She stared for a moment and then shrugged, as if the hand-off was what she would expect. 'He's had flowers from everywhere,' she said.

'I'm not surprised.' Erogenous was in the same funeral home as Lester Magellan. You could get this running together of police and villain lives sometimes, and deaths. Probably there had been days and nights when Erog tailed Lester, and now he was tailing him again: Erogenous's funeral was not until next week.

'Flowers even from Bixton's parents,' she said. 'I haven't thrown them out. Not yet. Will Iles be at Erog's funeral?' she asked.

'Of course.'

'Who'll tell Lane to stay away?'

'I will, if you like.'

'Thanks. But *you'll* come, Col?'

'If you—'

'He won't stop you?'

'Who?'

'Lane.' Suddenly, she sounded anxious, not aggressive. 'Look, if he stops you because he's excluded himself, well, he can come, too.'

111

'How could he stop me? Why should he? You weren't sure you wanted me there, anyway.'

'Erog would, regardless.'

Harpur decided not to ask her if she was inviting Sid Synott. She could do without that extra pain now.

Chapter Nineteen

At lunchtime, Iles said he thought the two of them should just slip along to the original very nice guy's funeral.

'They believe you killed him, sir,' Harpur replied.

'Well, *we* don't, do we, Col? And not in uniform, just modestly, unnoticeably among the mourners.'

'We're not unnoticeable, sir. They'll suspect you're rubbing it in.'

'We won't go to Lester's. That would be, well, overkill. I'll send Sam Oxford. And then, certainly, Erog's next week for both of us. Me, uniform, obviously, though only an ACC's. It's a sad, repetitive time, Col.'

'Death is—'

'Christ, not some *mot* about even-handedness.'

'I've others if you'd rather.'

They were in Lane's suite, Iles eating cereal and milk at the desk. He had had the long wall-mirror from his own room brought up and fixed here, so he could check his turn-out and features. 'Would I attend the original very nice guy's funeral if I murdered him, for God's sake?' he asked.

The question seemed to contain its own answer but this was Iles. 'That's certainly a point, sir,' Harpur said.

'When the Home Office and, or, Inspectorate hear we've been there together, Col, they'll very likely drop their stupid anxieties and despicable threats of an inquiry. They'll know you, C. Harpur, retarded by blistering rectitude, wouldn't be party to any ploy. They'll see our action as respect to a victim, although an out-and-outer. I've got black ties in the drawer.' He had on a marvellous solid navy double-breasted suit, a paean to any corpse, let alone the original very nice guy.

'Jane doesn't want Lane at Erog's funeral, sir,' Harpur said.

'Entirely reasonable. He'd bring piety. I'll tell him,' Iles replied.

'I said *I* would, sir.'

'This will require very sensitive handling, Harpur. The Chief can't take much more. I can speak to him with understanding. I love that man. Yes, she's right, it's quite possible the dim sick pompous old biscuit would imagine he ought to be there.'

The original very nice guy's was a chapel funeral, with great hymns, the sort Harpur remembered from his Sunday School, 'Build on the Rock' and that verse, 'When I tread the verge of Jordan'. The organ was playing a morose smooth pre-service piece as he and Iles entered and the music broke up hopelessly for a moment as the organist caught sight of Iles in the mirror over his keyboard. He would be used to amenable brides and coffins there, not this. The Acting Chief led towards the front, looking hard to left and right as he walked, pausing now and then, noting faces. He gave an occasional bad wince, maybe over people he had thought were still locked up, or someone's suit or woman. There was half a pew unoccupied immediately behind Mrs Brace and Iles stood at the end of it flicking his hand until the crew already there moved up, possibly relatives, nobody Harpur recognized. Mrs Brace must have sensed something and half turned. Eyes closed, Iles was well into the details of his arrival prayer and did not see her tremble. When he finished he leaned forward and whispered to her: 'We had to come, Mrs Brace. Raoul – a prince of sorts, always full of humour and ideas. Harpur was reluctant, thought it an invasion, but he's glad now. The Magellans here? Adore your scent. "Red"?'

The minister came in with the body following. He was

intoning something from Revelation, probably. Harpur could always get a kick out of these verses. Sometimes they actually made him feel there might be a system, and that good could pull through. *We give Thee thanks, O Lord God Almighty, which art, and wast, and art to come; because Thou hast taken to Thee Thy great power, and hast reigned.* The minister did a brief and friendly sermon, as if he actually knew the original very nice guy up to a point and liked him. Anyone could on those terms. One section dwelt on how the original very nice guy devotedly looked after his mother.

Iles said: 'Amen to that, padre.'

On the crematorium lawn later, as people dispersed, Mrs Brace, in dark blue and black, approached them: 'I'm glad you came,' she said. 'Some would not wish it, but Raoul, I know, would not object to your presence.'

'He had scope. Whenever I spoke to him, I was aware of character, unostentatious dignity,' Iles replied.

'Yet so young,' Mrs Brace said. 'But thirty-four and removed at his best. He had such happiness before him. Ah, Mr Harpur. So sorry about your wife. Marks on your face? You have another love life now, then?' She smiled, sadly, yet triumphantly: 'Can I tell you something, Mr Iles, Mr Harpur, which is, I must admit, in its way naughty. Yet also joyous. He and his lovely girlfriend were about to elope abroad. Yes.' She gave another deep, melancholic smile. 'Some warm, romantic, favourable country. I say naughty because, of course, technically the girl was rather under age, though not unwilling, and it could probably be assumed that consummation might, in fact, take place in due course. He was so full of it, so content, so certain of his choice.'

'This is Venetia Ember?' Harpur asked.

'So lovely in her crude way,' she replied.

'Did her father know?' Harpur asked.

'Ah, shrewd, Mr Harpur,' Mrs Brace replied. 'Yes, a sort of Romeo and Juliet situation – family hostility, though from his side only, let me stress. I do fear Panicking may have found out. He has his methods. In that sort of life. Of course, not all overseas countries pay so much attention to the age of consent thing, do they? These matters are very relative.'

'Now I see the Magellans,' Iles said. 'This is good. Even in their own pain they have time for Raoul.'

'I may well go to Lester's,' she replied. 'He was by no means a nobody.'

'And a charming flat,' Iles said. 'Why, here's the girl now, isn't it? Don't I recognize her from when they all lived at The Monty? Ah, almost a woman suddenly.'

Venetia Ember was running frantically towards them in jeans, denim jacket and what seemed a bold school scarf, long, trailing and garish for a funeral: reds, tangerines and yellows. She was weeping and shouting something Harpur could not make out. 'Venetia, child, what?' Mrs Brace called.

'Oh, I'm too late, too late,' Venetia said.

'We can tell you about the service,' Iles replied. They were standing among cut flowers and wreaths, which had been spread on the grass from all the day's funerals. He indicated them with a gentle movement of his arm. 'Raoul earned every one of these tributes.' He bent and looked at a card. 'Here's one from Alice and Dermot, "Profoundest lingering regrets". Probably Stan Stanfield and Beau.'

'Daddy sent me away. I sneaked out, but trains— It took me too long.' Venetia looked up at the crematorium chimney, and said nothing. Harpur thought she appeared even younger than fourteen today, lost, loud, very hurtable.

'You did well, love,' Iles replied. 'Raoul would have been proud of you. I would have expected Stanfield here, but he could be lying low for his reasons. Harpur wished to dodge out, Venetia, but, then, he's got a mini-soul. Raoul's mother was just telling us he was going to run away abroad with you permanently. This may come as news.'

She threw her arms in the air and clapped them above

116

her head, wonderfully astonished. Disturbed rooks cawed in elms.

'Oh, was he, was he, really?' she cried, suddenly beaming. 'Oh, the dear, dear one.'

'It was to be a surprise,' Mrs Brace told her.

'It *is*,' Iles said. 'This will be a lovely memory for you, Venetia. It will console you as you age, kid. He would have been extremely *persona grata* on the Continent with a name like that.'

'Yes, lovely,' she replied. 'Which country? At school – oh, they'll be so excited to hear. And jealous. I wish we could have run away in time.'

'Our Chief was the same,' Iles said.

Harpur saw a Rover he recognized pull into the crematorium car park. Nobody left it. 'I think your father's here, Venetia,' he said.

'That cow, my aunty. She must have phoned him at the university, when I was missing. He'd guess why.'

'Well, I expect you should go with him now,' Iles said. 'He's a good man and he loves you, too, you know. I'm certain of that.'

'Perhaps too much,' Mrs Brace said.

'Fathers,' Iles said.

'But how do you know?' Venetia replied.

'We'll talk to him, if you like,' Iles said. 'Harpur's sound on these things. He has a daughter of your age, emerging into the world. Isn't she, Harpur?'

'I'll come over to your dad with you, if you like, Venetia,' Harpur replied.

'No, it will be OK.' She stared up at the sky again, and then walked slowly to her father's car. They watched. Panicking got out of the Rover and stood waiting. Iles waved, but Ember did not respond.

'You think he did your boy, Mrs Brace, coal and all?' Iles asked.

'My son would hurt nobody, had only the most fervent respect for Venetia.'

'I'm surprised he would have left you and your lovely

117

home, for overseas, Mrs Brace,' Harpur said.

'Reluctantly, in a way, yes, agreed. Yet, one's children grow up, don't they, Mr Harpur? Thirty-four is thirty-four. Man's estate.'

'The original very nice guy would have given his best brogues to bang that for a year under a Med sky,' Iles replied. Harpur went for the car. On the way back to headquarters, Iles said: 'Why shoot us that horse shit about the planned overseas saunter, Col?'

'She wants to drop Panicking in it.'

'Savage – though, of course, he might certainly have done it.'

'He's offended her somehow, demeaned her boy.'

'Parenthood's so damn full time,' Iles replied. 'You'd better go up to The Monty tonight and take Ralphy's temperature, Col. I'd come, but mustn't go club-crawling now I'm supremo. Just make sure he's going to behave sweetly. We don't want that child persecuted. Hurt in any way.'

'Panicking's not like that.'

'We might not know what Panicking's like. This is the whole patriarchal thing in action. He sees himself as emblematic. That can produce jagged behaviour.'

'What an experienced man like the original very nice guy sees in a child of fourteen I cannot understand.'

'Oh, for fuck's sake grow up, Harpur.'

Chapter Twenty

'We went on fretting about you after the blockhouse, and not just that possible flat tyre,' Stanfield said. 'Popped down to your place to make sure you were definitely still in tune. No answer. Beau could get in, luckily – that way he has, you know. If you can do a safe, what's the door of a flat? And then he thought most of your stuff had gone from wardrobes or cupboards, either robbery or you'd run, Cyrus. Beau had to say then he believed a run, although he always backs you, as you know, and not just from positive discrimination. Too tidy for a burglary. Then I thought, this could be a misreading, all the same – harsh. Perhaps you never had much in your cupboards and wardrobes anyway. Life at the simple level, which many favour. Given all that you hath to the poor. Or you might be short of cash. And I said to Beau, it could be a night out, and why not? I knew you were a Monty member – isn't Panicking grand on race, though? – so up we come, in case. We didn't want to go into the club, for those reasons I mentioned, and we waited here in the car park.'

'Yes, that's it, a night out, Stan,' Cyrus said. 'I deserved a jolly, that's how I saw it.'

'Obviously, we knew you were inside when we spotted your vehicle here.'

'Yes,' Cyrus replied. His mind darkened a bit further.

'And then Beau opens the boot, that way he has. If you can do safes, what's a car boot? He finds two suitcases packed with your stuff, including evening smart gear, metropolitan touch, some of it, enough for weeks away.

Beau felt he had to believe the worst at that point again, Cyrus. This looked like a sincere flit.'

'I'm always packed ready to go, Stan,' Cyrus said. 'You open my boot any time, those cases would be there. Mobility. Sense of freedom?'

'I told Stan it was that. The gypsy urge.'

'A drink here, farewell to friends, then up the motorway to a hideout?' Stanfield asked. 'How we're bound to see it, Cyrus.'

Cyrus was pretty good at times like this – frightened, yes, but fright did not stop his mind working, and the more scared he was the more calm he seemed to become. The calm was only seemed, he knew that, of course he did, but he also knew the others would not know it, and he had already learned that's what this game was all about. This kind of moment was like in the woods with Stanley. Cyrus could imagine he glimpsed the pistol shape in Stan's pocket again, yet he kept his voice steady, and his legs seemed fine. They were near Stan's BMW, all of them standing in the dark at the edge of The Monty car park, Stan's hand not even in his pocket this time, so far. Cyrus knew the automatic was there, though. This was a hunt.

Stanfield said: 'I don't want to hang about too long in this car park.'

'They've got Panicking in the frame,' Cyrus replied.

'That right?' Stanfield said.

'Harpur is in there, watching, crowding, talking to him. You know his way – the matey smiles and heaviness.'

It was true. Cyrus's simple little experiment had worked. Well, up till now it had worked. If Harpur was there it must mean they thought Panicking, or thought they could load it on him good enough for a jury. Cyrus had been on his way back home when these two stopped him by his car. Forget London. He was ready for The Pines job. It could not have been Kenward who did those two.

'Harpur himself there?' Beau asked.

'Large as life,' Cyrus replied. 'It needs delicate, personal handling, to keep Iles clear. There's a tale out.'

'Which is that, then?' Stanfield asked.

'Motive for Ralphy.'

'I thought they had that already,' Beau replied.

'But stronger,' Cyrus said. 'The original very nice guy was going to take the girl abroad. Live together – some hot country, unniggly about a girl's age, even envious. And Ralphy found out just in time.'

'How?' Stanfield asked.

'You know Panicking. Ears all over, like a concert crowd,' Cyrus said.

'Let's get in my car,' Stanfield replied.

'Sure,' Cyrus said.

Beau went in the front and Stan climbed into the back with Cyrus. 'This yarn – how did it surface?' Stanfield asked.

'It's around the club.'

'People are talking about this when Panicking's there?' Stanfield said.

'Not so he can hear.'

'But where did it start?' Stanfield asked.

'You know how a buzz can begin, Stan,' Cyrus replied.

'No. Anyway, I can't run the future on a buzz.'

'What's it matter, Stan?' Beau replied. 'Harpur's there. Cyrus is right, it says everything. That's probably his vehicle, the beaten-up Orion from their pool for cover. Oldest thing in the car park. You know his ways.'

'He's not here for that. Panicking couldn't do it,' Stanfield said. 'He hasn't got the vim.'

'Maybe. But they use all this to turn it from Iles,' Beau replied. 'The real aim. Tough on Panicking, but nice for us. It means they don't think Kenward, or they'd go all out for him. Him they want more than any. So, he didn't do them. So, he won't be waiting for the replacements.'

'Right,' Cyrus said.

'I knew it already,' Stanfield replied.

'Not *knew*, Stan,' Beau said. 'You *felt* it. The famous educated instincts.'

'Same thing,' Stanfield replied.

Cyrus could see the arguments were beginning to flatten Stanley, except— Except there were still unquestionably the fucking suitcases full of exit gear. Stan had that kind of mousetrap mind, it would fix on something and there could be all sorts of other stuff floating around, but he would stay with that vital factor, hold it. This could be how he kept going and got bigger, stronger, richer, why it was not his funeral this afternoon. Stanfield did the thinking and Beau opened the boot. It was a bright confederation.

'So every time you want to change your boxer shorts you go out to the car in the road, do you, Cyrus?' Stanfield remarked. 'Beau says not a pair of pants in the place.'

'Plus I thought of cutting loose as soon as this job is over,' Cyrus replied. 'Smart take-off. Get a holiday.'

'That could be reasonable,' Beau said.

'Drive us somewhere, Beau,' Stanfield replied.

'What about his vehicle?'

'Just drive us somewhere,' Stanfield said.

Chapter Twenty-One

Denise said: 'Jack Lamb's really twitchy, Col, I mean really, well, *evil*, about some lad who makes the occasional pass at Helen, called Stanley Stanfield, no great harm. Even Helen's a bit scared at Jack's reaction. Do you know Stanfield?'

'Some name,' Harpur replied. 'His parents run out of sounds?'

They were in one of the hotels they sometimes used in the afternoons, The Tenbury. So far, both drew the line at going to his house, even when Harpur's daughters were at school. Strange. While Megan was alive, Denise would snarl about the precedence he gave his family. At times then she hated being a mistress, would stalk off and quit for a day or two. Now, though, she jibbed at the idea of coming any closer to his home life, not even by only entering the house. He did not object or press her, and found that strange, too. Did they both want to keep things free of domesticity? Christ, how immature. Christ, how effective. Christ, how expensive. Christ, how temporary. They were sitting on the bed, dressed still, having one of their pre-love picnics – wine, prawns and pasties. They both liked this slow build, Harpur particularly.

Denise said: 'Apparently some connection with a quite famous marine artist last century who knew Dickens, Clarkson Stanfield. He's a bit dishy – Stanley, that is.'

'Yes?' Harpur replied.

'In a big, slightly rogueish sort of way. Fair. Wide,

woolly moustache, like someone building the Empire. You don't know him?'

'You've met the lad?' Harpur said.

'Oh, he hangs around now and then when we're down the town hall doing ballet lessons, trying for a chat and so on – with Helen. Mainly with Helen. Well, he used to. He's dropped out of sight lately. Helen's a bit peeved. I don't mean she encourages him – but he's got something special.'

'It's gone that far?'

'Jack's getting on. Knocking fifty? Helen, not twenty. Stanley's, what, very early thirties? Yes, some considerable glam, I must say.'

'Must you?'

'Don't get ratty. It's Helen he wants. You don't know him?'

'How would I? I don't learn ballet,' Harpur replied.

'I get the impression – oh, I don't know, I could be doing him wrong – but the impression of—'

'Villainy?'

'How did you know? Or, on the edge of things.'

'We're all there, Denise.'

'Yes. A bit nearer to the wrong side than even you, though. Or even Iles. Helen thinks some sort of operator.'

'I've heard of such.'

'But not on your books?'

'Would I tell you?'

'Thanks, Col.' She munched for a while. 'Look, Mr Smug, what I'm telling you is I'm afraid. I think Jack could get very nasty about his girl.'

Jack had already. 'Afraid for Stanfield?'

'Is he a bit stupid, trying to make something with Helen, giving Jack the two fingers?' She systematically cleared the bed of the picnic debris and wine bottles. For someone of her age and a student she was astonishingly tidy. 'Anyway, that's enough Stan Stanfield.'

'True.'

Soon, she rejoined him and they lay straight out on their backs alongside each other, still in their clothes.

'I can tell you've missed me horribly,' she said.

'Yes.'

'I'm damn lucky to have this big, only marginally ageing, eternally secretive, probably not wholly bent copper devoted to me.'

'I think so.'

'What I would like to do is reciprocate and express in some way my gratitude. Not necessarily verbally.'

'This is a puzzler,' Harpur replied. 'On the other hand, I feel gratitude for the devotion of this brilliant, endlessly coarse, beautiful, sweetly titted nineteen-year-old to *me*, and would like to find some emphatic way of showing it . . . Reciprocate the reciprocity.'

'Lord, problems, problems,' she replied. 'Shall I get your trousers off – see if that helps? Else a great Prince in prison lies.'

'What's that?'

'From a poem pro the body.'

'Only part of the body is in the trousers.'

'We need to start somewhere.'

She got his shoes and socks off, then unzipped him and tugged his trousers and pants down.

'Great Prince?' he said. 'That rather strong? I always think of it as more like an acting corporal.'

'Yes, but he's into action. We might get him promotion in the field,' she said.

He removed the rest of his clothes, then started on her shirt and jeans, and began to kiss her. 'You taste of prawns,' he said.

'Depends where you go.'

'Don't rush things.'

'Why?'

'I'm marginally ageing,' he replied.

After a while she pulled back her head and rested it for a moment on his thigh. 'Well, you don't taste of prawns,' she said. 'Subtler.'

He drew her up so their faces were close. 'And did *you* miss *me*?' he asked.

125

'Don't miss me now,' she replied, wriggling under him. 'Hit the spot.'

'God, you mangle my words.'

'Not just your words.'

'No. I look at you sometimes, Denise – like now, for instance – and think you're really too lovely merely to fuck.'

'Merely fuck,' she replied.

He did, though he had meant what he said. That must be another sign of marginally ageing – to want to look at someone, at her, and enjoy the view, without always wanting to enjoy the body. He must conquer this.

'You have the most clutchable and communicative arse,' he said.

'Oh, but some bastard has shown you my headteacher's reference,' she replied.

When they were dressing to go, Denise said: 'Jack even put it around Stanfield tried violence on Helen. He's that ratty.'

'It's not true?'

'I doubt it. Helen has a giggle with Stan, that's all. Oh, perhaps some misunderstanding, an almost-unpleasantness at some stage, but not grave. I mean, would she be so upset he's dropped out of sight if he'd really tried to break into her pussy, Col?'

'Girls are funny. He could be working out of town.'

'Possibly. Yes, sometimes he acts as though he's going to roll up one day suddenly loaded and big, big wheel. You can see he envies Jack beyond – the property, the grandeur, the connections. You're a Lamb connection? Which aspect of me do you miss the most in the vacations, Col?'

'Your intellect.'

'Cruel, cruel sod,' she replied.

Chapter Twenty-Two

On Saturday, Stan Stanfield and Beau went out to look at Kenward Knapp's place once more. It had to be a two-job now, even Beau agreed. Or, what he agreed was, if they did the job at all it would be just the two of them. Impossible to replace Cyrus in the time left, and crazy if it was possible. You would have to take anybody, some bail bum. Trips to The Pines were getting like pilgrimages – Kenward snug in the holy of holies, so far.

Obviously, Stan had always had a two-plan in the cupboard, in case it had to be, and because he still thought it could be a two and ought to be, for reliability and bigger cuts: if you hoped to get to a girl like Helen Surtees, six or seven grand was certainly something but not something to last. That girl lived with money.

Now it definitely was changed to two, he needed to look at the actual site again and trace exactly how it would work. This was a thing about him, he could not plan from sketches or recollections like an ops room. He had to see the solids, live them and relive them – the fence, the property, maybe the dogs. Then he could visualize the movements for the night and get them exact and concrete in his head. There were other kinds of job planning, but this was his.

They went up again to that spot above and behind the house. As the car climbed, Beau's zing didn't: 'My own feeling is drop it now, Stan. Look, would I say this, knowing how you need it? But some jobs, they're jinxed from the start. Bright leaders spot it and accept. As useful as being at the head wagging your cutlass. Think if they'd said no to Vietnam.'

'Fuck jinxed.'

'When we've got plenty possible trouble as it is, but I'm not blaming.'

'Cyrus? I think I scared him enough, really extensive, Beau. He won't talk. Gone far, far away.' Stanfield parked as before and they stood shielded by trees again. There seemed to be no movement in The Pines or around. That must mean Kenward was inside, or the dogs would be prowling loose. With only Beau and himself working, there would be nobody to distract the Alsatians on the night, and they would have to be drawn to the entrance spot and killed. Also, there would be no sentry outside or driver ready with the engine running as soon as he saw them quit the house. These were difficulties, obviously, but they did not scare Stanfield. He still had the pistol as well as the crossbow. The gun remained unfired – he had been strict with himself about that, regardless – so no possibility of Ballistics matching bullets in the dogs with anything. True, the Alsatians would lie in view when killed, but they could easily be dragged out of sight from the road as Stan and Beau made for the house. No extra time needed. Beau might not like the idea, but he could not have everything. The dogs would be dead or very near.

Then, when it came to the sentry–driver, it could be a plus to be minus, especially someone as jumpy and thoughtful as Cyrus. Now, they knew as fact the car would be there when they came out with the funds. Today, Stan had to check what vision field he'd have from the house windows. That's where he'd do look-out. Beau hated being left alone when he worked. He was under enough stress now and must not get any more, or he would take an age on the safe, or fail. Stanfield reckoned there would be a pretty good all-round view from Kenward's windows, especially the gallery. In any case, only one view counted. That was the side road from the motorway Kenward would use coming home. Stanfield felt pretty sure this could be seen from the windows, and enough of it for plenty of warning if they had to run. Even if Kenward approached with lights off, which the smart bastard probably did, Stanfield reckoned the big Merc estate could be spotted in time.

And if it came to the worst— If it came to the worst, he would still have the pistol and enough rounds left. Kenward would be with Constance, his lady and possibly a driver to guard all the rubbish he bought for grandeur at the charity. Stanfield did not want to take them on, but thought it would go well if he did. He would have to do it alone, because Beau was useless in outright trouble, made of cringe, and, anyway, he did not have armament, refused to carry it, and would not know how to use it.

Stanfield did not talk over the hazards with him now. Beau would see a million of his own. He still needed persuading to be there. Christ, why couldn't he be reasonably money-mad? But Beau had this low-class satisfaction with things as they are, unless some way of making them better was slapped right on his plate, no peril. Stanfield put the binoculars away. 'It's more or less like it was, Beau. We go in at the same spot, leave the car at the same spot.'

'Has Cyrus got family?'

'Cyrus?'

'I've heard him talk about his father, as if he was all right. Perhaps that's where he's gone. He didn't say?'

'You drove us around, went back to your place and we left you there, Beau. I took him to the middle of the town and just told him to get lost for keeps. All I know. Who cares?'

'So, did he go back for his vehicle at The Monty – and the gear?'

'Can't say, Beau.'

They returned to the car. Stanfield drove a different way home. They had been buzzing around The Pines too much lately. 'Come on, Beau, it's going to be fine. We're

129

a full team without him.' All the same, for a couple of seconds, Stanfield wondered whether Beau had hit the word for this job – jinxed. But you could not start caving in to superstition or you were nowhere. Should he take off his moustache – too noticeable? Yet he thought Helen Surtees went for that, and her brainy friend, Denise.

Chapter Twenty-Three

Lamb wanted another urgent meeting and shocked Harpur by suggesting the foreshore defence post again. He never nominated the same rendezvous twice in succession. Jack was there first today. 'I hear a so-called informal inquiry, to start at once into that old Jamieson–Favard–Dessy Iles business,' he said. 'This is footling purists worried about law more than justice.'

'You mean that old Jamieson–Favard business.'

'Anyone could sympathize with Iles's motives,' Lamb replied. 'He was provoked beyond, poor sensitive ape. The Home Office are in a spot now he's Acting Chief. Procedures for someone of his rank are tricky, so they came up with the "informal" gambit. In the first instance. A retired chief to do it. Sir Clive Gambore, QPM, etc.? He gets to the root, they say.'

Christ, yes, they did say. Jack was the kind of informant who often knew more about police business than Harpur. London lay open to Lamb.

'You'll be all right, Col?'

'Of course.'

'I worry for you. Friendship. My future.'

Harpur could see now why Jack had chosen this meeting spot again. He had a new piece of army surplus tailoring, and would not waste it on a non-military background. This was an officer's tails-style mess-dress coat in dark blue, heavy with miniature medals and piping, spot-on for a filthy old blockhouse. Over the jacket he wore a thigh-length navy cloak that Harpur had seen before, and which might or might not be military – possibly from a racy foreign army sixty years ago, say Polish or Hungarian. Amazing he found stuff big enough. It was a sunny winter's day. The sea lay far out again, and the mud flats gleamed like fried liver. In the blockhouse it was freezing and Lamb hugged his cloak to him, once Harpur had appreciated the mess gear. 'Only the past,' Lamb said. 'Sir Clive can't take in the killings of the original very nice guy and Lester because they're still under investigation.'

'Quite,' Harpur replied. 'Very much so.'

'I believe it.' Lamb held out his arms wide from under the cloak in a Christlike come-unto-me gesture. He had on dispatch rider's red-brown gauntlets. 'You're implicated? Can I help you in any way, Col?'

'How would you do that, Jack?'

'A word here, there.'

'No.' God, no. 'No thanks.'

'It would be very possible for you, Col. Iles, no. That's too messy.'

'How's Helen?' Harpur replied.

'Another thing I wanted to mention is the disappearance of a lad called Cyrus Gordon Main. Late twenties, black. Know him? Some form. Nice kid in many ways.'

'Disappeared? How long?'

'Couple of days.'

'For God's sake, Jack. These kids go—'

'His car up at Panicking's place, full of clothes. Some forcefully interrupted flit?'

'By?'

Lamb shook his huge head a couple of times: 'Uncertain, but I hear a recent trip out Longdean way. Stan Stanfield's vehicle. Stan was in it – the moustache was spotted. Beau Derek possibly also there. This looks like a work party, wouldn't you say?'

'Christ, you're really hunting Stanfield.'

'He'd fuck mine, he'd fuck yours, Col. Bastard supposed to be descended from Clarkson Stanfield. Marine painter you'll have heard of, of course. Stan would use violence on a lovely post-punk girl, has.'

132

'Is that right, Jack?'

'Would I go after him if not?'

'Would you? Does Cyrus . . .?'

'Do crossbows? I shouldn't think so. But a good, healthy, all-round lad, vivid behind a wheel.'

'I saw him the other night at Ralphy's when I was checking Venetia was OK.'

'This is a sensible, careful, novice boy. Let's imagine they recruit him as fill-in for Lester but don't say what the job is. All enthusiasm at being with the biggies, and then they take him out to see it, and it's Kenward Knapp's place. Kenward has big collectables at home now and then. That's Longdean way, yes?'

'Possibly,' Harpur said.

'Oh, you've been there to look, have you? You're not ahead of me, for once?'

'Exploring many avenues,' Harpur replied.

'Say Cyrus is terrified, wants only to get out. This is some tender kid who suddenly hears they'll walk into Kenward's place. I mean, Col, Kenward Knapp. Who crosses Kenward? And the story around he's already done two. Cyrus would like withdrawal. He packs and tries.'

'Why hang about at Ralphy's?'

'Don't know. Perhaps some deal between them to be tidied.'

'He didn't speak to Panicking.'

'Because you were there, Col.'

'Possibly.'

'You're spottable. At any rate, Stan and Beau can't let him out, because for all they know he's a mouth. Myself, I've never heard anything from him, and never will now, you ask me. But they trace Cyrus to The Monty and greet him. They've probably seen his bale-out stuff in the car by then. Shouldn't you look around, Col? This could be a lad in a predicament, or past that, obviously. She's fine. Helen's fine. Lovely of you to ask. We make each other very happy.'

'Great.'

'Of course, I'm older.'

'I'd heard that.'

'Probably you and I have discussed this before. Yet this seems to trouble her not at all. Prostate's peachy.'

'Great.'

'Same with you and Denise, I imagine.'

'Will Kenward be waiting for these buggers, Jack?'

'But it's not an outing you'd want to stop, is it, Col? I mean, who gives a sod if one of them, all of them, are hurt, especially Kenward.'

'Or Stan, you mean?'

'If there's real trouble at The Pines a neighbour could do 999 and you'd have the chance to get in at last and look at Kenward's décor and assets and books. You might find something that would link him to the killings of the original very nice guy and Lester, and then, so beautifully, to Jamieson–Favard. Or could be bent to link him. What a let-out for Iles, Col. Stuff the Home Office.'

'All guess, Jack. This what you brought me out here for at a rush?'

Chapter Twenty-Four

Venetia's parents were both at the club, and she went up to their bedroom and one by one lifted four potted plants out of the bidet in the *en suite* and set them on some newspapers in case of soil dropping. She knew from way back that two of the pots had false bottoms, with money underneath in plastic envelopes so it would not be damaged by watering. She found the first envelope under lobelias in the second pot and took a fifty. Then she came on the rest in the geraniums' pot and took another fifty from there. She replaced the plants, but brought the lobelias out again and took another fifty. There must be a few thousand or even more in both pots, so her dad might not notice. If he did, it should be too late.

She must leave home. She thought London. Once, when she was supposed to be at Caroline's for the weekend, riding and playing Monopoly, Raoul had taken her in the Daimler to see some business friends at a house in Lewisham, London SE, which she knew she could find again. These were very nice people, very relaxed. She had thought perhaps some drugs, yes, but nothing wild and no fighting, just relaxed and jolly. She and Raoul did not sleep there, but they could have if they had wanted to, and she felt sure there would be a bed for her now. Instead, he had taken her to a quite nice hotel near King's Cross station, and asked her to make up a bit extra, so she would look older for Reception. It was fine and an adventure and a giggle, plus a meal out in a Thai restaurant, which was even better than Chinese, and wine.

Raoul knew his way around London, of course, and had many interesting business contacts there. Sophie told her she had been to London with her fireman friend including Soho itself, but this might be only fantasy and brag.

What Venetia would not do now was hitch lifts. Everyone knew how dangerous that could be, you were offering yourself. It would be a betrayal of everything she and Raoul had built. Caroline said she had hitched once, and it might be true, but she was very dumpy and a funny wide nose, though a lovely friend. Venetia would miss her most and would definitely send her a card from London. Venetia had some saved money in her special box upstairs, and had luckily also remembered where her father kept these reserve wads, cash from the club or elsewhere that he did not want known about for some reason, and could not place in the bank.

Venetia was sure she would have safety for a while at the Lewisham house. It was true Raoul had wanted to get into the hotel for comfort and because sometimes police victimized this house at night mob-handed, although definitely not a squat. Obviously, he could do without that kind of trouble, being with what the stupid law said was an underage girl, and the possible drugging atmosphere. He was always bothered about this kind of thing. Above all, he would have hated his name to be in the paper in a way that might hurt his mother, though in the end, of course, it was. Staying at that house now would not bother Venetia because the police would have nothing bad against her. When she was there, she met a couple of other quite young girls who seemed to have plenty of money, so there must be jobs, perhaps in that business organization which Raoul worked with. Anyway, they had very good clothes.

She folded up the newspaper and took it downstairs to the bin. One way of thinking of things was, she would be saving Dad money by leaving, such as food, and he could stop those school fees he moaned about and the cost of trips. She still loved him, he was still her dad, but now and then she could see why he was called 'Panicking' by some, as she had discovered from a bitchy kid at school named Grace, whose father belonged to the club. Dad had found out she went to the funeral, of course, and turned sweaty. He really frothed and eloquented – 'having been particularly told not to', all that sort of crap, and 'bringing the family down' before offal like Raoul's relations, especially his mother, that was his word, 'offal'. Of course, what he meant was not just the relations and Mrs Brace but all in that family were offal, including Raoul. Oh, God, God, wasn't this bound to make her wonder even more if he had killed Raoul? Was it her father's terrible way of making her free from him?

So, how could she stay here? This was going to go on and on, he was like that, and her mother would back him up always. She would say of course he did not harm Raoul and Lester, and say, too, that of course he was right to try to separate Venetia from Raoul, and now from the dear memory of him. How could Venetia stay even in this city or this school? Had she not become an outcast through forbidden love? At school, although her friends would be all right and jealous of this ill-fated yet very brilliant romance, some of the others, and those smirking staff hags, had their own ideas for certain about Raoul and would look down on him and on the precious memory of him. Now and then she would hear girls muttering that stupid name some gave him, 'the original very nice guy', which sounded quite friendly, yes, and much nicer than 'Panicking', but it was not really nice. That school was evil.

She packed a bag but not too much, just a couple of changes, because she did not want weight, in case she had some walking to do in London when looking for the house. With Raoul, she was in the Daimler, naturally, but now would have to find her way from the Tube station. She wrote a note:

Dear Mum and Dad,
    Do not think me bad or worry, but I have to go

137

because nobody understands the suffering that has come upon me since the terrible event you know of. I will not tell you where I am going, but it is to be with people who knew Raoul and respected him, and who mourn his death yet also glory in his life. I know these people will like me and will look after me, being Raoul's girlfriend.

Please do not search for me or inform the police, for it will be in vain. You can get rid of my school uniform and return all library books. I have taken a pork pie from the fridge and some apples for my journey and hope this is all right. Perhaps at Christmas and certain other festivals I shall telephone.

Your loving daughter,
Venetia.

She set out for the coach depot. She would have dearly liked a companion. To her surprise, she discovered that the girl she would have wanted to come with her was Hazel Harpur, not one of her school friends at all. So strange because she did not really know Hazel, who went to a comp, and lived down there in Arthur Street. But Hazel had seemed to understand her very quickly, and to want to help her in her terrible heartache. Of course, Hazel would never come. Why should she? She had her nice boyfriend, Scott, here, and her sister. In any case, Hazel's father was police, and the children of police would never do anything like this, they behaved. Perhaps it was best to go alone. One person could lose herself in London much easier, and the people in the Lewisham house would worry about a policeman's daughter. Venetia had the fifties in a money belt her father bought when she went abroad first on a school trip. She patted the pouch now and felt fine.

Chapter Twenty-five

Stan Stanfield went over to Beau Derek's place to do a team talk. Security would say it was mad to be calling on him so near the job, but it was because it was so near the job that Beau would need a lot of boosting, especially after Cyrus and because they were only two now. Well, it was a matter of would Beau turn up.

For the way he looked and his crummy lifestyle, Beau had quite a juicy woman with him these days, Melanie, a bit older than Beau, but her body holding together so well, and dark dye was still beating the grey. She had a good wide warm face, and her eyes would come on with a sudden blaze of brain. She would talk tough to Beau now and then but adored him, and this must be to do with the shits she lived with before. Beau had a lovely side to him, as long as you could keep him away from stress. Crazy to say that. How did a safe-breaker stay away from stress?

Stanfield did not know how much Beau had told Melanie, but he decided she had better know nearly everything, so they could both get the pressure on him to be positive and push out from under the shadows of those dogs and Kenward. When she heard this could be ten grand each for Stan and Beau, or even more, she would probably see the point, even if Beau couldn't. Stanfield took some brochures with him for great holidays abroad and cruises, so they could both smell the possibilities, but particularly Melanie. Beau made a career of doing without and he would not light up for a visit to the Sphinx.

Beau did not seem to mind when Stanfield said he wanted her briefed. Perhaps he'd told her most of it, anyway. She did not say so, yet Stanfield thought she seemed unsurprised as he gave her the outline and described how he became a crossbow star.

'Well, first thing, the information's all right, is it?' Melanie asked. 'Kenward's not going to be there?' She had a stringy, sharp Midlands accent, which made her sound like she wanted to believe you but had trouble.

'Watertight,' Stanfield said.

'I heard a rumour he might have done the original very nice guy and Lester,' she replied.

'Heard it where, Melanie?' Stanfield asked. 'Beau never told you that.'

'Around,' she replied. 'It's everywhere.'

'And it's rubbish,' Stanfield said. 'Police spread it, for their reasons.'

'Iles?' she asked.

'We keep him in mind for future treatment. Iles running loose – it could hit any of us.'

Melanie said: 'Because if it was Kenward—'

'Because if it was Kenward, it would show he was expecting something from those two and might be expecting something in its place, so we drop into another Arnhem,' Stanfield replied. 'Dead right. But that's not how it is.'

Beau said: 'Kenward's at a charity do.'

'Has to be,' Stanfield replied. 'The sod's after canonization.'

'But if it went quicker than we think, Stan? Not enough lots, not enough bidding,' Beau said. 'Kenward getting in there with big money, scaring the rest off. We've no eyes now.'

'My eyes,' Stanfield replied. 'It could even be better someone upstairs in that gallery. You get a sweep right over the terrain. This is often the thing with me, I can make something good out of a disaster. And then, the fatter shares, Melanie.' He pushed one of the brochures towards her, open at an unsinkable white liner and Far East cruise. 'Ever seen Java in April?'

Beau said: 'Stan's got this confidence, through a famous ancestor called Clarkson.'

He sounded completely wanked out. The flat looked a bit that way, too – the lights not bright enough, the furniture sad and rickety, the carpets hammered thin over the centuries. Christ, if only Beau would take an interest in Louis Quinze or Chippendale – anything pricey – he could be the greatest safesman ever.

'What happened to the number three?' Melanie asked. 'I mean, not Lester but subsequent?'

'Stan wasn't happy with him,' Beau replied. 'In the long run.'

'No,' Stanfield said.

'So?' Melanie was seated on the living-room table, showing off decent legs, thinnish but tolerable. She could perch on that bit of junk in a way that made you think some sort of saucy communication went on between the timber and her body. A few of these women wore well, no matter what kind of life they had previously. Obviously she had seen a lot of action before she met Beau. Melanie ought to be a nourishing experience for him but you did not spot many signs.

'We couldn't risk him, that's all,' Stanfield said. 'Not our type, we discovered.'

'Yes, but doesn't he know about—?'

'Oh, he's not the sort of lad who'll talk,' Stanfield replied.

'What sort of lad is he?' Melanie asked.

'We're both confident on this, aren't we, Beau?'

'A good lad,' Beau replied. 'But not good *enough*.'

Melanie stood, her eyes impressive. 'This auction public?'

'Of course. For a charity,' Stanfield said.

'Why don't I go and watch him?' Melanie asked. 'When he leaves, I get on the blower.'

Stanfield struck the arm of the Rexine chair he was in and felt it lurch. 'Christ, brilliant.'

'Ring Kenward's house while I'm working?' Beau said. 'He'll be ex-directory.'

Melanie went and brought the book. 'Yes, he is. So, you ring me when you get there. Give me the number.'

'Ring you where?' Beau asked.

'A phone box near the auction.'

'Great,' Stanfield said.

'Phone box? They never work,' Beau said. 'Will we have time to make phone calls?'

'Fuck off, Beau,' she replied. 'We can check the box out in advance.'

'I'll be waiting nonstop for that phone to ring while I battle that peter,' he said.

'That's all right, Beau. You'd still have a good twenty minutes after Melanie calls.'

'I don't like her getting involved,' Beau replied.

'Not involved. Just a call. She's a genuine part of the crowd. She could make bids. There might be some items in the flat needing replacement.'

'Nobody knows me, Beau,' Melanie said.

'You can't be sure,' Beau replied. 'His phone could be bugged – our voices on a record.'

'Keep it to a couple of words, Melanie,' Stanfield said.

'Maybe just a coded ring. Say six buzzes.'

'No,' Stanfield replied, 'someone else might call and give up after six.' These women could be clever, but never went the whole distance.

'If we were engaged,' Beau said. 'We've got to answer everything.'

'I'll say I'm the butler and end any other calls. "Mr Kenward Knapp is not presently at home." We could cut you in, Melanie – for at least a grand,' Stanfield said.

'I've earned money harder,' she replied.

Chapter Twenty-Six

Harpur returned from a dawnish trip to Dobecross woods and immediately had a call up to Iles's suite, the Chief's suite, as it had been. Mark Lane never used it much but would drift in to people's offices, shirt sleeves, no shoes, keeping matters as informal as he could. He loathed all things imposing or smart or army-like, dreaded what they might bring to a Police Force. Iles would run things differently. He regarded himself as a gem viewed best in its setting, and might consider the Chief's suite as just about adequate for that.

In civilian clothes today, the Acting Chief said: 'We're getting immediately what the Home Office puckishly term an "informal" inquiry into the state of the Force, Col, with special focus on the Jamieson–Favard episode you might recall. Double deaths? Something like that, wasn't it?'

'Who's doing it, sir?'

Iles, busy at the big mirror adjusting one of his lips, suddenly grew tense and stared at Harpur via the glass. 'You know all this, do you, you sod?'

'What does it mean, informal?' Harpur replied.

'You've even got this solemn has-been's name?'

' "Informal" – sounds like a sop to the politicos and media trouble-makers,' Harpur said.

'What I thought, Col. They're doing the minimum, damping down. No bother. But they'll give an appearance of urgency, so he flies in this morning. Or did you know that as well? We'll meet him at the airport. He'll want to see you early. And who's the dead black boy in the woods?'

'Found by children, I'm afraid, sir, in a negligible grave. Head wounds. Bit defaced and nothing in the pockets. We think Cyrus Gordon Main, minor but up-and-coming villain. Was. General duties. Nervy, thoughtful kid, smart with cars. Chat-up Charlie is looking at it.'

The Acting Chief, still in front of the mirror, dropped his trousers and underpants and examined himself both in the glass and direct. 'I could have picked up a dose, Col,' he said. 'You haven't had any trouble?'

'Might Lester have been doing something with that lady in the flat below him?' Harpur replied.

'I did press her on that, obviously, not just on account of infection,' Iles said. 'She swore not, and if he was she didn't seem very upset about losing him. But would people get upset about Lester, except a mother, possibly.'

'Do some of Personnel's windows overlook your mirror, sir?' Harpur replied.

The Acting Chief went on with his examination, moving himself about with one hand to get views from all angles, but did not ask Harpur for a verdict. In his other hand Iles held a print-out about the discovery of Cyrus. 'Lester AC/DC? Do I worry about HIV as well? Oh, it could be just acne,' he said, fixing his clothes again. 'Christ, how democratic clap is.'

Harpur said: 'You'll—'

'Steer clear of Sarah for a while? Why? Don't tell me you're still—'

'We ought to speak to the Chief about staying away from Erogenous's funeral, sir,' Harpur replied. 'It's tomorrow.'

'We? So tell me about this Cyrus.' He sat at his desk and with a slight shiver put the picture of Mrs Lane face down.

'Little known, beyond what I've said, sir.'

'Connections with any biggies?'

'Not that we can discover to date.'

'In woods?'

'We think he was killed there, not just dumped.'

'He'd gone voluntarily? Early primroses? Gang dispute? Which gang?'

'Some of them use the country for shooting practice. Perhaps that was the lure.'

'Why wasn't he shot, then? Easier, quicker. Or did they want the defacement?'

'We're only at the early stages yet, sir.'

'You're talking to me, Harpur, not the bloody Press.'

'We're only at the early stages yet, sir.'

'Vehicles seen there?'

'Chat-up's doing a trawl on that. We're only at the early stages yet.'

They went out in the Acting Chief's Senator to meet Gambore, Iles driving. 'This one's quaint and vicious, Col, the way they get when thoroughly mature. He wants to pay his respects first thing to Lane, meant as a smack in the chops for me. We'll take him there now and I can give the Chief my ban on the funeral, in the most tactful way, don't fret. You stay out of that, right? Right?'

'I'm sure you'll be gentle with him, sir, given he's ill.'

'That man's a treasure, sick or fit. If dear Lane's keen to keep up public appearances he can go to the charity auction in his diary for this week. Otherwise, I'll have to. We contribute unclaimed property. Do I fancy hobnobbing with dregs like Kenward Knapp, flashing cash to respectabilize themselves? Think how they tried to get Stalker for socializing.' His voice went high and took on long-suffering. 'Aren't I already persecuted enough, Col?'

'Possibly, sir,' Harpur replied. 'Which night is that?'

'Thursday, why?'

'Oh, I might look in for a bargain.'

'Why, Harpur?'

'Oh, I might look in for a bargain.'

'Interested in Kenward?'

'Of course, people bid generously at these charity things.'

'Out of your chicken-feed league. Seen Panicking?'

'He seemed mild enough, reconciled. Venetia will probably be all right, no victimization. He says he'll try to get her back to normal schoolgirl life.'

'Ah, nice. All-the-way love's a great competitor with that, though, once they've started. But you'd know. Ages since I was at The Monty. Anything interesting – not just women?'

'The usual crew.'

'Did Ralphy sound guilty as hell of doing the original very nice guy and Lester – the vengeful dad?'

'You know Ralphy, sir,' Harpur replied.

'Sir Clive,' Iles cried, as Gambore emerged into the airport concourse, 'I'm convinced you're going to love your time with us. The Chief is eager to see you again, and your visit will be a much needed tonic to him in his sadly progressive condition. Oh, yes, you'll still recognize him. In that sense, he's remarkably brave and resistant, but it's what's within in these cases, isn't it? This is Harpur, my head of CID, who spent so long on the Jamieson–Favard business, which I gather interests you, and quite naturally, too. Harpur's an ex-whizz-kid.'

In the car on the way to the Chief's house, Gambore said: 'But you, also, Mr Iles, sat very close to the Jamieson–Favard affair, I think.'

'Desmond, please, Sir Clive,' Iles replied. 'Sat? Close? One was head of Operations. Is that sat? You've seen the files, obviously.'

'A youthful undercover detective murdered, these two suspected and charged but acquitted. Some police evidence disbelieved by the jury. Suggestion of planted items?'

'Disgraceful smears by their gross lawyer,' Iles replied. 'Nobody gets that fat honestly.'

Gambore said: 'Desmond, you thought highly of this youngster, Raymond Street, and were very palpably moved at the service for him, I gather – his halo parade, as the culture has it?'

'Got a mole, have you?' Iles replied. 'Yes, total grief at the service. Wouldn't you? Street was one of our best. Ask Harpur – they say he's all integrity, more or less.'

'Well, I will, in due course,' Gambore said.

Far back in his accent, he had a touch of Scots, which would make Iles hate him much more. The Acting Chief often said how he got stomach cramps from kirk-type high-gloss posturing probity. Gambore was slim and faded, some of his hair still in place, but a seedy looking tint between ginger and grey. His eyes were blue and hostile, though possibly not hostile enough for what he was taking on here. He must be about sixty-six and had probably spent the last few years chairing some conservation outfit or youth leisure scheme. This would be unlike dealing with Iles. Gambore had a long, very strong face, still alert and occasionally cheerful, with a heavy straight nose and Queen's Police Medal chin. Harpur would spot him as a cop, just as everyone would spot Harpur as a cop. Iles was different: somebody meaning well told him lately he looked donnish, and Iles had struck her in the kidneys, though at the last moment pulling the punch.

'I suppose what I'm asking is whether you felt affronted by the acquittal of these two, Desmond,' Gambore said.

'I suppose you are,' Iles replied. 'The world should have been affronted, can't you see that? Lane swallowed it all right, naturally. The law took its frowzy course, so that's OK, is it? No wonder he breaks down. It's guilt. A late credit to him.'

'And you – did you swallow it?'

'This was a boy who'd got into bed with a gay for us, with Jamieson,' Iles replied. 'Talk of swallowing it.'

'You'd want to put things right for him?'

'The law needs to be in good hands.'

Gambore said: 'Yes, but who has—?'

'In good hands,' Iles said.

For a second, Harpur recalled Iles in front of his mirror, when only one hand was available to nurse the domain.

'And then some girl tied into it somehow?' Gambore replied.

He was sitting alone in the back. Iles snarled at him over his shoulder as he drove: 'I love your phrasing. You'll give even Lane a run for his money. She was *tied into it* through being burned to death by those maggots. Wilfully.'

'And the court didn't agree on that, either,' Gambore said. 'This was a girl close to you, I think. This was no casual piece of satisfaction?'

They were entering Lane's fine drive. 'Sir Clive, I'm probably poxed at this moment by some casual piece of satisfaction,' the Acting Chief replied. 'No doubt, you, too, are caught from time to time, despite galloping decrepitude, and so are most men. Harper no. He must have screwed through to immunity. I do know the difference between kinds of women. Celia Mars was not like that. No, not casual at all and, yes, very close to me.'

'Would you have killed for her?'

'I'd kill someone who called her a casual piece of satisfaction,' Iles replied. 'Which hotel are you in, Sir Clive? Ah, here's the Chief and his grand wife waiting for us in their very genuine old porch. She's a through thick and thin woman, believes in Lane whatever happens. Sometimes I envy him, never mind how she looks.' It was one of those moments when Harpur would detect real self-pity in Iles's voice. The Acting Chief pulled up and jumped out to open a door for Gambore. 'Mr Lane has well-etched views about the Jamieson–Favard business, too, Sir Clive, haven't you, sir?' he called. 'And possibly Mrs Lane, also. She very much shares her hubby's load.'

'Chief wants you to look at things with all your famed vigour and scrupulousness, Sir Clive,' Sally Lane replied.

They went into the big, light drawing-room with rural scene water colours and framed photographs of relatives around the high walls. The Chief had a former rectory at Baron's Hill, almost a mansion, with grand grounds and a paddock for the children's ponies. The boy and girl must be at their local Catholic high school now. Lane would have nothing to do with private education.

Sally Lane brought drinks and some party snacks on a glistening hostess trolley. Iles gazed at it, as he always did, horrified. She offered to withdraw then, but Gambore said: 'Not on my account, please, dear lady. My whole mission here is informal, and this is the least formal part of that informality.'

'Bravo,' Iles said.

'Two areas I'm told to look at,' Gambore said. 'Those killings and the present state of the Force.'

'Necessarily less good than it should be,' Iles replied, 'since the Chief is temporarily not in control. The rest of us do what we can, but where is the flair now, the deftness?'

On a sofa, with a glass of sherry at his feet, Gambore widened his eyes to indicate frankness. 'The real question that has to be put, I fear, is how seriously Desmond was investigated about those deaths. One sees the difficulty – an ACC.'

Lane replied at once, his doughy face momentarily criss-crossed by pink lines of excitement: 'I have absolute faith in Colin Harpur.'

'We all have,' Mrs Lane said.

'As a matter of fact, Col's always trying to get me for killings,' Iles said. He had stayed on his feet, as though reluctant to relax into full guest status here. 'There was some twopenny-halfpenny crook who'd been – well, Mrs Lane is present, so I'll be moderate – who'd been seeing a lot of my wife and was found nastily dead. I was aware of some ardent sniffing in my direction then as a suspect, too. That so, Harpur?'

Harpur did not reply.

'That so, Harpur?' Iles asked.

'I can't say what you were aware of, sir.'

'Absurd, absurd,' Mrs Lane cried. 'How *is* Sarah?'

'Bonny,' Iles replied. 'We've discovered mah-jong.' He had his usual old tart's drink, port and lemon, but with only a single port in it because of the driving. He looked about impatiently for another, and Mrs Lane poured. 'I mean, as you say, Sir Clive, what sort of a Force would we have here if an ACC, now Acting Chief, were reasonably suspected of such killings?' Iles gave a decent, incredulous chuckle.

'Right,' Gambore answered.

Lane was in a large black leather armchair that somehow made him look even feebler, like a fly trapped on sticky paper. For Gambore's visit he had dressed formally, or as formally as he could manage, in one of those dark suits that Iles reckoned were made by Zaire convicts as a minor switch from mail bags. Lane said: 'As to the Force now – fine, Clive. Fine, fine, fine.' He shouted the words, his voice loud, jaunty but thin, and much older than he was. 'Paradoxically, this will be brilliantly in evidence tomorrow at the funeral of one of our most valued officers, Inspector Jeremy Stanislaus Jones. I say paradoxically because, of course, another of our own officers has been charged with the killing. My feeling and that of most is this was a terrible, meaningless aberration. Tomorrow, the Force will close ranks and everyone will attend – no animosities, no coldnesses, a grand and solid turn-out for a fine man. A cleansing, healing ritual. It will do me no end of good to be present at this positive occasion. Yes, I do not hesitate to call it positive. That's the kind of Force we have here, Clive, and who says otherwise speaks evil lies.'

'Do you think you should submit yourself to such stress just now, sir?' Harpur asked.

'Ah, but Chief simply could not stay away,' Sally Lane replied. 'Why, the whole Force would expect him to be there, and he expects it of himself, demands it of himself. This is the leader his men and girls know.'

'But perhaps we must ask how far that death does indicate an appalling schism in the Force, Mark,' Gambore said. 'This would be another area I should look at. That possibility much concerns the Home Office and Inspectorate, I have to tell you. Funerals, yes – everyone's solid and forgiving for the moment at a funeral. I'm sure Mark and Desmond will be welcomed equally there. But does that really mean anything? Two or three hours after, are we back to a situation where one half of the Force is fighting the other?'

Harpur stirred: 'I think most of what you've just said is unintelligible to the rest of us in this room, Sir Clive. And offensive. You speak almost as though there were two camps – the Chief's and the Acting Chief's. Nobody in the Force would recognize that analysis.'

'Where do you stand, for instance, Mr Harpur?' Gambore replied.

'At the head of an efficient criminal investigation department, I hope,' Harpur said.

'Exactly,' Mrs Lane declared.

Harpur said: 'Tomorrow, the Chief and Mr Iles will sit together at the funeral service for our colleague and walk together behind the coffin. Of course you're right that this will be an exceptional moment, bonding all who loved Erogenous, which means everyone in the Force. But when our two senior officers sit and walk alongside each other like that, it will be no freak of the occasion, there will be no falsity in it. Simply, it will typify how the Force is run during its day-to-day existence, thank God. Certainly, grief over Erog unites them, but that unity is commonplace, the norm. How could we function otherwise?'

'Thank you, Colin,' Lane said.

'Thank you, Harpur,' Iles said, 'oh, thanks, you outright scheming fucker.' They had driven Gambore from the Chief's house to his hotel and left him there. Now, they approached headquarters. 'So Lane's my happy and eternal partner. This is the bugger who would have put Erog on my tail, but you took over instead. Yes, where *do* you stand, Mr Harpur? You worked it sweetly, I'll grant that. The gorgeously comic soul-mates' oration. After that, do I tell Lane he's not wanted at the funeral?'

'I knew you'd have been unable to do that to him, anyway, sir. In his condition, who could foresee the damage? Never in your nature.'

After a while, Iles gravely nodded. 'Sod off. But, yes, I can be fatally tender. Poor gibbering wreck. His wife's loyalty to him makes me cry.'

'Besides, would you want to put it all on a plate for Sir Clive?'

'Well, you could be right there, Col. I'll settle that vicary prick. Harpur, I think I can say you've never heard me call you a total fool, I mean, total?'

'That's a tricky one, sir.'

Later, Harpur drove to the Incident caravan they had established at Dobecross, then walked up into the woods with Chat-up Charlie for another look at where Cyrus was found. He had been moved now, of course, though the spot remained tented and under guard.

It was another good, sunny afternoon, with the first feel of spring warmth about. Harpur did not think much of the countryside, but this particular area could generally bring cheerful memories. As a child, he used to be ferried out by special train to a field at the foot of these hills for the Sunday School Treat on Whit Mondays. They would play cricket and baseball and touch-rugby, get fed tea and cake in a big marquee, and some of the older boys and girls would slink off in pairs to the woods. On the way back in the train they all chanted gospel choruses, most looking forward to the hereafter: *Will there be any stars in my crown?* A grasping faith, really: not only a crown for playing right in life, but top scorers rated a bonus. He used to wonder whether those in the woods still qualified for stars, or even their crown? Harpur stopped attending Sunday School before he was old enough to discover if the present pleasures of what went on among the trees was worth trading for afterlife promises. Gazing at the rough, stony grave, he wished he could still believe in future crowns and stars. It would help him forget sights like Cyrus with half his face pulped.

Chat-up said: 'Two things, sir. A couple of farm families report seeing a car parked at odd times in various places around the base of this hill. At first, it was always in the day but then an apparent switch to night visits. Two thought possibly a red Cavalier or Peugeot, two others said a BMW, but also red. They were viewing from a long distance.'

Stanfield's file might settle that. They had reached the tent and Chat-up held the flap open for Harpur to enter and came in afterwards. Both had to stoop, but especially Chat-up. Sergeant Charles Hill was about six foot eight and thin enough for anorexia. His wellington boots looked absurdly wide on his skinny legs and absurdly short. His voice, though, was fat and forever friendly. He wore small, rimless, Himmler-style glasses and was possibly almost as good an interrogator as Iles himself. Erogenous had been better than both, unparalleled at getting suspects to abandon their right to silence.

'Then there's the Mountain Centre on the other side of the hill,' Chat-up said. 'For climbers, survival courses and so on. The warden says a lad who'd been out night orienteering in the woods last week came on somebody practising crossbow.'

'In the dark?'

'Apparently. This character didn't like the look of things very much and stayed out of sight watching. There were at least two people, apparently, and he thought one might be black. An arrow flew wide and this sidekick went to search. For a moment then, our observer feared the man with the crossbow was going to do him some damage.'

'With the bow?'

'He put down the bow and approached him from behind. The spy says it looked as though the – of course, sir, this is in the dark, in a wood and from a good way off, so we have to wonder – but to him it looked as though the bow man was pulling a hand gun from his pocket. He even believes he saw a glint of moonlight on metal. He felt so sure that he was about to shout a warning, never mind

153

his own safety. But then the moment seemed to pass. He took his hand off the gun, if that's what it was. Not long afterwards the two left together, seemingly mates again, possibly making for the Cavalier-Peugeot-BMW.'

Harpur said: 'The warden's recounting what he was told? Can we reach the observer direct?'

'I'm trying. There were two groups in the Centre around that time. They book in the names of their clubs, not individually, and the warden can't give me a name.'

'No description of the bow man?'

'Biggish. Dungarees. His back was to our boy the whole time.'

So, Stan Stanfield, in his resourceful way, learning how to replace Lester, and doing it in the dark to match job conditions? Was Stan already in two minds about Cyrus then? Then they'd caught him with a car full of getaway clothes and that clinched it? Harpur revelled in the idea of this possible gun. If there were a break-in at The Pines and trouble, conceivably Kenward would catch a bullet. Only conceivably, but you took what was offered, and even helped things along where you could. Now and then, unsolved crimes might be conveniently loaded on to someone dead and past hiring a smart defence. It was a bit like the scapegoat he often heard of in Sunday School – that poor old beast elected to carry all the sins of the Children of Israel. Perhaps it got stars in its crown as reward for the sacrifice. Possibly, late in his career, Kenward Knapp could pick up some, too.

Chapter Twenty-Seven

This was getting crazier and crazier, but Beau wanted another meeting, so urgently the poor dab could hardly speak when he phoned Stan Stanfield. Beau was not supposed to phone at all so near a project, and they weren't supposed to meet so near a project, either, but Stanfield stayed beautifully tolerant, agreed to a get-together. Beau was artistic temperament. You had to respect it. Stan reckoned he sympathized with artists owing to descent from Clarkson Stanfield. Why couldn't Melanie open safes? She had the balls.

Obviously, Stanfield knew what it was about. Beau would feel a bit betrayed. That discovery of Cyrus came much too soon, and the media spread. The papers gave very unnecessary descriptions of his injuries. You'd think a body could lie at peace in the countryside, without kids messing. What the hell were kids doing out alone in a thick part of Nature, anyway? They should be vandalizing cars. Beau said not the blockhouse this time, it was getting too regular, so they did one of their alternatives, Marks and Spencer's shoe department. You could sit there back to back on the rows of chairs, and talk while trying on the trainers or suedes. Because of these positions, nobody saw both faces at once. How to get an unobserved conversation in a crowd, a real skill. You could buy something or not, nobody served you or pressured. Take as long as you liked. It might be quite long with Beau in the state he was. The other beauty of the M and S shoe section was CID boys always went for class footwear, wanted celebrated modes with renowned names, and never bought in a multiple.

'Christ, Stan, you did him,' Beau said.

'Has Melanie sorted out the phone box?' Stanfield replied. It was not too busy in the shoe section, but he watched his voice level.

'Harpur's looking at this Cyrus death himself,' Beau said.

'Nothing leads anywhere. It could be a useful smoke screen.'

'But only a kid, Stan. Black, yes, but still only a kid.'

'Old enough to talk, Beau, and pack a bag.'

'You said it was all right – he wouldn't chatter. You said he had gone to his parents.'

'No, you did.'

Stanfield went to fetch a pair of green and purple loafers. When he returned, his chair behind Beau had been taken by a woman with two children, who had to be fitted with sports shoes, so communication was suspended. Beau glanced back, troubled by the interruption, a sweat patch on the skin of his scalp. After ten minutes, Stanfield resumed his place and tried on the loafers. He thought as fun things they worked. The colours were lively, but all right. That could be something else he had from Clarkson, colour awareness. Many had remarked on this in Stan.

'You went out there with him in your own car, for Christ's sake?' Beau asked.

'It was very late, wasn't it? Not much about.'

'But you've been around there before, yes, practising?'

'I changed the parking spot every time, obviously. Absolutely nothing noticeable. Try some shoes, Beau. You might be obvious otherwise. Maybe security cameras here. Big Brother's bothered about your feet.'

Beau stood and went to fetch some black lace-ups. When he came back, he fiddled with them for a while and pushed out his legs to inspect. 'Those injuries, Stan.' He was near to sobbing. An emotional job, choosing shoes. 'You gave me lies.'

'I hoped unrecognizable, especially if he'd been there a while. Cleared the pockets. But, of course, they had prints. What I would not do is use the gun. I knew that would bother you, Beau, if he was found, and you'd start worrying about bullets there and maybe at The Pines.'

Beau sat back hard in his chair so their heads knocked. 'The Pines is dead, Stan. Deader than Cyrus. Why I called you. Why we're here. It can't be, not now.'

'So, a heavy mason's chisel,' Stanfield replied. 'It was instant, Beau, and from behind. The rest of it, well after death. And he came out there without too many worries, because we'd been before with the bow. You don't have to feel bad about him. He never knew. He thought just another practice. Basically, I liked him. It wasn't such a big mistake choosing him. Don't blame yourself.'

'It's off, Stan.'

'Oh, I doubt it,' Stanfield replied. 'No need to feel uneasy about the chisel. I lost it in one of those little dark water lakes up there immediately afterwards, and bought a replacement. Try them walking, Beau. Show you're serious.'

Beau had a pace about.

'Comfy?' Stanfield asked when Beau sat down again. 'We've got too much invested in this now – time spent, the thinking. Look, I can understand your first reaction, Beau – not panic, leave that to Ember, but nice consideration in you for your chosen lad, and, I admit, the shock of finding out like that, through the Press, when I'd let you think he'd done a runner. That was from consideration, too, though. I knew you'd be disturbed. Jesus, this is one hell of a discussion to be done back to back.'

Beau said: 'If Melanie—'

'No need to tell her this unpleasant case in the papers was our number three, Beau. My own feeling, she'd understand the necessity, anyway. You've got a rare one there. And she'd probably feel there could be a similar – how do I say it? – similar risk for yourself, Beau, in view of how far on we are. The thing is, I can't let you out now.

I couldn't let Cyrus out, and same for you, Beau, only much, much more so, obviously. You're the heart of this job. You're the fingers, but you're the heart. I can replace the chisel but not Beau Derek. I'm proud to know you, and hope that can go on and on.'

'Harpur—'

'Does Harpur care about some villain dead in a wood? One less to fuck him about, disrupt his sex life. Would Harpur care about Kenward's place being done, if Harpur had any idea of it? Someone grabs Kenward's trafficking loot. That upsets police? Iles will need hospital through laughing. This discovery of Cyrus could be a real plus, Beau, that's how I've come to see it. I'm going to get these loafers. A purchase gives us cred here. And they'll merge with some of my riper moods. So, see you at the pick-up spot with all your magic keys and brilliance.'

'I—'

'Beau, if I could do it alone, I swear I'd leave you out and free from pressure. Can't be, though, can it?'

'I—'

'Can it, Beau?'

Chapter Twenty-Eight

There were food and drinks back at the bar in head-quarters after Erogenous's funeral. Iles had convinced Erog's girl, Jane Vanteaux, that their flat would not be big enough to take the crowd. Harpur saw the Acting Chief wanted recognition for Erog and had concocted this official party. Erog did not rate a plaque on the so-called Halo Wall – for officers murdered on duty. To be stabbed in a jolly at Iles's house by a brother cop was different, and not even he could swing that. Iles had decided on this get-together, instead. 'We trumpet our pride, Col.'

There had been no protest from Jane at Lane's presence, not so far. The Chief had even tried to comfort her, as would be his decent way, and she appeared to take his words and the arm around her shoulders almost gratefully. She liked to hear Erogenous praised, of course she did. And if the testimonial came from someone she thought an enemy of his it could seem even more valuable. She was wrong to believe Lane did not love and admire Erog, and just as wrong if she thought Erogenous hated Lane. Not the time to tell her, though. Sarah Iles, with a neat gin in her hand, said: 'What's wrong with Desmond, Col? Will they get him at last for those killings, Jamieson and Favard?'

'You talk as if he did them.'

'He has his own way of settling things.' She was in a dark blue outfit with a ruff-collared cream blouse, and looked as she generally did: combative, very bright, very breakable, gorgeous, uncertain. Sometimes he wondered why he had let it die with her. Or had she let it die with him? Anyway, it was good and dead, except for a very occasional hurried nice resurrection for old times' sake. Christmas could start ancient longings, somehow.

'I thought things went all right at the funeral,' Harpur said. 'He was mild with Lane. Still is.' He waved a hand to indicate Iles, the Chief and Mrs Lane talking on the other side of the room with Jane and what could be relatives of Erog. Harpur had put Sid Synott on the Cyrus case with Chat-up, to keep Sid away. No need to remind Jane of that slip, especially with Erogenous's sad kin around.

Sarah said: 'Oh, I'm not talking about today. That's easy for him. Des can find any face for a couple of hours, even friendliness, even respect, you know that. Deeper, Col. He's crippled. Is he frightened? Des frightened? Christ, it ought to be unthinkable.'

'Frightened of what? I hadn't noticed anything,' Harpur replied.

'He doesn't want me, Col. Sleeping separate. Is that an answer?' She gripped his wrist, tugged at his arm to demand concentration, but controlled her voice, thank God.

'There's some stress for all of us just now,' Harper said.

'Usually, he eats stress.'

A lot of people were in uniform this afternoon, including Iles and Lane, and the big panelled room gleamed with silver buttons, pain and white collars. Police dressed up and in numbers always convinced Harpur he had picked the right career. Even in disaster you sensed they knew how to look after themselves and might get round to looking after the public. Drinks had begun to bring many out of their grief, and the noise level rose and grew more hearty. Almost all of them, not just Harpur, saw too many job funerals, and they had learned to scramble back fast from sorrow, or swim back. Iles had said a free bar, though Harpur did not know where the money might come from. Perhaps it was Iles's own. That would be like him. One aspect of Lane Iles found incomprehensible was meanness.

Sarah said: 'Can this invading sod get him, Col?'

'Gambore?'

'Gambore and whoever's behind Gambore.'

'It's just a ritual, Sarah.'

'Who's driving it, Col? How high in the Home Office? They'll finish him.'

'You talk like a cop. It's all totally informal.'

'What's that mean – get everyone off guard?'

'There's nothing he can find. No need to be on guard.'

She grabbed his wrist again and stuck her nails in, let them sink, so he could inventory each. Her breath struck him like a flail. '*Get* on guard, you soft, smug sod. This is my husband we're talking about. This is big power hunting him.'

'Your husband himself thinks the inquiry is just a gesture.'

'So why is he destroyed?' Francis Garland joined them. 'I was just telling Colin, Des doesn't fuck me any more. What's happening, Fran?'

Some situation. Two men who had had affairs with Sarah while she was married to Iles now asked to help with her home sex life. How did you explain that Iles was being noble, getting his sordid sickness into isolation? Of course, Garland was the sort who would tell her right out, if he knew Iles was off colour. He said in that big metallic voice: 'We all go through these phases, Sarah,' so he did not know.

'There's the bastard,' she replied and nodded towards Gambore. He had attended the funeral with Iles and Lane and now stood alone, in a fine, dark suit and tie, gazing about, reading things as he wanted to read them, painting dark pictures in his dark, rapid brain. Yes, who'd sent Gambore? 'Can you beat him, Col?' Sarah asked.

'If anybody can, Colin will,' Garland said.

Normally, egomania stopped Garland giving compliments, just as career arrogance prevented him admitting mistakes. He must be frantically worried about Iles, too, and driven to put trust even in Harpur.

'But can anybody, even Col?' Sarah asked.

'Suddenly you're in love with your husband?' Garland replied. 'That's fine.' He moved off.

'Yes, *are* you?' Harpur asked her.

Sarah swigged the gin. She seemed to need that before speaking. 'He's mine. This is marriage, Harpur. Heard of it? This is a husband. He's strong. He's my daughter's father. I don't let him get hurt. He wiped out those people, didn't he, Col?'

She meant this as another of Iles's assets? 'Which?'

'In the very best of causes, but he did them. Because nobody else would, including you, you legalistic prat.'

'Watch what you say to Gambore,' Harpur replied. He went and brought her another double gin and himself a mixed cider and gin. Harpur began to think his life even more than most around him now was too taken up with funerals: Megan's, the original very nice guy's, now this. His dark suit would start to shine.

'Of course I'm in love with him,' Sarah hissed when Harpur returned. 'According to my style. I won't see him made less, made pathetically scared and gutted, by some back-room cop/politician conspiracy, Col. Lane in on it? Col, *you're* not in on it? You want him out of the way? Why? Career?' She paused, then blurted: 'Not you and me? That's not really active, is it, is it?' The last 'is it?' went down not up, a finality, not hope or invitation.

'We've got some things moving,' Harpur replied.

'I should bloody hope so,' she said. 'Do I ask what?'

'This is Sarah Iles, the Acting Chief's wife, Sir Clive,' Harpur said. Gambore had approached briskly, but looking a bit lost, his long powerful face showing amiability for a while, or close.

'Who sent you here?' Sarah Iles asked Gambore.

'Why, the Home Office, Mrs Iles.'

'But who?'

'These decisions are often committee, consensus,' Harpur replied.

'Colin's the great placator,' Sarah said. 'It's sweet in him, and feeble. Why Des says he'll never move up.'

'I stand across this room and see a beautiful woman and Harpur talking and am sure they are talking unfavourably about me,' Gambore replied. 'My role here, seemingly so masterful, even sinister, is also unpleasant and appallingly lonely, with perhaps that loneliness underlined by the obvious hostility of a lovely woman.'

Harpur said: 'Oh, Sir Clive, Sarah would never—'

'Go fuck yourself, Gambore,' Sarah replied. 'You took the role, didn't you? You'll never crack it here.'

He had no drink with him and raised his arms as though in surrender then walked on, into further loneliness.

'Does Des talk to you about me, Col? I mean, sexually?'

'Never.'

'Why not? You had me in common.'

'A privilege. I remember. Perhaps that's why. He worships you, Sarah. So he should. He knows you only shagged around in search of love. Nothing cheap.'

'Yes. Did I find some love, Col?' But she did not pause for an answer. 'You say things moving? What kind? Not details, just what kind?'

'If we could get someone for these two later ones, the original very nice guy and Lester, it might help douse interest in the others.'

'How? Proving one couple doesn't prove the other.'

'We don't have to prove the early ones full scale. I told you, this inquiry's a show. We need just enough to shake Gambore. Not a court matter. A wrap-it-up-quick-Clive-and-forget-it matter.'

She put her brisk, educated brain to it for a while. 'You mean drop the lot on a dead – the old police way? You've got a dead? A potential one?'

'We have some things moving.'

'We? Who?'

'Me.'

'That's better, Col,' she replied. This time when she took his wrist it was almost a fondle.

Across the room, Mrs Lane suddenly moved in front of her husband, as though he had been threatened, like a cat protecting its kitten. Perhaps Jane's tolerance had gone. A little while afterwards, the Chief and his wife left, waving to all, mostly ignored. Iles and Jane with what might be three of Erogenous's relations began drifting over towards Harpur and Sarah, pausing now and then to talk to others.

'There are wars inside the drugs game all the time, worse than police,' Harpur said. 'So it's feasible that whoever finished the original very nice guy and Lester also had Jamieson and Favard.'

'I like feasible.'

'These people – drugs people – they adore the violence. Youngsters especially, but right through to old hands. Always chance of a death. Violence is status. Ornate killings are routine, a laugh – like US inner city posse rule. Or Moss Side, Manchester.'

'Would you say I'm still screwable, Col?' she replied. 'Although you, of course, want it much younger?'

He tossed a coin and caught it. 'Yes,' he said, without looking. He repeated that with the same answer.

'It must be Des in a bad way then. How young *is* she, Col? Why didn't you bring her? She and I could chat.'

'There's more than one way of being in a bad way,' Harpur replied.

She had another think. 'Oh, I see. Just that? Like when he went all hidden away and celibate for his secret vasectomy – to conceal the bruising.' She stared at Gambore's back. 'Little boy bloody lost. To me, Sir Clive seems stuffed with honour and guile. How will you cope, Col? You're short of both.'

'It's grand in him, really – old, but still has to check policing's in good hands.'

Iles and his group reached them. 'The Chief's due his

little nap now,' he said. 'Frail. The idle sod won't do the auction at Chanter Hall, of course, Harpur. Jane wants to talk to the Bixtons.'

'Their boy kills my man, but they wished to come, and it's brave and good,' Jane replied.

Iles pointed: 'This is Inspector Jones's mother and father and his brother, Gareth, not a cop. Here's my wife, Sarah, talking to a dear friend of hers, Chief Superintendent Colin Harpur, and, of course, a friend of mine. Despite everything.'

Sarah asked: 'So, has Des persuaded you to speak to the Bixtons, Jane – a unity and forgiveness display for Sir Clive?'

'I don't even think about him,' she replied.

'Nor me,' Iles said.

'Jesus,' Sarah said.

'Why is he here?' Mrs Jones asked. She was big, square, small-voiced, dressed in full mourning, including a hat. The two men had on dark jackets and dark, striped trousers.

'As a clean-up instrument, he thinks,' Sarah replied. 'He believes the Force is rotten right through.'

'I'd say his mind is open,' Harpur replied.

'Balls,' Sarah said.

'And Jeremy's death is part of the rottenness?' Mrs Jones asked. The two men with her, narrow faced, alert looking, followed the talk yet seemed uneager to speak.

Iles said: 'But Harpur's going to fix the bugger. Looking at Col you wouldn't think it, but he's got nasty talents.'

'Shall I bring the Bixtons now?' Harpur replied. They were seated alone at a table, not drinking. He crossed the room and, when he explained, they silently followed him back. They looked young to be Ned Bixton's parents, both in denim and jeans, both small and dumpy and fair-headed. Harpur made the introductions this time.

'We felt obliged to share your sadness, that's all,' Mr Bixton told the Joneses. He had a West Country accent, slow and warming. He put out a hand like a faith healer, as though about to touch Mrs Jones, then did not go through with it.

'But why did it happen?' she replied.

'They learn these terrible skills, have these terrible weapons. And so, terrible accidents,' Mrs Bixton said. She came from somewhere else, a hard town voice, maybe London, Reading.

'Accident?' Jane muttered. 'Enough force to kill?'

'These terrible skills are needed,' Iles said quickly. 'Sometimes they go wrong, even maverick. I'm guilty myself. Yes. The other side has even worse terrible skills. They will not win.' He brushed some speck off the shoulder of his fine blue uniform.

'Erog's skills were so damn useless at the end,' Jane said. 'Tailing, interrogating. He didn't know about self-preservation.'

'Erog?' Mr Jones asked. His eyes shone with curiosity, perhaps resentment.

Sarah said: 'A code name that stuck to Jeremy, wasn't it, Des, after some operation? Meaning, Emergency Reserve Officer. The G says gun-trained.'

'That's it,' Harpur said.

'I like that name,' Mrs Jones said. 'It indicates he did well in the operation – there was something to commemorate. A victory?'

'He always did well,' Harpur replied.

'Jeremy sounds a wonderful person,' Mrs Bixton said.

'He was, he was,' Jane said fiercely. 'I never wanted anyone else, believe me.'

Afterwards, Harpur went to his room and sent for Beau Derek's file. It was a while since Beau had done anything they knew about, and Harpur's memory needed a shake. He read Beau's previous and studied the pictures. Then he drove down to near his flat and watched. He liked to get an early look at people he might be coping with soon, an early look at them in actuality, not pictures – the way some villains could not do a job from plans and maps, had to see the reality. Occasionally, Harpur was able to read in the face some indication that a job was imminent. It might be excitement, it might be anxiety, it might be greed, it might be too much calm. With Beau it would be super-anxiety.

In about half an hour, Beau came out and Harpur turned his back and watched in the car mirror. There was a woman with him, probably a bit older than Beau, good body, pleasant wide face, tough jaw. She could be what Beau needed. They called a cab and Harpur followed, trying to recall all he had learned once about staying unobserved, and all the tricks he had seen in Erogenous. Near the centre, they paid off the taxi and walked. Harpur pulled in on some double yellows to watch. They were near Chanter Hall. The woman glanced about and then made for a pay phone opposite, leaving Beau to trail. She went inside, picked up the receiver but did not appear to make a call: possibly only checking that it worked. Beau stood outside looking jumpy. But he always looked jumpy. The woman replaced the receiver and made a note on her wrist, presumably the phone number. She rejoined Beau and they strolled over to Chanter Hall and went inside. A traffic warden tapped Harpur's side window and he rolled it down.

'You imagine you're a law unto yourself, mate?' the warden asked.

'Right,' Harpur said. 'Keep an eye on it for me.'

He left the car and, as he stood up, the warden must have recognized him. 'Yes, you are, aren't you?'

Harpur went very gingerly into the building. He was not made for tailing. In the vestibule, he studied some notices and tried to locate Beau and the woman from the corner of his eye. They reappeared soon, from the direction of the general hall. It seemed to him they had been giving the place a quick once-over. He tried to crouch a bit and shoved his face even closer to the notices. Erog would probably have pointed out this display made him three times as obvious. But Beau seemed too caught up

167

in his worries to see much around him. The woman had charge of this sortie. From what Harpur could recall, whoever was with Beau always took charge, except when it came to the safe.

Chapter Twenty-Nine

Venetia went into Victoria by coach and then took a Tube train to New Cross and walked. She loved London, felt she really belonged. There were so many young people about, all sorts and colours. You could tell this was a place that really attracted youth from throughout the world, and it excited her to be answering that call, too. Also you could tell these interesting persons would not let themselves be messed about by a school or parents. Loud guffaws would be what they greeted that idea with.

She was pleased at how well she remembered the buildings and big central road towards Lewisham, and it did not take her long to find the area she used to visit with Raoul on business matters, despite darkness. She knew that if she had stopped some of these girls or even boys around the coach depot or in the street now and told them that she had had a wonderful and mature business-man lover but that he was dead in bad circumstances which might even involve her own father they would listen and be helpful – not in some sentimental or miserable way, but in the mature way people dealt with these things in capital cities – there would be feelings, there would be strong, brief, deep, good wishes for the future. Like her, they knew well how things were in this life, sometimes brilliant, sometimes tragic.

This certainty that they would understand meant she felt no loneliness or fear at Victoria or on the Underground or now at the edge of Lewisham by night. When she came before it had been in the big car with Raoul.

That was better, that was lovely, of course. But she liked it this way, too, the closeness to people and the bustle of it all: the posters for gigs, a fat woman with a white cat on a lead, food shops catering to various races and a mad dwarf trying to direct traffic. Obviously, there were things going on everywhere. If she had talked to folk in the street about Raoul and so on, she probably would not have mentioned the Daimler, because it would have seemed a brag, a bit Lady Muckish. Londoners were well known for knocking that kind of person off their perch with a few Cockney sayings, such as 'ark at 'er.

The house had heavy wooden street doors always closed and a peephole because of persecution by police at all hours, whenever they itched to be heavy. It was quite a time since she visited last, but she felt sure there would be some people who would remember her, especially when she mentioned Raoul, who had been so vital to them. In London there was none of that stupid nickname people gave him at home, they did not know it here, and they had more respect, anyway.

You had to knock very hard with your fist and wait. You could see where one panel of the door had been smashed in with a police axe, probably, now repaired with a slab of wood and long nails that came through to this side and were bent over, still unrusted it was so recent. Windows had thick curtains on or were boarded from inside, again to make sure of privacy and stop interference by all kinds, but especially police. Many of the houses in this street were like that. People kept separate. After she knocked she had to wait a long while, but then heard someone moving and she could tell she was being looked at through the peephole, although you could not see any eye or anything like that. Then she thought she heard somebody move away, back into the house, but the doors stayed shut. She knocked again and called out, 'It's Venetia, that's all. I came with Raoul?' She was still not frightened, but this was what her father would call a very mixed sort of region and she had an idea there would be eyes

170

watching her from other houses, stuck here, banging the door, shouting, with her bag at her feet. London was a great place, but you also had to be grown up and realize it definitely had unknown elements. She touched the money-belt pouch again.

She heard more movement inside and then after a minute the door was opened a bit on its chain and a man said: 'Christ, Venetia. We thought you might. You by yourself, you really by yourself.'

She knew it was Mark and felt really great again to hear his voice. 'Yes, by myself, of course.' Hadn't they heard about Raoul? It was on TV.

'Well, I don't know, Venetia,' he said, and did not undo the chain.

'What?' Venetia said.

'What do you want, kid?'

'I've got some trouble.'

'We heard that. But what do you want?'

'So I got out of it at home. I thought, come here. Only for a while. Until I look around.'

'I ought to ask the others, but most are out now. It's the busy time.'

'Can I come in and wait?' she replied. 'I've got so much to tell you all.'

He moved again and she could see something of his face now. He had his big round glasses on and looked as pale as ever. He still did not undo the chain and she could tell that he had shifted position so he could see past her into the street and make sure she was alone. If that was suspicion, it hurt her, but she knew they were very touchy, through being messed about all the time. You could not turn up from nowhere and expect them to understand everything was all right. If it was not police it might be troublemakers or the giro people, even late.

She heard Mark undo the chain and one of the doors opened a little. Picking up her bag she went inside. Mark closed the door at once, as if still expecting a police army to charge in after her. This was the kind of nerves that

171

affected a menaced community. When she came with Raoul, Mark had always seemed what he called her just now, a kid, not part of any of the business talks or with a girl of his own. Raoul used to tease him and say he was so pale from jerking off, like boys.

But tonight Venetia realized Mark must be years older than herself, maybe even twenty. She had not noticed this because Raoul was so much more mature and had made her feel mature, also, in a way, wifely.

'They're afraid of your father,' Mark said.

'Who?'

'Everybody here. He must be very big deal, Venetia.'

They went into the long downstairs room she remembered. In a way it was definitely rubbishy, and she knew her mother and father would think it a real tip, with a smell of grass, scraggy red curtains across and a couple of dim lights always on. At school they had a video of a play called *The Caretaker*, which was about a place full of junk, and this room reminded her of it a bit. This furniture came from everywhere, some of it on its last legs. Armchairs had springs showing and there was a great big old sideboard with no doors on the cupboards and only one drawer out of four. She had seen that drawer open and it was full of ball bearings, old playing cards and ancient cutlery. Greasy mats and bits of lino covered parts of the boards, no proper carpet. But she liked this room, all the same. You could see it was where people really lived, and they were people who did not care about anything very much. Well, it was dirty, yes. You could feel the muck under your shoes like gravel, and the top half of the wall mirror was covered in dust. The thing was, though, the room could look great when some of the people were here in the chairs, talking, relaxed, maybe smoking, some, and the sound system on. The sound system was new and grand in the corner, and it was in this room she first heard the Red Devils. She thought Raoul used to regard this house as grubby, but you had the idea when everyone was in this room that these people had picked a life for themselves and nobody could spoil it or alter it. Well, yes, the police came in now and then, and once they tried to get the sound system, saying it had been nicked, probably after it for themselves, but one of the girls here then, Carrie, knew a full lawyer via some of her own trouble leading to a relationship, and that sound system had to be brought back, plus compo for damage.

There was a girl in the room now, one Venetia did not recognize, a bit older than herself, maybe sixteen, shorts and a khaki blouse, no shoes, cleanish feet, and Venetia thought this was the one who came to the door first and went back to fetch Mark. She probably did not know who Venetia was yet, and the connection with Raoul. The girl was sitting on the floor mending another blouse, not smoking, and she gave Venetia a good wave with the hand holding a needle and a trail of yellow thread. 'You the one whose old man did your boyfriend, coal in the mouth, all that? This is a grief, Venetia. He Sicilian or something, your dad? You don't look like that.'

'They won't let you stay, Venetia,' Mark said. 'They talked about that, in case you showed, didn't they Tess?'

'How did you know – I might show?' Venetia replied.

'How could you stay home?' Tess said. 'Can a girl stay with a man who killed her man – if you understand me? Was your dad doing anything with you?'

'What?'

'That's the worst jealousy there is, the father against the boyfriend,' she said. 'But you know. Because the daddy knows he's got no rights at all, only habit, and he sees this youngster bloke come on the scene, and it makes him feel like the far off past, his mouth goes dry. They can't take that.'

'No,' Venetia replied. 'Nothing like that.'

'You're lucky.'

'Well, obviously, I heard of it in school. But no.'

'If he came here, someone like that – I mean garotting, coal in the mouth, that's terrifying. Christ, Venetia,' Mark said.

'It's not certain he did it,' Venetia replied.

Mark had on a long grey calico coat, the kind some people wear in shops, over a grey jersey and black trousers. He wore slippers that seemed to be a woman's, green and gold, with a gold bobble on one. They were breaking up on the sides and could have been found in a throw-out bin.

Venetia said: 'Raoul—'

'Everyone here thought Raoul was a real prince and timeless,' Mark said.

'Oh, yes, yes,' Venetia replied.

'I heard of him, I think. Nice, was he?' Tess asked.

'This only happens to any woman once in her lifetime,' Venetia replied.

'Really a prince, a timeless prince,' Mark said. 'I mean powerful, supreme, with élite shoes, a Daimler and his domain back there. Then along comes this Ember and does him just like that and his confed at the same time. Just, *You touch my daughter, I kill you, and your minder.* I mean, Jesus, Ven, if Ralph Ember traced you here what happens? You thought of that? People snorting, smoking, dream-soft and no hope of defending themselves.'

'How did you hear it was my dad, could be my dad? That's not in the Press. They could not say that. It isn't proved.'

'We read about this death, these deaths, but above all Raoul, owing to the business connection, so we have to put out feelers, don't we? We're scared of repercussions this direction. One lad has a friend living your way and he gets on the phone to him one night and what he hears is Ralph Ember. He hears Ralph Ember, and hears that Ralph Ember is still free regardless and working to get the whole thing stuck on to a cop, some foremost cop, not just a bobby, and we hear it's happening. He can do it! That's one hell of an old man you've got, Venetia. Framing an Assistant Chief. An inquiry. R. Ember is the real prince – got to be. Clever, hard, hard.'

'And he wasn't even having you?' Tess asked. 'Christ,

174

this is real majesty then. This is quality rage, now been's spite. I can see why they're scared here.'

'He can't find me,' Venetia replied.

'Someone princely like that – info flows their way,' Mark said. 'People want to feed them, keep in good with them. How did you get here?'

'Coach.'

'Jesus,' Mark replied. 'Hanging around the bus station? *Thanks very much, lady, you're painting arrows on the ground.* Your bloody dad could be here any minute.'

Venetia heard what might be two or three more people enter the house from somewhere at the back. She wanted to tell these two, and all of them, that her father was empty and a giggle, was called 'Panicking' at home or Ralphy, like someone's retarded nephew, and could probably never kill Raoul and Lester and would have no network to trace her to London. They ought to give her somewhere to sleep and need not worry. Although some said her father looked like Charlton Heston younger, others thought Cardew the Cad on TV, a real daftie.

But she could not bring her dad down like that. She found when Mark was talking about him, calling him a prince, and more a prince even than Raoul, that she grew proud of her father. Tess was thrilled by his anger. These two did not regard him as someone who went into a dreary pong sweat every time things turned a bit bad. These were people in the capital city, yet they felt real awe of her father, made him sound like Godzilla. In a way it was terrible, of course, to regard him as so important because they thought he killed her lover. Terrible, horrible, cruel. Yet it used to make her sick when she thought of people calling him Panicking or Ralphy, making out he was nothing, a joke but with cash. The people in this house would soon say something about that.

Another good side of him was he had never touched her, although this girl thought that would be the usual fatherly thing, obviously. Venetia came to think her father was quite a father. This did not take away from what she

грief was still all-through real and
...ner father seemed greater than she used
...o determined. There was a battle inside her
...now she should think of these two, her father and
Raoul. It confused her, even gave her pain, yet thrilled
her, too. She had been fought over by two great men, one
a father, one a lover. The father had won. This did not
mean he was better than her lover, just that was how it
had happened. There could not be many girls even in
London who were the cause of hatred and violence
between two such notable men. She had no need to brag
to these people here about it, because they had seen it,
even before she saw it herself. They knew how badly
those two men had wanted her, in their different ways.
Tragedy, in fact, had attended her from a remarkably low
age. Few girls had been made such a target for severe woe.

Two men and a girl came in. Venetia knew them all.
These two men were older, Gary and Willy, and they
could be who the house belonged to. Gary usually looked
like he had cares and he talked like a boss.

'There was a wreath from us, Venetia,' he said. Gary
had on a black leather bomber jacket and she always
hated seeing this kind of garment with baldness such as
his, monk baldness with the bits around the edge ginger.
The jacket had such a good warm glow and smoothness
and then this mess above, although he was only about
thirty-six.

'I know his mother's going to write thanks to everyone,'
she replied.

Willy said: 'No names or address on the card. Just
"Friends, deeply saddened." '

'Oh, I saw it,' Venetia replied. 'I can give you personal
thanks now, instead. Oh, yes, lovely.' It was a way of
building some goodwill with them. Raoul used to talk
about always doing that in business, especially with anxious people.

'What flowers did they do, Ven?' Willy asked. 'This was
Interflora. You never know.'

'Great carnations. And lilies.' Take your pick.

'Mark told you you can't stay here?' Gary replied. 'Regrets. But don't worry. We won't kick you into a Bond Street shop doorway.'

'This is quite a current problem, the homeless,' Venetia replied.

'I've had a word with someone in case you came, and he's prepared to give you a base, backed by our recommendation,' Gary said.

'You'll like these people,' the new girl said. She was about nineteen in a man's dark overcoat, not completely slaggy but her hair cut by a drunk.

'Who's going to take her?' Tess asked.

'Kenneth,' Gary replied.

Tess shrugged.

'Well, we told him you know what's what, Ven,' Willy said. 'Going on fifteen?' He was about Gary's age and used to be a partner with him in all the business talks with Raoul. Willy had on an old anorak and jeans, with trainers. In this poor light, he looked quite good, with a small black moustache, neat nose and very dark eyes. He touched his face a lot, maybe checking it was all still there. You could believe Willy had a great future, starting any time now – that kind of cockiness, not needing smart clothes.

'I'd rather stay here, Gary,' Venetia replied. She felt like crying but didn't, not in front of this lot. One thing her school taught you was only cry when you could trust the company. The staff so despised all that wailing at Mid-East funerals. 'This is the spot I was thinking about all the way on the coach. Well, almost as a sort of home.'

'But Mark explained, did he? Actually, Ven, you shouldn't even be in here now. We're very exposed. Mark – a softie. But I don't hold it against him.' They all sat down, yet it did not seem like the old times, not so relaxed. This could be because Raoul was absent, who was so good at getting everyone at ease because of his maturity.

She said: 'What I thought all the way on the coach was I knew exactly where Raoul would want me to go if he knew my plight, and was bereft of him. Raoul really believed in this place. And I thought you would understand this.'

'Darling Raoul screwed us for every last tenner,' Willy replied. It was like an animal's snarl. 'This was top-quality stuff every time, and he's always looking for how to knock the price, finding fault with perfection. Freighting dangers? He didn't want to know. Maybe you two had a giggle about it, how he ripped us off. You could have stayed here then, couldn't you, but bloody Raoul wants silk sheets and a boots? Tonight, another story. We live in this tip, Ven, and he was driving a Daimler – could buy himself a sweetie from a private school, plus those shoes.'

'You in a private school?' Tess asked. 'Straw hats? I love all that.'

'Willy's sour today, that's all,' Gary said. He turned and really snarled back at him. 'There's no need to talk like that, for Christ's sake. This was a fine relationship. Raoul always spoke of it respectfully, very long-term. Why vulgarize? Get a respectful vocab, Willy. You're dealing with a sensibility.'

'Thanks, Gary,' Venetia said. 'I know it. Nothing Willy can say will change that.'

Willy leaned across and fondled her elbow. She did not pull away. 'All right,' he said, 'I spoke out of turn. Sorry. True, we won't see another Raoul and all's fair in a dirty business. But Kenneth will fix you up, and everything will be fine over there, believe me. You'll have the absolute right to veto anyone nauseating. And good friends, girls your own age, with troubles. Some of them on the run to London just like you. They'll help you along.'

'But Gary,' she cried – 'just for Raoul's sake. Please.'

'Can't be done, Ven. I've got to think of the general welfare. Your father—'

'My father's just a laugh. He's so soft.' She screamed this betrayal. 'He couldn't do any of that. He's yellow

178

right through. Even if he knew I was here he'd never have the guts to come after me.'

'That's not what we hear,' Mark replied.

'One of us close to you and that mad giant gets in, where are we?' Willy said. 'And even if not, he'd think it. I don't eat coal.'

Chapter Thirty

Stan Stanfield had driven about half a mile down into the city when he suddenly had the idea of something on his tail, a big old blue Granada, maybe with two blacks in the front, one under a navy fedora. It was the kind of grey-patched, war-torn car you would remember, and he didn't, and they were the kind of faces you would remember, and he didn't. He kept himself from staring too much in the mirror, a giveaway that you'd spotted them. But the occasional glance said, yes, two blacks, one fifties with the hat on, a younger lad driving. Well, there was a drill, and he kept his speed as it was and did a couple of turns off, signalling very nicely, and the Ford stayed, not making much attempt to hide, the faces dead-set, eyes on nothing but the BMW, like an altar or a target.

He was on his way to the town hall Arts Centre, a change of mind. Earlier, he had thought of one more session with the crossbow. It was a few nights since his last practice, and he wondered about a refresher before the job tomorrow. Obviously, he could not go back to Dobecross woods. But there were other quiet spots, say that strip of shingle between the foreshore blockhouse and the mudflats, deserted enough in the day and totally at night. There would be no trees to fix his bit of cardboard to but plenty of cans washed up. Good idea to practise on a downward angle like that. He had to hit these dogs in the throat or eye, and even if they were leaping at him, they would not be at any real height.

But then he had decided, sod that. It would be only

bad nerves to do more practice, and he switched to the Arts Centre for his outing. The point was, you could stick at things too long. Last session with the bow, he decided he was as good as he could be, and it was useless training any more – like a boxer leaving it all in the gym. He needed relaxation. Usually, he was pretty good at that and always took the night off before a project, got his soul out from under the stress. So, he had thought slip down to the Arts Centre bar with a chance of seeing Helen Surtees, Jack Lamb's girl. They did their ballet class at the Centre tonight, Helen and her friend, Denise.

The Ford dropped back a bit, but was still there. Those two thought they had discovered subtlety. Stan very gradually took his speed up and made the turns faster, no indicating now, and a sharp acceleration afterwards. The Ford kept with him, getting nearer again, roaring like a Sherman or vengeance. His second thought like his first was this had to be a couple of Cyrus's people, maybe dad and brother. Of course, they'd think police would not give a shit for a dead black in a wood, so these two came looking personally, asked around and picked up a whisper somewhere. That meeting in The Monty car park could have been spotted, identifications made, the last time anyone else might have seen Cyrus alive.

Anyway, this pair were a genuine worry. He thought only a pair, but it was night and there could be others in the rear, sitting right back or crouching. His third thought was that Kenward really had killed the original very nice guy and Lester and had now hired a unit to make sure Stanfield did not raid The Pines, either. This crap vehicle was just right for the cheapo way Kenward would try to get it done.

Had the Granada been with him from the flat? Did they know where he lived? That could be a peril. Well, of course they knew. How else would they have picked him up? Christ, he had been dozey, maybe could have spotted this tail earlier, or even seen them from the flat window, waiting for him. He had been thinking of so much, wondering whether Helen had noticed his absence lately at the Centre. The practising and crises had taken a lot of time. What he did not want was for her to forget him, or think he had moved on and write him off, especially now, for God's sake with the Knapp money so near.

Suddenly, Stanfield really gave the BMW some speed and some manoeuvring. They were around the Sabre Park area, one or two good long straightish quiet roads, and a nice criss-cross of side-streets off, some closed with bollards to stop through driving. He thought he knew the lay-out pretty well. These boys behind, probably no. The car registration was out of town, and he never heard Cyrus had local relations. He got up to seventy along the park, then pulled hard into a one-way street, going the wrong way, out into another good wide half-main one, Banner Drive, off again into a narrow lane by a builder's yard, under the rail bridge and across a patch of waste ground, back on to Lake Way, so where's the lake? He did not want too much of this mad motoring. If he was picked up it was the end of the job, and Beau could get his pulse down again and Helen Surtees would stay distant.

There was a decent flow of traffic on Lake Way and he slotted in and went back to normal driving. Then he studied the mirror hard and did not find the Ford. That could mean it was lost in the side-streets a mile back or was tucked in somewhere three or four behind, still in touch, still capable of trouble.

Of course, most would say he'd never even get started with Helen. But that could be so wrong – the way she chatted sometimes and fooled about with him at the Centre, touching et cetera, and how she glanced at him, and once or twice fingered the moustache, that cheeky style some women had, though respectable. Christ, Lamb, the lad she lived with, had to be twice her age and a slab more, and he looked it. She must need something else. A lot had the idea Lamb talked to the police, which accounted for the fat, untroubled art business that helped him buy her. But Lamb would not have a bloody thing to say to them about Stanfield, except Helen had the hots for him, no felony. Of course, the story was around that Lamb said Stanfield had tried something forcible with her, which *would* have been a felony. That was fright, exaggeration, jealousy. It excited Stanfield to bite at Lamb's edges like this, nibble at his girl and eventually maybe more, fool those famous fucking antennae just before a job. And it would be stupid to let Helen cool when tomorrow he would have a grand new status for a while through new funds. In the kitchen just before setting out, he had done a couple of dexterity exercises with the crossbow for luck – not firing any arrows, obviously, just getting the feel and balance again, checking its savage mechanism. Then the same with the pistol: aiming, reminding himself of the weight and shape, enjoying the coldness of the metal. He had put both weapons out of sight under spare bedclothes and left. It would be wrong to have a gun aboard when meeting someone as refined and sweet as Helen.

He drove on. One by one, vehicles following turned off at junctions and he could still not see the Granada. He took a left into another wide road, Cork Street, and found a parking spot, put his lights out and waited. After ten minutes the Ford had not shown. He lit up and started again, went round the island and back into Lake Way, this time running in the opposite direction. Clear. But, Jesus, he had been dim leaving that gun behind.

He could make his way to the Arts Centre now. When he arrived, Helen and Denise were in the bar, showered and relaxing after probably nonstop pirouettes. Helen looked like she always did on these nigh_s, great and clean and pale but shiny, and unavailable, so far. Those ten-ners and twenties brought from Kenward's tomorrow would be grubby, for sure, real back-street notes, and he would hate to pull that kind of money out if he was with a shining girl like Helen. Somehow he must change it for new stuff, as though he had just drawn his weekly spending wad from the bank, like a happy businessman. She would be used to that. Jack Lamb was old but he would not have old notes.

'Here he is,' Helen said. 'Where've you been all our lives? Denise and I want to go to a club. You can take us if you like. We just decided, if you showed up.' Perhaps she had had a drink or two already. She was full of noise and spurt.

'Right,' he said. Yes, right. It was happening. He would have bet it would. Helen knew art and this could be what helped set up this quick, powerful, subconscious draw between them, because of Clarkson Stanfield, not just the moustache, for God's sake.

'We don't mean just any club,' Denise said.

'No?'

'A notorious club,' Helen said. 'The Monty, Shield Terrace. Heard of it? Where they found this black guy's car, full of escape clothes. The murdered guy in the papers. This has to be an interesting place. Why haven't I ever been there?'

'The Monty?' Stanfield replied. 'Where did you say?'

'Not scared, are you?' Helen asked.

Yes, in a way scared. Those lads in the Granada might have traced him through The Monty, and could be waiting there, now they'd lost him. The police might be there, too, because of the car and the body. In any case, he still did not want any problems with Ralphy or Ralphy's cohorts at the moment. 'There are clubs much nearer, better,' he replied.

'The Monty,' Helen said.

'Kind of mystery spot, Stanley,' Denise said. 'Exploration. Do you know it?'

'Probably members only, that kind of place,' Stanfield replied.

'You sound really snobby, Stan,' Helen said. 'Well, we're going. You want to come or not?'

Suddenly, he saw himself losing her almost as soon as she had seemed nearer. Girls like this, living with bags of money and freedom, did whatever they felt like whenever they felt like it. It was the best chance with Helen he had ever had and he was going to turn it down, wasn't he? Wasn't he? And it got better, or worse.

Denise said: 'I can't stay there long. I'm meeting my boyfriend when he comes off work.'

'Work at this hour? What the hell does he do?' Stanfield asked.

'So it would be just you and Helen,' Denise replied.

'All right with you, Stan?' Helen asked.

'Not there,' he said.

'Just for the fun of it,' Helen said.

'No,' Stanfield replied. He turned his face blank. He had this way of seeing what counted and sticking to it. What counted was he should be around tomorrow night to take Beau to The Pines and get him past the dogs and to work, then bring him and the takings away. That would not be helped by going to The Monty now. In fact, it could destroy everything. Weren't there enough hazards already? Kenward might know and have defence forces waiting. Perhaps those two or however many in the Granada were just getting a look at the enemy in advance. There was a duty to Beau although Beau was shaky, and there was a duty to himself. He needed those takings to make his name with Helen, long-term – or at least not as short-term as this jaunt tonight, just a whim. He knew she would see this if he could explain later.

'You're a flop, Stanfield,' Helen said. She stood up, slight and beautiful, full of aggro. 'You look so game, and you're a pussy cat.'

Stanfield said: 'I—'

'Come on, Denise.' In a minute they had gone. Denise waved, not Helen. Stanfield thought of following, but only for a second. His work plan held him like a faith, or like chains. In a while he went home. He took it carefully, parking a couple of streets away from the flat and walking the rest very alert. He saw nothing to trouble him, though. Inside, he brought out the automatic and checked the action once more. He would sleep with that close, if he slept at all. He made a window check front and rear but could not see the Granada. As to sleep, revenge slept? Hit teams slept? What he had done was right. Pussy cat? In less than twenty-four hours this pussy cat would be killing a couple of big Alsatians. This was a lovely kid who saw nothing and thought she knew everything because she mistook money for experience.

Stanfield had seen a lot more, did what was necessary and kept quiet about it all. If you had a mission, you had a mission, and could not let women get in the way, not even Helen.

Chapter Thirty-One

Reading the pointers, Harpur guessed there would be movement at Kenward Knapp's place tonight. Kenward himself was due at the charity auction with Iles and the rest in Chanter Hall, so The Pines might be empty: dog-girt but alarmless. It was a collection day and people like Kenward avoided banks: there should be a few bucketfuls of big, grubby notes in his safe. Beau and his girlfriend had been down to the Hall taking a scan and apparently checking communications. Perhaps she would monitor Kenward while Beau worked his magic in the house, nannied by Stanley Stanfield, tooled up. Only a two-man? Two-man and a girl assistant. That surprised Harpur, but fatter pickings. Because of the marine art lineage, Stanfield did think big, though nowhere near big enough to compete with Jack Lamb.

Harpur planned to take a glance at the auction himself, and then get out to The Pines. On the whole, he wanted to watch what happened but not interfere. A bit of luck, a bit of firepower, might resolve everything there tonight. He would like to spectate, but stay unseen, and he told nobody how events might shape, especially not the Acting Chief. If Iles knew, he could foul the prospects by some-thing impulsive at Chanter Hall. In any case, Harpur would not choose Iles as a secret partner. Obviously, he always had to be looked after as far as possible, for Sarah's sake and standard cop reasons. It went no further. He was Iles, and was best alone, like Scotch or mastur-bation. Most people were best alone, and that meant Harpur, too.

Sir Clive had said he would like to see Harpur one-to-one 'for a general chinwag about the past, old son', and they had arranged a late morning meeting. It could be another chance to look after Iles, as far as possible. Gambore preferred to do his interviewing away from headquarters, which made sense when his job was to take the place apart, and especially the man running it now. Not too logically, though, Gambore suggested they should talk in what the world knew as 'the police pub', Basil's, right opposite headquarters. Like Lane, he was keen on informality, plus his brief was to keep the inquiry at that level, for the moment.

Gambore bought. He was in a grey hacking jacket and flannels today, possibly his tap-room gear. They did not suit him, but did not suit him in an aggressive, not a pitiful way, say like Stalin in cub's uniform. Harpur thought he looked altogether formidable: the chin, the effortlessly unfriendly blue eyes, his swift, delicate movements, eerily good at that age: some elderly, scraggy ferret still up to holding throats. Now and then Harpur wished he had Iles present to help deal with Gambore, but only now and then.

There were a few people from across the road already in the bar for lifters, including Laissez-Faire Rowles, Carl Diamond and Bob Tarr. They would wonder and try to eavesdrop and lip-read. Some would be worried about themselves, some about Iles, some about Iles and themselves. One or two might be in Iles's Lodge, which would give brotherly bulk to the fret. Harpur was not pleased to be seen drinking on this wise prejudicial old snoop.

They took a reasonably secluded table and Gambore chucked any attempt to come gently at the subject. 'What puzzles me, you see, about the deaths of those two, Jamieson and Favard, is that you'd had them under surveillance after the acquittals and then, very suddenly, arbitrarily, this was lifted. If it had stayed on they could hardly have been reached and murdered, could they, Colin? Not even by someone with rank rights to go anywhere.'

Harpur said: 'We had them under watch for a while, yes. Arson suspects. We thought they'd fired the house where a woman called Celia Mars was burned to death.'

'Mr Iles's good friend.'

'He did know Celia.'

'Why was the surveillance ended?'

'We found both Jamieson and Favard had unbreakable alibis. They'd have claimed victimization.'

'Whereas what happened to them wasn't victimization at all?' Gambore replied.

'Some gang thing,' Harpur said.

'Who lifted surveillance?'

'I'd have to check the notes for that.'

'Might it be Mr Iles?'

Harpur let that go.

'Would you have the rank to do it?'

Harpur let that go.

'Iles then. Would this be the situation, Colin: suspicion that Jamieson ordered nobodies to torch the house, having provided himself and Favard with this "unbreakable alibi"?'

'All kinds of suspicions at that time, Sir Clive.'

A tough-looking woman of around forty wearing a smart suit came in and, standing near the door, stared about. Harpur thought he ought to recognize her, but not police. She moved away towards the lounge bar, obviously unhappy, obviously trawling for someone special.

Gambore said: 'In the totally understandable rage of the moment, a sort of rough justice might decide, "Sod the alibi, we know the brain behind this pyre. So, pull the surveillance, leave them exposed, settle with the bastards for Celia Mars and Street. Coal in his gob to give the fire motif." Personal touch. No gang, Colin.'

Harpur nodded. 'Rough justice might indeed say this. Thank God we're not in that game, though, are we, Sir Clive? We're for justice tied unswervingly to law. We live by that.'

'Nice,' Gambore replied. 'Where's that voice come

from, Harpur – the Methodist Conference? *Who* lives by that?'

'The police. What police are for.'

'All police?'

'All police worthy of the job,' Harpur said. 'Surely.'

Gambore gazed at him over his whisky glass. 'Do private feelings sometimes smash through the fine rules of the job?'

'Whose private feelings?' Harpur replied.

Gambore kept the stare on, old eyes evil and punitive. 'Harpur, as I find, you were screwing his wife all ways known to Masters and Johnson on a regular twice-weekly basis at one stage, yet now this insane, culpably obstructive loyalty to Iles. How can it square? Garland's the same. Or perhaps the loyalty is to her? She's very lovely, classically noble, wonderfully durable. But it's over, isn't it? You're giving it to some student now, I hear. Denise Something? Glittering mind and a sublime arse.'

'And how's *your* sex life, Sir Clive?' Harpur replied.

'This bond with him: are you Lodge?'

Harpur began to feel shredded. He fought to keep Gambore at bay, yet every other officer here now would speculate on how many of them Harpur was betraying to this jaunty old nose – for a gin and cider sweetener. You could see it in the desperate set of their faces – particularly Tarr and Diamond – and simply in the way they stood leaning on the phoney panelling, for God's sake, rigid with distrust. As professionals they would all fully recognize that Gambore had his very worthwhile job to do, and all would agree he could do it without their sodding help. They believed some episodes were nicely wrapped up, as tidily finished as possible. The Ray Street–Celia Mars episode was one of them.

'Your Jamieson–Favard investigation said probably only one killer, I think?' Gambore asked. 'Who other than someone immensely resourceful and fiendishly ruthless could manage to see off two accomplished villains like these on his own?'

190

'Or her own,' Harpur replied.

'You see which way I'm pointing?' Gambore asked.

'Towards someone unknown, immensely resourceful and fiendishly ruthless.'

Gambore groaned. 'Did any names leap into the reckoning – I mean, given motive and so on? Doesn't one name above all strike you?'

'We had a good short-list,' Harpur replied. 'But nobody we could nail. One of the most gifted was already inside.'

'All right, who was on the short-list?'

'I'd need to look at the file.'

'But you knew we'd be talking about this today. Haven't you prepared yourself?' Gambore asked. He gave a comfortable smile, to counter what his eyes said.

'I couldn't anticipate the direction of your questions,' Harpur replied. 'I thought a general inquiry into the Force.'

'As general as I'm compelled to make it. But we start with specifics.'

The woman had come back and once more gazed hungrily around the bar. Harpur waved a hand towards the headquarters building. That could have been a mistake. She saw it and seemed to fix on him but stayed where she was. Harpur said: 'Rest assured, Sir Clive, people over there will co-operate, to the best their memories will allow. Above all, we want to be positive.'

Harpur bought. He must look pretty bad because Philemon, the South African barman, said: 'High-jump time, Col?'

'Could be.'

'Avenging angel in town, we hear. Do you want I poison him?'

'Leave it to us.'

Then Carl Diamond came and stood close to Harpur as he waited for his drinks: 'Gambore getting anywhere, Col?'

'Nowhere to get.'

'As long as you know that. Sir.'

'Know anyone who'd know it better? Prick.'

When Harpur went back to the table, Gambore said: 'And then I understand Jamieson was leaking a yarn that Desmond Iles, you and possibly others were on his pay roll – all connived at the killing of your undercover man, Street, because he unearthed this and his mouth had to be shut, fast in both senses. You pianissimoed the case against them.'

Yes, Harpur recalled this. At times he had considered killing Jamieson himself. 'Jamieson was known as You Know Who – as if people feared speaking his name. He was capable of anything.'

'Who else was capable of anything, Colin? This was the kind of monstrous slur that could turn some mad.'

'Yes, it was a monstrous slur,' Harpur replied.

'And might produce colourful retaliation? For instance, Mr Iles seemed to regard Street as not only a protégé but a friend. He was angry?'

'Certainly. All of us.'

'To what degree?'

'We wanted the people who killed Ray. That fucking degree. But our suspects had been acquitted after due process.'

'Wanted?'

'Wanted to bring them to trial, of course.'

'Other people?'

'Obviously. Jamieson and Favard were not guilty.'

'You accepted that? Did Mr Iles accept that?'

The woman standing near the door seemed to make up her mind suddenly and walked towards Harpur. Now he remembered the Thatcher hair style and junk jewellery. This was Elaine from the flat beneath Lester Magellan's.

'You were with Des that day on my landing?' she asked him hesitantly. 'He around? I heard all you people come here. You part of this crew, too?' She had turned to Gambore. 'I gather Des got a leg up, then. Where is the sly sod?'

Harpur said: 'The Acting Chief doesn't use Basil's.'

With her dark business suit she had on a male type striped shirt and scarlet cravat, and looked marvellously spruce, whatever a check-up might find. She remained standing, not quite as sure of herself as her big voice seemed to say. 'The bastard gets what he wants, then disappears. When I say gets what he wants, I'm not talking just about all the usual. No, I mean information.'

Gambore sharpened: 'Please, join us. Drink?'

At once she sat down at the table, giving Gambore a great, thankful smile. Harpur felt sorry for her: would have felt sorry for any woman hooked enough by Iles to stalk him. 'You knew about me?' she asked Harpur.

'Of course.'

'Did Desmond speak of me?' It was almost girlish, the bold face suddenly sad and anxious.

Christ, Iles, you shouldn't mess about with people.

'What shall I get you?' Gambore stood.

'Something soothing,' she said. 'You choose, my captain.'

Harpur made introductions. Gambore went to the bar and came back with what looked like a brandy and port, more whisky for himself and another gin and cider for Harpur. Tarr watched it all with grand and blatant hatred. He muttered something to Diamond, though without turning his head away. He would not want to miss any second of the treachery.

She said: 'I open my door to him, this is to a cop, despite everything – the perils, the shunning, name-calling by neighbours – and then, "Hail and farewell, Elaine." I was in a very vulnerable state at the time, Clive, losing Lester. You know about Lester?' she asked Gambore.

'Enough.'

'A lovely, long-term thing and it's grossly untrue he and the original very nice guy were banging each other on even days. Oh, Lester might have little relationships here and there, but nothing of significance, rest assured. He was someone with great flair and sweetness. Then, so suddenly, snatched from me like that, I mean, horrifically.

193

It was natural I'd be susceptible to someone with – well, Desmond is charming, and marvellous clothes – that long overcoat – and wit.'

Harpur said: 'I could possibly take a message to him, if you want to get away now, Elaine. He's so busy – the new job.'

'What information?' Gambore asked.

'Elaine lives near a man who was murdered,' Harpur replied.

'This is the copy-cat killings?' Gambore said.

'Right,' she replied. 'That's why I said horrifically. The fact it was like the previous killings – like it was, well, a pleasantry.'

'Horrific,' Gambore said.

'You a detective, too? At your age? Like a very senior detective? But not with Des and this lot? Your Scotch accent. From away?' She had finished her drink. It was Harpur's turn, but he would not offer. This had to end. Too much was being said. After a moment, Gambore bought another round. More people from over the road had come in: Seabourne, Jane Bish, Chat-up. The atmosphere did not lighten. Elaine went on: 'What people say is that these killings – Lester, the original very nice guy – are to suggest it was some sort of gang war, and some sort of gang war for the last ones, also. In case there was trouble, an investigation, even so long after. It's possible – to help someone get himself clear of those early ones.'

'As a matter of fact, I've heard this,' Gambore said. 'How do you see it, Elaine?'

She leaned across the table, confidingly to him. 'Lester was never a gang person. This was above all a very individualistic gem. What information? Well, asking if I'd seen anyone around the flat block, or near Lester's place.'

'Had you?' Gambore asked.

'Dessy kept on and on questioning,' she replied.

Gambore said: 'Might he have been asking in a subtle way if you'd seen him, Mr Iles himself, near Lester's place before?'

'Desmond? Why? What the hell are you saying?' she asked. Elaine's long, unlined face went sad again. 'One day he's heard all he wants, and he's going to call me tomorrow. I never hear a squeak then or since. Suddenly, unreachable, like emigration. Dessy has very various bed tastes, but I can put up with that. What I hate is the blankness suddenly. The insult of it, Clive.'

'The damn coldness,' Gambore said.

'Exactly that,' she replied. 'You understand so well.'

'Some of it,' Gambore said.

'I noticed that in you from the start. A kind of empathy.'

'Thank you,' Gambore replied. 'So easy to feel with someone like yourself.'

'Kind. You down here alone, Clive? I mean, the Scotch accent. It can be very lonely, can't it? Even in a crowd,' she asked.

'Damn lonely,' Gambore replied. He surveyed the bar, met full-on any eye contact offered. You did not make his kind of career by fearing the troops. He stood to get another round, but Harpur said he really had to leave.

'Clive and I will be all right, I expect, Colin,' she said. 'I don't think I'll go back to the office today. One of those headaches?'

'I hope not,' Gambore said.

'Oh, not one of *those* headaches,' she replied. 'But you're brisk for your age, isn't he, Colin?'

Late in the afternoon, too late for repairs, Harpur went down to the telephone booth near Chater Hall and put the receiver out of operation with a couple of smart blows on the shelving, hidden by his body. He walked to the next nearest booth and waited until a man came out and then did the same there. Both instruments still looked all right from a distance and would give no early warning they were dead.

Now he was single-parenting he liked to get home reasonably early and did not return to headquarters. When he reached the house, Jill was alone there, still in her school stuff, fiddling with some homework in the

195

kitchen, head low. 'Hazel had to go out,' she said. 'This was urgent.'

'Gone where?'

'It could be some distance. We had a phone call from that girl – the one with the big, tragic romance? Widow at fourteen.'

'Venetia Ember?'

Jill looked up and sat back from her books, as though she had decided to level. 'I answered first. She wanted *you*. She really needed help, Dad, still talking a treacle storm about that man, but real fright behind it.'

'Where? She's at their house? The club? Her father's giving trouble?'

'I don't think so.'

'You know so?'

She did not answer that. 'Hazel took over the call then. She told Venetia she'd come right away.'

'But she wanted me,' Harpur said.

'You know what Hazel's like about police, Dad,' Jill replied. 'She told Venetia you were not necessary. Well, "a waste of time" were the words. Hazel said she could handle whatever the situation was.'

Harpur made some tea for them both. 'So, gone where?'

Jill turned back to the books for a few moments, then said: 'Well, actually, it's London, I think. Yes, London. Can't you understand why?'

'Why what?'

'That girl would want to put distance between herself and her father, if he killed Raoul. Poor kid.'

'Some children have to grow up fast,' Harpur replied.

'Yes. I'm glad you see that, Dad, because Hazel said she wouldn't be back tonight. She *is* fifteen, you know.'

'Where in London?'

'I don't know.'

'Jill, where in London?'

'I told you, I don't know.' She grew tearful. 'Stop getting heavy, will you? Is that why you made the tea, to soften me up? I can see what Hazel means about police.'

196

'What urgency?'

'She's having difficulty with some people, I gather.'

'What people?'

'This is people the great Raoul used to deal with. Probably not the Queen Mother's household. Venetia thought they were in love with him, too, and would be thrilled to welcome her, as his precious one. But no it seems.'

'Some names? Even first names only?'

'No.'

'But you've got an address, Jill?'

'No, honestly. Haven't I told you? Hazel has. She said better not give it, or you'd rubber-hose it out of me.'

'By train, coach or what?' Harpur asked.

'Listen, Dad, she said don't come looking. Twice she said it. She said give you the basics so you wouldn't worry, and that's all.'

'Great. Naturally, I won't worry. She's got money?'

'She's always got money hidden around, that one. Or perhaps hitching.'

He drove at once to the train and bus stations but could not see her, then checked the motorway link for a hitcher, with no luck, either. Of course, she might be lying low, certain he would search, watching the car from somewhere right now. She could travel later. Also of course he could put out a call to have her picked up, but that was not something you did to your daughter. It would strengthen the anti-police evil she already felt. He called the Control Room to see whether Ralph Ember had reported Venetia gone, but this was negative, too. Should he ring Ralphy, find what he knew and what he thought of it? This was the kind of stress that might make Ember sing. He was called Panicking, wasn't he? Yet the girl herself could have rung there if she had wanted his help. It might be a kind of treachery for Harpur to tell him what he knew. In a way, they were linked: two fathers with missing daughters. Harpur did not fancy the idea of being bracketed with Panicking like that, though, so he kept quiet.

Chapter Thirty-Two

Driving to pick up Beau for the job, Stanfield watched the mirror again. So, two uncertainties, both high grade. Would the old Granada show up once more, and would Beau's worries let him show up at all? Stanfield could do without those two blacks tailing him, and especially tailing him to Kenward's place. He could not do without Beau.

But, after a couple of miles through the town, Stanfield saw no Granada, and here's Beau as arranged and looking almost solid in the kebab shop doorway, a few tools and the key collection like his supper in a brown paper carrier-bag. Yellow light from the shop gave his cheeks a grim, daffodil glint. Obviously, Stanfield did not find actual fight or hope on Beau's face now, but there was no terror or collapse, either. Melanie must really have worked on him, told him how money would plump up his charisma.

Beau did not clink at all as he climbed into the car. His tools were always carefully wrapped in rag and the keys greased. As to his trade, he was unbeatable. What let him down was a sick lack of grab. Stanfield drove gently out towards The Pines, still doing his mirror drill, but not too earnestly, scared of unsettling Beau.

After they had been driving a couple of minutes, Beau said in that tinny, slippery voice: 'The tale is Panicking's daughter's run, Stan. Heard it? She's so sure he did the original very nice guy. She must really know something, as fact. This is only a kid of fourteen. Ralphy confessed to her, boasted to her? It could not have been Kenward killed them. He won't be waiting for us after all.'

He said it like he had personally done the analysis about Kenward. Dim people told you what you had told them and believed they had just thought of it. But let's keep Beau happy, he had a sweaty night ahead. Stanfield replied: 'Is that right? Run? Yes, maybe Panicking, then. But, in any case, definitely not Kenward.'

'Why I feel good,' Beau replied. 'It happening just the right moment – could be a sign. You still say Iles? Well, I don't know. But you've got this faith in your judgement, Stan. Beautiful.'

'You see anything like a real investigation into those deaths? I mean not just the original very nice guy and Lester, but the earlier models. Harpur's not even handling these last himself. Garland. Garland's promising but where's the clout? Beau, they don't want to solve it, them. It's a cull. Police thin out the opposition now and then. Their own methods, sort of backhanded help for the courts.'

'Christ.'

'You'll be all right. They're fond of you. And your mouth's too petite for coal.'

'Fuck that.'

'Melanie down there?'

'We ring the box with Kenward's number first thing. I've got the booth number. Any luck, she might be able to tell us then that he's arrived. She'll stick with him and give the warning suppose something's wrong. Stan, I feel it's like having three on it, after all.'

'Well, it is. It could be better than. More tactical.'

'Yes. That Cyrus – talented or I definitely wouldn't have started him, Stan. But edgy. I still don't know about that out-and-out remedy, though.'

'He'd have talked. Or he might have talked. Same thing. We couldn't rely. Let's thank the good God we found him and the suitcases, or the job would have been off.'

'Yes, very edgy,' Beau replied.

A couple of miles from The Pines they stopped in a hedged lay-by and Stanfield went to the boot and brought the crossbow into the car. Then he checked the action of the automatic again and transferred it from the holster to his waist belt, for speed. If it came to it he would have to drop the crossbow and go for the pistol. More and more he thought it *would* come to it. Getting off one bolt would be easy, but the reloading, the re-aiming under stress – that could be beyond. OK, Lester must have thought it would work. Owing to death, though, no results were to hand on that experiment. Of course, everyone knew a gun pointing down in the waistband was dicey because in a rush drawing it you could shoot your cock off. He had had a foul vision of it actually dropping from his trouser leg and on to his trainers while they were still outside the house and maybe those meat-eating dogs about. But the thought of all that Alsatian breath and fur up around his neck also really scared him, and he must make sure it never happened. So, the waistband. Beau, sitting alongside him and watching the preparations with the crossbow and pistol, seemed to lose a bit of glow, reminded of the opposition. He had his carrier-bag on the floor in front of him and crouched over it, very still, like a drunk with a bottle. 'Pity we've got to be in before we can ring Melanie. No way she can tell us now, I mean right now, that Kenward's really there, not lurking in the house with friends. You should have a car phone, Stan. Maybe we should ring the box from a box.'

'And then ring again to give the number? Too fussy, Beau. And making her conspicuous, the bell going off twice in a phone booth while she's hanging about. I thought you'd dropped that idea about Kenward. He's there at the Hall all right because he wouldn't miss it. It's glory. Top company advertising itself, scoring for generosity. Even the Chief goes, or maybe Iles if Lane's still palsied. Kenward will love to bid for police stuff and then put it back in, to show contempt.'

'How did he get so far so fast?' Beau asked.

Not by being a wet dream like you. 'Kenward's had the luck,' Stanfield replied. 'We'll kick a hole in it tonight.'

He drove on to the motorway for a short stretch, then off again. They passed a pay phone and Stanfield felt Beau's little heart flutter up like a demented thrush on a window, trying to get to it. But Stan kept driving. Once, when they were quite near the house, he thought he glimpsed a vehicle in the mirror, unlit and too far back to identify, but moving, and moving this way. Had those blacks learned how to do it? He turned into the lane that led off the road to The Pines and its fence. They could see that the house was lit here and there inside behind curtains, and all the security lights were on. That would be normal for a deserted property. To leave every room dark was an invitation.

Stanfield stepped from the car at once, carrying the crossbow. He did not say anything to Beau. This was not a time for orders or prodding. Beau had to do it from inside himself. And he did, only a second's delay. As he got out, the dogs arrived at the fence, galloping and frisking that powerful way Alsatians do, so you might think they were just playful if you were mad, and if you could not hear the snarling and barking and see the teeth and foam. They hurled themselves in turn against the mesh fence, like an act Kenward had made them rehearse. Disturbed, Beau dropped the bag and when he bent to pick it up kept his eyes on the animals all the time, as though they could somehow crash their way through the fence and reach his entrails.

'See, it's good, Beau,' Stanfield muttered.

'Is it?'

'They're loose. It means he's out.'

'You said you knew he was already.'

'I did. This is so *you'll* know. Get the cutters. Come on.' He had them with his tools in the bag.

'Can't you do them here, through the fence?' he replied.

'I told Cyrus, the mesh might foul an arrow.'

'Use the gun.'

'No silencer. Neighbours not all that far. There's a plan, Beau, and we stay with it. Get the cutters.'

201

And he did. He pulled them out of the bag and stripped the rag away. The plan said he did this work, so Stanfield could stand ready with the bow in case the dogs tried to force their way through the gap at Beau. Christ, they should have practised something like this, but how did you do it? Cutting wire was easy, it was the sodding dogs that made the problems, and how did you mock them up? Now and then Stanfield thought it might have been easier to climb a section of the wooden fence and jump into the grounds. But you would be right off balance when you landed, and the dogs would hear and be on you before you could do anything – definitely before you could aim a crossbow.

Beau started cutting, from the top down. That was his own good instinct. Open the bottom and the dogs might force a way out. Not like this. Once he began working with tools, Beau was somebody different and worth a pilgrimage to watch. His brain and drive were in his fingers. He did things right immediately – the quickest, the cleanest, the safest. That's why he was worth his half. That's why you put up with the spells of bleating despair. He cut from just above his own height. Stanfield would have to stoop to get in and would be a bit unready, but not much. It would not be as bad as leaping from a fence. As Beau came low with the cutting and neared the ground, he was crouched over, working very fast, very straight, the bald head with its rim of dark hair bent forward in concentration. Now, he looked not like a drunk but an artist, dealing with some tricky bit in a fine work. Picasso was bald, wasn't he? Stanfield, standing alongside him with the crossbow nestling ready, felt like the guardian of a rich talent. At this kind of moment on a job, it was as if Beau had become main man and Stanfield just a heavy. Stanfield never minded that. Because of his link to art he could appreciate these deep skills, even reverence them.

Well, of course one of these fucking dogs, Fluffy, the long-haired, darker one, somehow got its muzzle through the hole Beau had made and had him with a bite high up the cheek, near his eye, and would not let go. Beau screamed like a girl, and suddenly all that artisan and art stuff had gone again. He was Beau, who knew defeat was always waiting for him, and if it was not waiting he'd go and find it. He tried to strike at this animal with the cutters, but they were weak shots, like he was beaten already, done by Fate not dogs, and in any case the blows were hindered by the fence. Beau tried to lift his face and look up to Stanfield in appeal, making a bigger tear in his skin as he tugged against the teeth. The Alsatian was on its hind legs like a circus pooch to reach Beau and the other animal longed to get at Beau's face, too, but could not find room for its head in the fence gap.

Stanfield pulled back the flap of cut wire above Beau and got the crossbow pointing almost direct down at the head of the darker dog. It was no real angle for aiming but he let an arrow go. It missed the animal's face and head. Maybe Stanfield had unconsciously pointed wide for fear of hitting Beau. But the arrow took the Alsatian in its left shoulder and sank in good, maybe even nudging the heart. The creature released Beau at once and spun around with its mouth, trying to get at the source of pain and remove it. Beau lay flat against the fence groaning, his head on the bag of tools. A half-moon of blood spread fast on that.

Stanfield saw it was a crux moment. Was the job dead? Would Beau be able to work? Christ, would he be willing to? If it was all over, Stanfield ought to get him to the car and vanish. Forget the other dog. It had taken fright and was standing back, behind the injured one, still snarling and occasionally surging a few steps forward, but keeping away from the fence now and watching Stanfield and the crossbow. The wounded dog had stopped trying to lick at the wound and lay silent, flat on the ground, not dead but very poorly. This was a win, for God's sake. No retreat now. Stanfield reloaded, forced the flap of wire down a bit further, so he could use it like a platform to support the crossbow, and fired at the lighter dog's throat as it made one of its cagey skips forward. Too high for the throat but it took the Alsatian in the open mouth. Stanfield heard a tooth snap. The dog yelped once – again like playfulness, *throw me a ball* – and then its front legs went out under it like ruptured undercarriage, and the animal fell forward hard, breaking the arrow in half with a nice crack.

'You did well there, Beau,' he said, 'slashing him with the cutters. I only had the finishing.' Stanfield helped him to his feet and picked up the carrier-bag. Blood had weakened it too much and the tools and keys fell through the bottom. Stanfield gathered these and distributed them among his pockets. 'Are we right, then?'

'Let's get clear,' Beau said. He was shivering and had a handkerchief up to his face. The dark dog snarled once more, twisted its head violently towards the arrow again and then sank back, finished.

'Melanie's waiting for a call from us, remember?' Stanfield replied.

'I'm never going to be any good now, Stan. And my blood all over the place.'

'It's just Kenward's carpets.' Stanfield picked up the cutters, stood the crossbow against the fence and pulled the gap wide. He went through. 'Only three minutes altogether, Beau. We're on schedule.'

He saw Beau look towards the BMW, but what could he do there, except sit in it and wait? Stanfield had the keys. 'Lovely silent operation, Beau.' Except for the screaming and the death groans. Maybe they wouldn't carry. Stanfield held the flap open for Beau. In a moment he followed Stanfield inside and kicked the dead, dark dog four times in the head.

'Good lad,' Stanfield said. 'You take that one.' They dragged the animals by their tails away from the fence and the patches of security lighting to some bushes. Then they broke into the house and made for the gallery.

'I'm dripping,' Beau said. 'They identify from blood?'

'Who? Kenward? He's no path lab. And he's not going to the police. I might do a bit of vandalizing while you're getting it open, Beau. Teach the sod to keep savage beasts like that.'

'Just watch, Stan, and keep watching.'

'Don't forget we've got a sentry.'

While Beau looked for the floor safe, Stanfield went to the telephone at the other side of the gallery and, as Beau sang out the number, dialled the public booth near Chanter Hall. He got an unobtainable. He dialled again and got another unobtainable. 'That you?' he said. He slowly read Kenward's number twice from the phone base into the receiver. 'Got that? We're in place. No trouble. Not much, anyway. Your partner saw it off good. Our friend has arrived? Grand. Clockwork. Hope you don't have to call. If no answer, we're away and a lot heavier. See you back there.' He put the phone down quickly, before Beau could hear the howl of a dud line.

'Here we go,' Beau said. He had pulled back a big black and yellow Afghan carpet and lifted a square of floorboards. He stared at the safe. Stanfield went and joined him. 'I've seen worse, Stan.' Stanfield laid the tools and keys out near the hole in the boards. They were a bit stained. Two drops of blood from Beau smacked on to the silver door of the safe and spattered the handle. 'She all right?' he asked.

'Fine,' Stanfield replied. 'Kenward's there and she thinks such a stack of stuff it will go on for hours.'

'He might not stay till the end.' Beau was already trying some keys.

'She's prepared for that.' This was one of the rooms where the lights had been left on, making the work a little easier. Stanfield went to the window and gingerly looked around the edge of the curtains. As he had expected, it was a good view, better than anything that would have been possible from the car. He could see the lights of the motorway and most of the road and lane to The Pines. Except on the motorway, nothing moved. He would need to be very careful now the phone link was out. What a country! You checked a booth one minute and it was fine. The next, buggered. A nation of Huns. He took another good look and then did a quick survey of the upper floor. In the three bathrooms he fitted the tub and hand basin plugs, jammed the overflows with flannels, and turned the taps on full. The pictures did not seem up to much, probably bought at some charity binge, but he slashed them with the wire cutters and did the same to all the clothes in the principal wardrobes, his and hers. Ornaments he mashed underfoot. With lipstick he drew a few murals twice life size of the dead Alsatians, plus arrows, in the two main bedrooms. He unhitched the vacuum-cleaner bag, emptied it into what seemed to be the chief double bed and moistened the mix with some very superior cologne: those sitting close to Kenward at the auction might have a treat.

The destruction thrilled him and he had a great hard on. In two shakes he could come. Time for two? As well as the gorgeous deaths of the dogs, he exulted in the rich roar of water tanks, and the sound of cascades in the bathrooms, and now tumbling down the stairs. In addition, was the thought of Melanie, frantic in the city, waiting hopelessly, tearfully to hear from him, and this sweetly sharpened his excitement. Those exorbitant thighs: this was Woman reaching out eternally for Man, wanting him, kept from him by Fate or a barren, envious enemy. He brought himself off in a quite decent china vase somehow overlooked, then flung it to shatter against a wall. This was the life.

When he returned to the gallery and squinted around the curtains again, Kenward and his woman were drawing up outside the fence. There seemed no driver-guard. Beau had the safe open and was swiftly transferring notes into the plastic sacks brought in his pockets. Stanfield did not disturb him, yet.

'No phone calls, Beau?'

'Not a tinkle,' he said. 'You got it absolutely right again, Stanley. But shouldn't I have known?'

'Thanks, Beau.'

'I'd say nearer thirty grand than twenty.'

'It's a real growth industry. You'll need some extra for plastic surgery.'

Kenward came from the Mercedes in his evening clothes and walked quickly to Stanfield's BMW, unlocked for a quick exit. He sat in the driving seat, then bent forward, obviously looking for the bonnet release, so he could do a little immobilization. Probably he had already called up a few employees by car phone to help him deal with whatever was here, and wanted whatever was here to be still here when they arrived. Perhaps he could hear the water system. Only the top of Kenward's head showed. He stayed low like that a little while, maybe unfamiliar with a BMW's controls. It was a distance, but Stanfield drew the pistol and was about to aim when he saw someone move out from the trees near by. Immediately, he recognized the Fedora but not the big old revolver. Three shots were fired through the BMW open side window and Kenward went down out of sight. The Fedora slipped back among the trees. They must have parked the Granada a long way off for silence. The avenger had walked the rest, arriving at just the beautiful moment to get things wrong.

Beau had finished and was standing behind Stanfield holding the two sacks: 'God, shooting? What, Stan?' His voice was at its tinniest.

'Cyrus's daddy thinks he's killed me. He knew my car.'

Kenward's Constance, in a long white evening gown, climbed out of the Merc and walked slowly across to the BMW, tall, very elegant, like a TV ad for any good-class vehicle. She pulled open the driver's door, bent down and looked in. Then she straightened and glanced about. Possibly she saw the former dogs. Turning, she went much faster back to the estate car, started it, turned and drove away. Stanfield could watch her almost until the motorway.

He and Beau left the gallery. Water was trickling through the ceiling there and deluging in the hall and dining-room. The ceilings must start coming down soon.

Kenward could not be upset by that now, though. They left by the kitchen door forced for entry. Stanfield pulled Kenward out of the BMW and dragged him to a different resting place from where the animals lay. He deserved some respect, regardless. Quickly, Beau went through his pockets. This was Beau's kind of finger work, too. He would have emptied the wallet, but Stanfield said no. That would be shoddy. In Kenward's breast pocket Beau found a piece of paper, perhaps torn from a notebook, which he handed to Stanfield. He could read it in the glare of the security light. The words were in pencil:

> *Ladybird, ladybird, fly away home*
> *Your house is on fire.*

'What is it, Stan?'

'Someone tipped him. Why he's early.' He tore the paper up and let the bits fly.

'Who? Who knew?'

'Who knows who knew?' Stanfield said.

'Why didn't Melanie ring?'

'Things don't always go as planned, Beau. For instance, the money's more.'

'Melanie tipped him? That cowing girl – I've only known her a year.'

'Don't be so bloody stupid. Melanie still gets her grand. I know she did her best. And a bit for Mrs Brace.'

'Who did tell him, then?'

Stanfield was trying to clean up the BMW's front seats with a duster. 'There are some very fly people in office, Beau. Christ, but this car's a mess. I'll keep it out of sight for a little while, do some valeting.'

'But you'll be wanting to squire Helen about now you're in funds.'

'That's true. Oh, I'll hire. Plus I'll need a new suit. Water, your blood, Kenward's. Yet, on the whole it went very sweetly, wouldn't you say, Beau?'

'I relocked and put everything immaculate,' he replied.

208

'Nobody would know the safe's been done, except Kenward.'

Just before they left Stanfield thought he heard the nice crash of a ceiling.

Chapter Thirty-Three

Some evenings, Iles called in on Harpur at home. It was probably to get a look at Hazel again and talk to her, but as pretext he would generally bring some bit of business for discussion. In the old days, he could also chat about books with Megan, though she had never been keen on chatting to Iles about anything, especially as he knew so bloody much.

'What interested me, Col, was Kenward received a note brought by an attendant during the auction and left immediately,' the Acting Chief remarked. 'Just before you went.'

'That right?' Harpur replied.

'I was watching him off and on, naturally. Vast bids for total crap, all smiles and big-heartedness. Then he reads this bit of paper and a sudden switch, dragging his floozie out with him like luggage on wheels.'

They were in Harpur's big living-room drinking tea, the wall shelves still rich with Megan's books. There was no real point in keeping them now, and Hazel argued all the time they should go. But Harpur had not managed to make the decision yet: they had helped make Megan what she was, and although he had not always liked what she was they did add up to a memorial. Jill used to say she wanted the Joe Orton *Diaries* kept and a boxing book, *The Sweet Science*, not the rest.

'You sent him that fucking note, Harpur,' Iles said. 'To get him up there for possible execution.'

'Ah, here's Hazel and Panicking Ralph's kid,' Harpur

replied. He had seen them on the front garden path, Ember's child with a haversack on her back and carrying a case. Jill must have spotted them from upstairs and clattered down to open the door. They all seemed to go through to the kitchen, not joining Iles and Harpur yet.

'They've been on some sort of ramble?' Iles asked.

'Like that.'

'You were up at The Pines were you, Harpur, slimy, secretive bastard, watching all that, whatever it might be?'

'Timberlake has neighbour sightings of an old Granada in the vicinity with two blacks aboard, one in a Fedora. Must be Cyrus Main's people, looking for a reckoning. Nifty with guns and crossbows. We found the bow.'

'Reckoning? Kenward did Cyrus?'

'Destroying a face makes relatives very ratty, sir. We're assuming Cyrus was recruited as replacement for Lester Magellan. Kenward heard and got to him, as well. Another bit of pre-empting. Like Kenward to go for the easiest ones.'

Harpur thought he would not tell Iles about the outdoor man's sighting in Dobecross woods of the big crossbow artist and a black. That witness had never been found, so the description was only secondhand and unreliable, useless in court. Soon it would certainly be necessary to fix Stanfield convincingly for something else very major. That should even things out and make Jack Lamb happy again and once more unafraid of age, especially if Stanfield made strides with Helen now. But the current priority was to look after Iles, as far as possible, even if, as ever, he acted ungrateful.

'Cyrus's people vandalized the house as well as doing the dogs,' Harpur said. 'Message: don't offend the Mains. Pure vengeance. Kenward still had more than five hundred quid on him, and as far as we can tell the safe hadn't been opened, though it turns out to be empty. We're investigating whether daddy Main or a brother has a Granada. And we're looking for Kenward's Constance in case she saw something.' Might Main Snr. say he thought he was killing someone else? Meet that when it happened. He'd probably say nothing.

The girls came in. 'Here's a wondrous treat,' Iles exclaimed. 'Hazel, you're looking – well, mature. Wouldn't you say so, Harpur?'

'They wanted Venetia King's Cross whoring, that's all,' Hazel replied.

'But you rescued her,' Iles said. 'You're your father's daughter, Hazel.' He put a hand apologetically to his mouth and spoke rapidly: 'Oh, but that's the very least to be said about you. I don't want to offend. Do tell us how you managed to get Venetia away.'

'I thought you'd ask,' she said, and left it at that.

'Yes, your father's daughter,' Iles replied.

Venetia said: 'Those people, London people – so interesting on the surface, yet unable to understand about a great unique love relationship.'

'I can believe it,' Iles replied. 'People generally are poor on that.'

'This was a man named Raoul, now dead,' Venetia told him. 'But perhaps you know. Don't I remember you at the funeral?'

'Raoul, certainly,' Iles replied.

'Perhaps under another, foolish name,' Venetia said. 'They think if a girl has had such a mature relationship that girl is now available for – for anything, for anyone.'

'It's hurtful,' Iles said.

'I wouldn't say hurtful,' Venetia replied. 'Stupid.'

Harpur said: 'Our view is you needn't run again. We believe your father is unimplicated in all these terrible events, Venetia. We have the man, though unfortunately he is dead.'

'Did you say *un*fortunately, Dad?' Jill asked.

'These rolling gang wars,' Harpur replied. 'Jamieson, Favard, Raoul, Lester – all tied up.'

'But will the old Home Office sleuth-fox accept that?' Jill asked.

'I think he must,' Harpur replied. 'Don't you, sir?'

'Unquestionably,' Iles said.

The three girls left. Hazel and Jill would take Venetia home.

'Do you really think Gambore will swallow it, Col?' Iles asked.

'Of course. It's irresistible. Even Tobin will be satisfied. Obviously recurrent gang slaughter, with Kenward repeatedly victorious, until now.'

The Acting Chief stood and walked to the book shelves. 'Ah, here's *The Character of a Trimmer*, Harpur.' He pulled the volume out. 'Remember the bit about laws needing to be in good hands? Then that other sweet chunk: *if it is true that the wisest men generally make the laws, it is true that the strongest do often interpret them.*'

'I think Gambore was nibbling at Elaine,' Harpur said.

'Elaine?'

'The flat under Lester's.'

'Oh, *Elaine*,' Iles said. 'The octopus brooch? He might be at some hygiene hazard there. I thought he was here to purify.'

'It's not something you can warn a retired very senior officer about in the presence of the woman,' Harpur replied. 'How are things with you, sir?'

'Didn't I mention something about it to him in the car to Lane's place that day, Col?'

'He might think another source, sir.'

'Or it could be a deep-down sense of solidarity and common destiny with us all, and to hell with risk. Even Sir Clive is bound to have that somewhere. In any case, he's so damn ugly can he pick and choose?' Iles asked. He pondered. 'Cyrus, the original very nice guy, Lester. What about the others who would have been in this job, Harpur?'

'We think they called off, sir. This is probably Stanfield and Beau Derek. Perhaps they had a tip there would be no cash in the house. Perhaps they had been scared off.'

Iles replaced the book. 'Sod, you saw them there, did you? If Beau Derek opens and closes a safe, nobody could tell.'

'Tricky getting a decent examination of it, because the

ceiling's down in that room and the whole place awash. In some ways, it's all a considerable tangle.'

'Yes. Thanks, Harpur.'

'In some ways, it's remarkably neat.'

'Yes. Thanks, Harpur.'

Bill James
Take £3.99

*'What police did not like, what Harpur and Iles did not like, were
people living on their ground who had a record of armed robbery . . .'*

On this occasion, Chief Superintendent Harpur and ACC Desmond
Iles were almost prepared to forget their differences and get on with
the job in hand.

Once Panicking Ralph started panicking they were doubly sure. It
finally looked like Ron 'Planner' Preston was about to make his first
mistake . . .

A mistake big enough to lead Harpur and Iles straight to the source
of the crime . . .

'Excellent . . . an absolutely corking ("must see what happens") story.'
H.R.F. KEATING

'Subtle and riveting to the last page.' THE TIMES

Bill James
Club £3.99

To coppers like Harpur and Iles, there is no such thing as good or bad, just the shadows where the villains meet the law.

The last thing Assistant Chief Constable Desmond Iles expected from the police force was an easy life. But if your wife gets pregnant and the chief suspect becomes the subject of a murder enquiry, even a top cop is entitled to feel nervous . . .

With DCS Harpur this time taking a back seat, Panicking Ralph out of retirement from villainy and whispers about a bank raid on the street, time is rapidly running out for ACC Iles . . .

'Savagely comic, expertly choreographed . . . dialogue and black comedy cast still among the choicest. Wickedly entertaining.' GUARDIAN

'Excellent on the seamy side with few illusions about human nature, in or out of uniform.' OBSERVER

'Bruisingly good.' SUNDAY TELEGRAPH

Bill James
Astride A Grave £4.50

*'Now and then Harpur had to deal with graves – mostly shallow,
hastily made, ineffective – though he had never encountered a
woman standing astride one . . .'*

After the news from Exeter, Chief Superintendent Harpur and ACC
Desmond Iles can only pretend to be surprised at their colleagues'
tale of woe.

First a daring bank raid, netting £1.8 million in cash. Then a vicious
fight over the share of the spoils. A fight that doesn't stop at kidnap
– or murder.

Whatever happened to honour among thieves, wonders Harpur,
leaving his scruples behind to enter the fray . . .

'Cops and villains belong to one family . . . Quietly, subtly, Bill James
is compiling a brilliant portrait of a society which few writers have
penetrated.' MARCEL BERLINS, THE TIMES

'Only too convincing, and quite unputdownable.' IRISH TIMES

'Wickedly entertaining.' GUARDIAN

All Pan Books are available at your local bookshop or newsagent, or can be ordered direct from the publisher. Indicate the number of copies required and fill in the form below.

Send to: Pan C. S. Dept
                  Macmillan Distribution Ltd
                  Houndmills Basingstoke RG21 2XS

or phone: 0256 29242, quoting title, author and Credit Card number.

Please enclose a remittance* to the value of the cover price plus £1.00 for the first book plus 50p per copy for each additional book ordered.

*Payment may be made in sterling by UK personal cheque, postal order, sterling draft or international money order, made payable to Pan Books Ltd.

Alternatively by Barclaycard/Access/Amex/Diners

Card No.

Expiry Date

_____
Signature

Applicable only in the UK and BFPO addresses.

While every effort is made to keep prices low, it is sometimes necessary to increase prices at short notice. Pan Books reserve the right to show on covers and charge new retail prices which may differ from those advertised in the text or elsewhere.

NAME AND ADDRESS IN BLOCK LETTERS PLEASE

. . . .

Name _____

Address _____

_____

_____

_____

6/92